FAIRY LEGENDS

AND

𝕮𝖗𝖆𝖉𝖎𝖙𝖎𝖔𝖓𝖘

OF

THE SOUTH OF IRELAND.

———•———

Second Edition.

"Come l' araba Fenice
Che ci sia, ognun lo dice;
Dove sia, nessun lo sa."—METASTASIO.

LONDON:

JOHN MURRAY, ALBEMARLE STREET; AND
THOMAS TEGG & SON, CHEAPSIDE.

MDCCCXXXVIII.

PREFACE

The erudite Lessing styles a preface " the history of a book." Now, though there can be no necessity for a preface in that sense of the word to the reprint of a work of mere whim, which has been nearly ten years before the public, yet a few words are requisite to prevent the present condensed and revised edition from being considered an abridgment.

However compact may be the mode of printing adopted, the act of compressing into one volume the three in which the " Fairy Legends" originally appeared, involved to a certain extent the necessity of selection, perhaps the most difficult of all tasks judiciously to perform; but the following statement will show the system proceeded on.

Forty tales descriptive of Irish superstitions now appear instead of fifty. All superfluous annotations have been struck out, and a brief summary at the end of each section substituted, expla-a2

natory of the classification adopted, and in which a few additional notes have been introduced, as well as upon the text. It is therefore hoped that this curtailment will be regarded as an essential improvement; some useless repetition in the tales being thereby avoided, and much irrelevant matter in the notes dispensed with, although nothing which illustrates in the slightest degree the popular Fairy Creed of Ireland has been sacrificed. At the same time, the omission of a portion of the ten immaterial tales will sufficiently answer doubts idly raised as to the question of authorship.

CONTENTS.

TO THE
DOWAGER LADY CHATTERTON, CASTLE MAHON.

Thee, Lady, would I lead through Fairy-land (Whence cold and doubting reasoners are exiled), A land of dreams, with air-built castles piled;

The moonlight Shefros there, in merry band

With artful Ci.uricaune, should ready stand To welcome thee—Imagination's child 1 Till on thy ear would burst so sadly wild

The Banshee's shriek, who points with wither'd hand.

In the dim twilight should the Phooka come, Whose dusky form fades in the sunny light, That opens clear calm Lakes upon thy sight,

Where blessed spirits dwell in endless bloom.

I know thee, Lady—thou wilt not deride

Such Fairy Scenes—Then onward with thy Guide.

The Wood Engravings after Designs by Mr. Brooke, R. H. A. Mr. M'Clise, and the Aithob.

FAIRY LEGENDS.
THE SHEFRO.

' Fairy Elves

Whose midnight revels, by a forest side Or fountain some belated peasant sees, Or dreams he sees, while over-head the Moon Sits arbitress, and nearer to the earth Wheels her pale course "—

MILTON.

LEGENDS OF THE SHEFRO.

THE

LEGEND OF KNOCKSHEOGOWNA.

I.

In Tipperary is one of the most singularly shaped hills in the world. It has got a peak at the top like a conical nightcap thrown carelessly over your head as you awake in the morning. On the very point is built a sort of lodge, where in the summer the lady who built it and her friends used to go on parties of pleasure; but that was long after the days of the fairies, and it is, I believe, now deserted.

But before lodge was built, or acre sown, there was close to the head of this hill a large pasturage, where a herdsman spent his days and nights among the herd. The spot had been an old fairy ground, and the good people were angry that the scene of their light and airy gambols should be trampled by the rude hoofs of bulls and cows. The lowing of the cattle sounded sad in their ears, and the chief of the fairies of the hill determined in person to drive away the new comers ; and the way she thought of was this. When the

harvest nights came on, and the moon shone bright and brilliant over the hill, and the cattle were lying down hushed and quiet, and the herdsman, wrapt in his mantle, was musing with his heart gladdened by the glorious company of the stars twinkling above him, she would come and dance before him,—now in one shape—now in another, —but all ugly and frightful to behold. One time she would be a great horse, with the wings of an eagle, and a tail like a dragon, hissing loud and spitting fire. Then in a moment she would change into a little man lame of a leg, with a bull's head, and a lambent flame playing round it. Then into a gTeat ape, with duck's feet and a turkey-cock's tail. But I should be all day about it were I to tell you all the shapes she took. And then she would roar, or neigh, or hiss, or bellow, or howl, or hoot, as never yet was roaring, neighing, hissing, bellowing, howling, or hooting, heard in this world before or since. The poor herdsman would cover his face, and call on all the saints for help, but it was no use. With one puff of her breath she would blow away the fold of his greatcoat, let him hold it never so tightly over his eyes, and not a saint in heaven paid him the slightest attention. And to make matters worse, he never could stir; no, nor even shut his eyes, but there was obliged to stay, held by what power he knew not, gazing at these terrible sights luitil the hair of his head would lift his hat half a foot over his crown, and his teeth would be ready to fall out from chattering. But the cattle would scamper about mad, as if they were bitten by the fly; and this would last until the sun rose over the hill.

The poor cattle from want of rest were pining away, and food did them no good; besides, they met with accidents without end. Never a night passed that some of them did not fall into a pit, and get maimed, or may be, killed. Some would timible into a river and be drowned: in a word, there seemed never to be an end of the accidents. But what made the matter worse, there could not be a herdsman got to tend the cattle by night. One visit from the fairy drove the stoutest-hearted almost mad. The owner of the ground did not know what to do. He offered double, treble, quadruple wages, but not a man could be found for the sake of money to go through the horror of facing the fairy. She rejoiced at the successful issue of her project, and continued her pranks. The herd gradually thinning, and no man daring to remain on the ground, the fairies came back in numbers, and gambolled as merrily as before, quaffing dew-drops from acorns, and spreading their feast on the heads of capacious mushrooms.

What was to be done ? the puzzled farmer thought in vain. He found that his substance was daily diminishing, his people terrified, and his rent-day coming round. It is no wonder that he looked gloomy, and walked mournfully down the road. Now in that part of the world dwelt a man of the name of Larry Hoolahan, who played on the pipes better than any other player within fifteen parishes. A roving dashing blade was Larry, and feared nothing. Give him plenty of liquor, and he would defy the devil. He would face a mad bull, or figlit single-handed against a

fair. In one of his gloomy walks the farmer met him, and on Larry's asking the cause of his down looks, he told him all his misfortunes. " If that is all ails you," said Larry, " make your mind easy. Were there as many fairies on Knocksheo-gowna as there are potato blossoms in Eliogurty, I would face them. It would be a queer thing, indeed, if I, who never was afraid of a proper man, should turn my back upon a brat of a fairy not the bigness of one's thumb." " Larry," said the farmer, " do not talk so bold, for you know not who is hearing you ; but if you make your words good, and watch my herds for a week on the top of the mountain, your hand shall be free of my dish till the sun has burnt itself down to the bigness of a farthing rushlight."

The bargain was struck, and Larry went to the hill-top, when the moon began to peep over the brow. He had been regaled at the farmer's house, and was bold with the extract of barleycorn. So he took his seat on a big stone under a hollow of the hill, with his back to the wind, and pulled out his pipes. He had not played long when the voice of the fairies was heard upon the blast, like a slow stream of music. Presently they burst out into a loud laugh, and Larry could plainly hear one say, " What! another man upon the fairies' ring ? Go to him, queen, and make him repent his rashness j" and they flew away. Larry felt them pass by his face as they flew, like a swarm of midges; and, looking up hastily, he saw between the moon and him a great black cat, standing on the very tip of its claws, with its back up, and mewing with the voice of a water-mill.

Presently it swelled up towards tlie sky, and turning round on its left hind-leg, whirled till it fell to the ground, from which it started up in the shape of a salmon, with a cravat round its neck, and a pair of new top-boots, " Go on, jewel," said Larry; "if you dance, I'll pipe;" and he struck up. So she turned into this, and that, and the other, but still Larry played on, as he well knew how. At last she lost patience, as ladies will do when you do not mind their scolding, and changed herself into a calf, milk-white as the cream of Cork, and with eyes as mild as those of the girl I love. She came up gentle and fawning, in hopes to throw him off his guard by quietness, and then to work him some wrong. But Larry was not so deceived ; for when she came up, he, dropping his pipes, leaped upon her back.

Now from the top of Knocksheogowna, as you look westward to the broad Atlantic, you will see the Shannon, queen of rivers, " spreading like a sea," and running on in gentle course to mingle with the ocean through the fair city of Limerick. It on this night shone under the moon, and looked beautiful from the distant hill. Fifty boats were gliding up and down on the sweet current, and the song of the fishermen rose gaily from the shore. Larry, as I said before, leaped upon the back of the fairy, and she, rejoiced at the opportunity, sprung from the hill-top, and bounded clear, at one jump, over the Shannon, flowing as it was just ten miles from the mountain's base. It was done in a second, and when she alighted on the distant bank, kicking up her heels, she flung Larry on the soft turf. No sooner was he

thus planted, than he looked her straight in the face, and scratching his head, cried out, " By my word, well done! that was not a bad leap/or a calf!"

She looked at him for a moment, and then assumed her own shape. " Laurence," said she, " you are a bold fellow; will you come back the way you went ?" " And that's what I will," said he, " if you let me." So changing to a calf again, again Larry got on her back, and at another bound they were again upon the top of Knocksheogowna. The fairy, once more resuming her figiire, addressed him: " You have shown so much courage, Laurence," said she, " that while you keep herds on this hill you never shall be moleated by me or mine. The day dawns, go down to the farmer, and tell him this; and if anything I can do may be of service to you, ask, and you shall have it." She vanished accordingly; and kept her word in never visiting the hill during Larry's life : but he never troubled her with requests. He piped and drank at the farmer's expense, and roosted in his chimney comer, occasionally casting an eye to the flock. He died at last, and is buried in a green valley of pleasant Tipperary: but whether the fairies returned to the hill of Knocksheogowna* after his death, is more than I can say.

* Knocksheogowna signifies " The Hill of the Fairy Calf."

LEGEND OF KNOC^FIERNA *.

It is a very good thing not to be any way in dread of the fairies, for without doubt they have then less power over a jjerson; but to make too free with them, or to disbelieve in them altogether, is as foolish a thing as man, woman, or child can do.

It has been truly said, that " good manners are no burthen," and that " civility costs nothing;" but there are some people foolhardy enough to disregard doing a civil thing, which, whatever they may think, can never harm themselves or any one else, and who at the same time will go out of their way for a bit of mischief, which never can serve them; but sooner or later they will come to know better, as you shall hear of Carroll

* " Called by the people of the country ' Knock Dhoinn Firinne, the movintain of Donn of Truth. This mountain is very high, and may be seen for several miles round ; and when people are desirous to know whether or not any day will rain, they look at the top of Knock Firinn, and if they see a vapour or mist there, they iramedi-. ately conclude that rain will soon follow, believing that Donn (the lord or chief) of that mountain and his aerial assistants are collecting the clouds, and that he liolds them there for some short time, to warn the people of the approaching rain. As the appearance of mist on that mountain in the morning is considered an infallible sign

that that day will be rainy, Donn is called ' Donn Firinne,' Donn of Truth."—^IR. EdwarpO'Reillv.

O'Daly, a strapping young fellow up out of Con-naught, whom they used to call, in his own country, " Devil Daly."

Carroll O'Daly used to go roving about from one place to another, and the fear of nothing stopped him; he would as soon pass an old churchyard or a regular fairy ground, at any hour of the night, as go from one room into another, without ever making the sign of the cross, or saying, " Good luck attend you, gentlemen."

It so happened that he was once journeying, in the county of Limerick, towards " the Balbec of Ireland," the venerable to^^Ti of Kilmallock ; and just at the foot of Knockfiema he overtook a respectable-looking man jogging along upon a white pony. The night was coming on, and they rode side by side for some time, without much conversation passing between them, further than saluting each other very kindly; at last, Carroll O'Daly asked his companion how far he was going?

" Not far your way," said the farmer, for such his appearance bespoke him; " I'm only going to the top of this hill here."

" And what might take you there," said O'Daly, *' at this time of the night ? "

" Why then," replied the farmer, " if you want to know ; 't is the good people."

" The fairies, you mean," said O'Daly.

" Whist! whist!" said his fellow-traveller, " or you may be sorry for it;" and he turned his pony off the road they were going, towards a little path which led up the side of the mountain, wishing Carroll O'Daly good night and a safe journey.

" That fellow," thought Carroll, " is about no good this blessed night, and I would have no fear of swearing wrong if I took my Bible oath that it is something else beside the fairies, or the good people, as he calls them, that is taking him up the mountain at this hour. The fairies!" he repeated, " is it for a well-shaped man like him to be going after little chaps like the fairies! To be sure some say there are such things, and more say not; but I know this, that never afraid would I be of a dozen of them, ay, of two dozen, for that matter, if they are no bigger than what I hear tell of."

Carroll O'Daly, whilst these thoughts were passing in his mind, had fixed his eyes steadfastly on thfe mountain, behind which the full moon was rising majestically. Upon an elevated point that appeared darkly against the moon's disk, he beheld the figure of a man leading a pony, and he had no doubt it was that of the farmer with whom he had just parted company,

A sudden resolve to follow flashed across the mind of O'Daly with the speed of lightning : both his courage and curiosity had been worked up by his cogitations to a pitch of chivalry; and, mixt-tering, " Here's after you, old boy!" he dismounted from his horse, bound him to an old thorn-tree, and then commenced vigorously ascending the mountain.

Following as well as he could the direction taken by the figures of the man and pony, he pursued his way, occasionally guided by their partial appearance : and, after toiling nearly three hours over a rugged and sometimes swampy

path, came to a green spot on the top of the mountain, where he saw the white pony at full liberty grazing as quietly as may be. O'Daly looked around for the rider, but he was nowhere to be seen; he, however, soon discovered, close to where the pony stood, an opening in the mountain like the month of a pit, and he remembered having heard, when a child, many a tale about the " Poul-duve," or Black Hole of Knockfierna; how it was the entrance to the fairy castle which was within the mountain; and how a man whose name was Ahern, a land-surveyor in that part of the country, had once attempted to fathom it with a line, and had been drawn down into it and was never again heard of; with many other tales of the like nature.

" But," thought O'Daly, " these are old woman's stories: and since I've come up so far, I'll just knock at the castle door and see if the fairies are at home."

No sooner said than done; for, seizing a large stone, as big, ay, bigger than his two hands, he flung it with all his strengih down into the Poul-duve of Knockfierna. He heard it bounding and tumbling about from one rock to another with a terrible noise, and he leant bis head over to try and hear when it would reach the bottom,—and what should the very stone he had thrown in do but come up again with as much force as it had gone down, and gave him such a blow full in the face, that it sent him rolling down the side of Knockfierna, head over heels, tumbling from one crag to another, much faster than he came up. And in the morning Carroll O'Daly was found

lying beside his horse; the bridge of his nose broken, wliich disfigured him for life; his head all cut and bruised, and both his eyes closed up, and as black as if Sir Daniel Donnelly had painted them for him.

Carroll O'Daly was never bold again in riding alone near the haunts of the fairies after dusk; but small blame to him for that; and if ever he happened to be benighted in a lonesome place, he would make the best of his way to his journey's end, without asking questions, or turning to the right or to the left, to seek after the good people, or any who kept company with them.

THE

LEGEND OF KNOCKGRAFTON.

III.

There was once a poor man who lived in the fertile glen of Aherlow, at the foot of the gloomy Galtee mountains, and he had a great hump on his back : he looked just as if his body had been rolled up and placed upon his shoulders; and his head was pressed down with the weight so much, that his chin, when he was sitting, used to rest upon his knees for support. The country people were rather shy of meeting him in any lonesome place, for though, poor creature, he was as harmless and as inoffensive as a new-bom infant, yet his deformity was so great, that he scarcely appeared to be a human being, and some ill-minded persons had set strange. stories about him afloat. He was said to have a great knowledge of herbs and charms ; but certain it was that he had a mighty skilful hand in plaiting straw and rushes into hats and baskets, which was the way he made his livelihood.

Lusmore, for that was the nickname put upon him by reason of his always wearing a sprig of the fairy-cap, or lusmore*, in his little straw hat, would ever get a higher penny for his plaited-work than any one else, and perhaps that was the reason why some one, out of envy, had circulated

* Litenllj, the great herb—Di^alit purpurea.

the strange stories about him. Be that as it may, it happened that he was returning one evening from the pretty town of Cahir towards Cappagh, and as Httle Lusmore walked very slowly, on account of the great hump upon his back, it was quite dark when he came to the old moat of Knockgrafton, which stood on the right-hand side of his road. Tired and weary was he, and noways comfortable in his own mind at thinking how much farther he had to travel, and that he should be walking all the night; so he sat down under the moat to rest himself, and began looking mournfully enough upon the moon, which,

" Rising in clouded majesty, at length, Apparent Queen, unvell'd her peerless light, And o'er the dark her silver mantle threw."

Presently there rose a wild strain of unearthly melody upon the ear of little Lusmore; he listened, and he thought that he had never heard such ravishing music before. It was like the sound of many voices, each mingling and blending with the other so strangely, that they seemed to be one, though all singing different strains, and the words of the song were these :—

Da Luan^ Da Mort^ Da Luan^ Da Mort^ Da Luan, DaMort, when there would be a moment's pause, and then the round of melody went on again.

Lusmore listened attentively, scarcely drawing his breath, lest he might lose the slightest note. He now plainly perceived that the singing was within the moat, and, though at first it had charmed him so much, he began to get tired of hearing the same round sung over and over so often without

THE lege:«d of knockgrafton.

any change; so, availing himself of the pause when the Da Luan^ Da Mort, had been sung three times, he took up the tune and raised it with the words augus Da Cadine, and then went on singing with the voices inside of the moat, Da Luan, Da Mort, finishing the melody, when the pause again came, with aufftis Da Cadine*

Da Lu-an, da Mort, da Lu-an, da Mort, da

i

E&

-g—g— n —a*—

Lu - an, da Mort, au - gus da Ca - dine. Da

i

^^

Lu - an, da Mort, da Lu - an, da Mort, da

S

^

I

a

^^

—m — n #

Lu-an, da Mort, au-gus da Ca - dine.

i

^

P

» Correctly written, Dia Luain, Dia Main, agut Dia Ceadaoine, i. e. Monday, Tuesday, and Wednesday.

The faries within Knockgrafton, for the song was a fairy melody, when they heard this addition to their tune, were so much delighted, that with instant resolve it was determined to bring the mortal among them, whose musical skill so far exceeded theirs, and little Lusraore was conveyed into their company with the eddying speed of a whirlwind.

Glorious to behold was the sight that burst upon him as he came down through the moat, tvdrling round and round and round with the lightness of a straw, to the sweetest music that kept time to his motion. The greatest honour was then paid him, for he was put up above all the musicians, and he had servants tending upon him, and everything to his heart's content, and a hearty welcome to all; and in short he was made as much of as if he had been the first man in the land.

Presently Lusmore saw a great consultation going forward among the fairies, and, notwithstanding all their civility, he felt very much frightened, until one, stepping out from the rest, came up to him, and said,—

"Lusmore! Lusmore! Doubt not, nor deplore, For the hump which you bore On your back is no more !— Look down on the floor, And view it, Lusmore ! "

When these words were said, poor little Lusmore
felt himself so light, and so happy, that he
thought he could liave bounded at one jump over
c
the moon, like the cow in the history of the cat and the fiddle; and he saw, with inexpressible pleasure, his hump tumble down upon the ground from his shoulders. He then tried to lift up his head, and he did so with becoming caution, fearing that he might knock it against the ceiling of the grand hall, where he was; he looked round and round again with the greatest wonder and delight upon everything, which appeared more and more beautiful; and, overpowered at beliold-ing such a resplendent scene, his head grew dizzy, and his eyesight became dim. At last he fell into a sound sleep, and when he awoke, he found that it was broad daylight, the sun shining brightly, the birds singing sweet; and that he was lying just at the foot of the moat of Knock-grafton, with the cows and sheep grazing peaceably round about him. The first thing Lusmore did, after saying his prayers, was to put his hand behind to feel for his hump, but no sign of oni* was there on his back, and he looked at himself with great pride, for he had now become a well- shaped dapper little fellow; and more than that, he found himself in a full suit of new clothes, which he concluded the fairies had made for him.

Towards Cappagh he went, stepping out as lightly, and springing up at every step, as if he had been all his life a dancing-master. Not a creature who met Lusmore knew him without his hump, and he had great work to persuade every one that he was the same man— in truth he was not, so far as outward appearance went.

Of course it was not long before the story of Lusmore's hump got about, and a great wonder was made of it. Through the country, for miles round, it was the talk of every one, high and low.

One morning, as Lusmore was sitting contented enough at his cabin-door, up came an old woman to liim, and asked if he could direct her to Cappagh.

" I need give you no directions, my good woman," said Lusmore, " for this is Cappagh; and who do you want here ?"

" I have come," said the woman, " out of Decie's country, in the county of Waterford, looking after one Lusmore, who, I have heard tell, had his hump taken off by the fairies: for there is a son of a gossip of mine has got a hump on him that will be his death; and may be, if he could use the same charm as Lusmore, the hump may be taken off him. And now I have told you the reason of my coming so far: 't is to find out about this charm, if I can."

Lusmore, who was ever a good-natured little fellow, told the woman all the particulars, how he had raised the tune for the fairies at Knock-gi'afton, how his hump had been removed from his shoulders, and how he had got a new suit of clothes into the bargain.

The woman thanked him very much, and then went away quite happy and easy in her own mind. AVhen she came back to her gossip's house, in the county Waterford, she told her everything that Lusmore had said, and they put the little humpbacked man, who was a peevish and cunning c2

creature from his birth, upon a car, and took him all the way across the country. It was a long journey, but they did not care for that, so the hump was taken from off him ; and they brought him, just at nightfall, and left him under the old moat of Knockgrafton.

Jack Madden, for that was the humpy man's name, had not been sitting there long when he heard the tune going on within the moat much sweeter than before; for the fairies were singing it the way Lusmore had settled their music for them, and the song was going on: Da Luan^ Da Morty Da Luan, Da Mort, Da Luan, Da Mort, augus Da Cadine, without ever stopping. Jack Madden, who was in a great hurry to get quit of his hump, never thought of waiting until the fairies had done, or watching for a fit opportunity to raise the tune higher again than Lusmore had: 80 having heard them sing it over seven times without stopping, out he bawls, never minding the time, or the humour of the tune, or how he could bring his words in properly, auffus da Cadine augus Da Hena*, thinking that if one day was good, two were better; and that, if Lusmore had one new suit of clothes given to him, he should have two.

No sooner had the words passed his lips than he was taken up and whisked into the moat with prodigious force; and the fairies came crowding round about him with great anger, screeching and screaming, and roaring out, " AVho spoiled our tune? who spoiled our tune?" and one stepped up to him above all the rest, and said—

* And Wednesday and Thursday.

" Jack Madden '. Jack Madden! Your words came so bad in The tune we feel glad in;—This castle you're had in, That your life we may sadden ; Here's two humps for Jack Madden !"

And twenty of the strongest fairies brought Lus-more's hump and put it down upon poor Jack's back, over his own, where it became fixed as firmly as if it was nailed on with twelvepenny nails, by the best carpenter that ever drove one. Out of their castle they then kicked him; and in the morning when Jack Maddens mother and her gossip came to look after their little man, they found him half dead, lying at the foot of the moat, with the other hump upon his back. "Well, to be sure, how they did look at each other! but they were afraid to say anything, lest a hump might be put upon their own shoulders: home they brought the unlucky Jack Madden with them, as downcast in their hearts and their looks as" ever two gossips were; and what through the weight of his other hump, and the long journey, be died soon after, leafing, they say, his heavy curse to any one who would go to listen to fairy tunes again.

THE PRIESTS SUPPER.
IV.
It is said by those who ought to understand such things, that the good people, or the fairies, are some of the angels who were turned out of heaven, and who landed on their feet in this world, while the rest of their companions, who had more sin to sink them, went down further

to a worse place. Be this as it may, there was a merry troop of the fairies, dancing and playing all manner of wild pranks on a bright moonlight evening towards the end of September. The scene of their merriment was not far distant from Inchegeela, in the west of the county Cork—a poor village, although it had a barrack for soldiers; but great mountains and barren rocks, like those round about it, are enough to strike poverty into any place: however, as the fairies can have everything they want for wishing, poverty does not trouble them much, and all their care is to seek out unfrequented nooks and places where it is not likely any one will come to spoil their sport.

On a nice green sod by the river's side were the little fellows dancing in a ring as gaily as may be, with their red caps wagging about at every bound in the moonshine; and so light were these bounds, that the lobes of dew, although they trembled, under their feet, were not disturbed by

their capering. Thus did they carry on their gambols, spinning round and round, and twirling and bobbing, and diving and going through all manner of figures, until one of them chirped out—

" Cease, cease, with your drumming.
Here's an end to our mumming ; , ^
By my smell
I can tell A priest this way is coming!"

And away every one of the fairies scampered off as hard as they could, concealing themselves under the green leaves of the lusmore, where, if their little red caps should happen to peep out, they would only look like its crimson bells; and more hid themselves in the hollow of stones, or at the shady side of brambles, and others under the bank of the river, and in holes and crannies of one kind or another.

The fairy speaker was not mistaken ; for along the road, which was within view of the river, came Father Horrigan on his pony, thinking to himself that as it was so late he would make an end of his journey at the first cabin he came to. xVccording to this determination, he stopped at the dwelling of Dermod Leary, lifted the latch, and entered with " My blessing on all here."

I need not say that Father Horrigan was a welcome guest wherever he went, for no man was more pious or better beloved in the country. Now it was a great trouble to Dermod that he had nothmg to offer his reverence for supper as a relish to the potatoes which " the old woman," for so Dermod called his wife, though she was

not much past twenty, had down boiling in the pot over the fire: he thouglit of the net which he had set in the river, but as it had been there only a short time, the chances were against his finding a fish in it. " No matter," thought Dennod, " there can be no harm in stepping down to try, and may be as I want the fisli for the priest's supper, that one will be there before me."

Down to the river side went Dermod, and he found in the net as fine a salmon as ever jumped in the bright waters of " the spreading Lee;" but as he was going to take it out, the net was pulled from him, he could not tell how or by whom, and away got the salmon, and went swimming along with the current as gaily as if nothing had happened.

Dermod looked sorrowfully at the wake which the fish had left upon the water, shining like a line of silver in the moonlight, and then, with an angry motion of his right hand, and a stamp of his foot, gave vent to his feelings by muttering, " May bitter bad luck attend you night and day for a blackguard schemer of a salmon, wherever you go ! You ought to be ashamed of yourself, if there's any shame in you, to give me the slip after this fashion ! And I'm clear in my own mind you'll come to no good, for some kind of evil thing or other helped you—did I not feel it pull the net against me as strong as the devil himself?"

" That's not true for you," said one of the little fairies, who had scampered off at the approach of the priest, coming up to Dennod Leary, with a whole throng of companions at his heels;

" there was only a dozen and a half of ns pulling against you."

Dennod gazed on the tiny speaker with wonder, who continued: " Make yourself noways uneasy about the priest's supper ; for if you will go back and ask him one question from us, there will be as fine a supper as ever was put on a table spread out before him in less than no time."

" I'll have nothing at all to do with you," replied Dermod, in a tone of determination ; and after a pause he added, " I'm much obliged to you for your offer, sir, but I know better than to sell myself to you or the like of you for a supper; and more than that, I know Father Horrigan has more regard for my soul than to wish me to pledge it for ever, out of regard to anything you could put before him—so there's an end of the matter."

The little speaker, with a pertinacity not to be repulsed by Dermod's manner, continued, " Will you ask the priest one civil question for us ?"

Dermod considered for some time, and he was right in doing so, but he thought that no one could come to harm out of asking a civil question. " I see no objection to do that same, gentlemen," said Dermod; " but I will have nothing in life to do with your supper,—mind that."

" Then," said the little speaking fairy, whilst the rest came crowding after him from all parts, " go and ask Father Horrigan to tell us whether our souls will be saved at the last day, like the soiils of good Christians; and if you wish us well, bring back word what he says without delay."

Away went Dennod to his cabin, where ho

found the potatoes thrown out on the table, and his good wife handing the biggest of them all, a beautiful laughing red apple, smoking like a hard-ridden horse on a frosty night, over to Father Horrigan.

" Please your reverence," said Dermod, after some hesitation, " may I make bold to ask your honour one question ?"

" What may that be?" said Father Horrigan.

" Why, then, begging your reverence's pardon for my freedom, it is, if the souls of the good people are to be saved at the last day?"

" Who bid you ask me that question, Leary ?" said the priest, fixing his eyes upon him very sternly, which Dermod could not stand before at aU.

" I'll tell no lies about the matter, and nothing in life but the truth," said Dermod. " It was the good people themselves who sent me to ask the question, and there they are in thousands down on the bank of the river waiting for me to go back with the answer."

" Go back by all means," said the priest, " and tell them, if they want to know, to come here to me themselves, and I'll answer that or any other question they are pleased to ask, with the greatest pleasure in life."

Dermod accordingly returned to the fairies, who came swarming round about him to hear what the priest had said in reply; and Dermod spoke out among them like a bold man as he was : but when they heard that they must go to the priest, away they fled, some here and more there; and some this way and more that, whisking by

poor Dermod so fast and in such numbers, that he was quite bewildered.

When lie came to himself, which was not for a long time, back he went to his cabin and ate his dry potatoes along with Father Horrigan, who made quite light of the thing; but Dermod could not help thinking it a mighty hard case that his reverence, whose words had the power to banish the fairies at such a rate, should have no sort of relish to his supper, and that the fine salmon he had in the net should have been got away from him in such a manner.

THE

BREWERY OF EGG-SHELLS.

It may be considered impertinent, were I to explain what is meant by a changeling; both Shakspeare and Spenser have already done so, and who is there unacquainted with the Midsummer Night's Dream * and the Fairy Queen ? f

Now Mrs. Sullivan fancied that her youngest child had been changed by " fairies' theft," to use Spenser's words, and certainly appearances warranted such a conclusion; for in one night her healthy, blue-eyed boy had become shrivelled up into almost nothing, and never ceased squalling and crying. This naturally made poor Mrs. Sullivan very unhappy ; and all the neighbours, by way of comforting her, said, that her own child was, beyond any kind of doubt, with the good people, and that one of themselves had been put in his place.

Mrs. Sullivan, of course, could not disbelieve what every one told her, but she did not wish to hurt the thing; for although its face was so withered, and its body wasted away to a mere skeleton, it had still a strong resemblance to her own boy ; she, therefore, could not find it in her heart to roast it alive on the griddle, or to bum its nose off with the red-hot tongs, or to throw it

♦ Act ii. sc. 1. t Book 1. canto 10.

olit in the snow on the road side, notwithstanding these, and several like proceedings, were strongly recommended to her for the recovery of her child.

One day who should Mrs. Sullivan meet but a cunning woman, well known about the country by the name of Ellen Leah (or Grey Ellen). She had the gift, however she got it, of telling where the dead were, and what was good for the rest of their souls; and could charm away warts and wens, and do a great many wonderful things of the same nature.

" You're in grief this morning, Mrs. Sullivan," were the first words of Ellen Leah to her.

" You may say that, EUen," said Mrs. Sullivan, " and good cause I have to be in grief, for there was my own fine child whipped ofi" from me out of his cradle, without as much as by your leave, or ask your pardon, and an ugly dony bit of a shrivelled-up fairy put in his place; no wonder then that you see me in grief, Ellen."

" Small blame to you, Mrs. Sullivan," said Ellen Leah; " but are you sure 't is a fairy ? "

"Sure!" echoed Mrs. Sullivan, " sure enough am I to my sorrow, and can I doubt my own two eyes ? Every mother's soul must feel for me !"

" Will you take an old woman's advice ?" said Ellen Leah, fixing her wild and mysterious gaze upon the .unhappy mother; and, after a pause, she added, " but may be you'll call it foolish ?"

"Can you get me back my child,—my own child, Ellen ?" said Mrs. Sullivan with great energy.

" If you do as I bid you," returned Ellen Leah,

" you'll know." Mrs. Sullivan was silent m expectation, and Ellen continued. "Put down the big pot, full of water, on the fire, and make it boil like mad; then get a dozen new-laid eggs, break them, and keep the shells, but throw away the. rest; when that is done, put the shells in the pot of boiling water, and you will soon know whether it is your own boy or a fairy. If you find that it is a fairy in the cradle, take the red-hot poker and cram it down his ugly throat, and you will not have much trouble with him after that, I promise you."

Home went Mrs. Sullivan, and did as Ellen Leah desired. She put the pot in the fire, and plenty of turf under it, and set the water boiling at such a rate, that if ever water was red hot— it surely was.

The child was lying for a wonder quite easy and quiet in the cradle, every now and then cocking his eye, that would twinkle as keen as a star in a frosty night, over at the great fire, and the big pot upon it; and he looked on with great attention at Mrs. Sullivan breaking the eggs, and putting down the egg-shells to boil. At last he asked, with the voice of a very old man, " "What are you doing, mammy?"

Mrs. Sullivan's heart, as she said herself, was up in her mouth ready to choke her, at hearing the child speak. But she contrived to put the poker in the fire, and to answer, without making any wonder at the words, " I'm brewing, a tick" (my son).

"And what are you brewing, mammy?" said the little imp, whose supernatural gift of speec4i

now proved beyond question that he was a fairy substitute.

" I wish the poker was red," thought JMrs. SuUivaii; but it was a large one, and took a longtime heating: so she determined to keep him in talk until the poker was in a proper state to thrust down his throat, and therefore repeated the question.

" Is it what I'm brewing, a vick" said she, " you want to know ?"

" Yes, mammy : what are you brewing ?" returned the fairy.

" Egg-shells, a vick" said JMrs. Sullivan.

" Oh!" shrieked the imp, starting up in the cradle, and clapping his hands together, " I'm fifteen hundred years in the world, and I never saw a brewery of egg-shells before !" The poker was by this time quite red, and Mrs. Sullivan seizing it, ran furiously towards the cradle; but somehow or other her foot slipped, and she fell flat on the floor, and the poker flew out of her hand to the other end of the house. However, she got up, without much loss of time, and went to the cradle intending to pitch the wicked thing that was in it into the pot of boiling water, when there she saw her own child in a sweet sleep, one of his soft round arms rested upon the pillow— his features were as placid as if their repose had never been disturbed, save the rosy mouth which moved with a gentle and regular breathing.

Who can tell the feelings of a mother when she looks upon her sleeping child ? Why should I, therefore, endeavour to describe those of Mrs. Sullivan at again beholding her long-lost boy ?

THE BREWERY OP EGG-SHELLS.

The fountain of her heart overflowed with the excess of joy — and she wept!—tears trickled silently down her cheeks, nor did she strive to check them—they were tears not of sorrow, hut of happiness.

LEGEND OF BOTTLE HILL.

VI.

" Come listen to a tale of times of old, Come listen to me "

It was in the good days, when the little people, most impudently called fairies, were more frequently seen than they are in these unbelieving times, that a farmer, named Mick Purcell, rented a few acres of barren ground in the neighbourhood of the once celebrated preceptory of Mourne, situated about three miles from Mallow, and thirteen from "the beautiful city called Cork." Mick had a wife and family: they all did what they could, and that was but little, for the poor man had no child grown up big enough to help him in his work : and all the poor woman could do was to mind the children, and to milk the one cow, and to boil the potatoes, and carry the eggs to market to Mallow; but with all they could do, 't was hard enough on them to pay the rent. Well, they did manage it for a good while; but at last came a bad year, and the little grain of oats was all spoiled, and the chickens died of the pip, and the pig got the measles,— she was sold in Mallow and brought almost nothing; and poor Mick found that he hadn't enough to half pay his rent, and two gales were due.

" Why, then, Molly," says he, " what 'll we do?"

"Wislia, then, mavournene, what would you do but take the cow to the fair of Cork and sell her ?" says she; " and Monday is fair day, and so you must go to-morrow, that the poor beast may be rested again the fair."

" And what 'll we do when she's gone?" says Mick, sorrowfully.

" Never a know I know, Mick ; but sure God won't leave us without Him, Mick; and you know how good He was to us when poor little Billy was sick, and we had nothing at all for him to take, that good doctor gentleman at Ballydahin come riding and asking for a drink of milk ; and how he gave us two shillings; and how he sent the things and bottles for the child, and gave me * my breakfast when I went over to ask a question, so he did: and how he came to see Billy, and never left off his goodness till he was quite well ? "

" Oh! you are always that way, Molly, and I believe you are right after all, so I won't be sorry for selling the cow; but I'll go to-morrow, and you must put a needle and thread through my coat, for you know 't is ripped under the arm."

Molly told him he should have every thing right; and about twelve o'clock next day he left her, getting a charge not to sell his cow except for the highest penny. Mick promised to mind it, and went his way along the road. He drove his cow slowly through the little stream which crosses it, and runs by the old walls of]\Ioume. As he passed he glanced his eye upon the towers and one of the old elder trees, which were only then little bits of switches.

" Oh, then, if I only had half the money that's

buried in you, 't isn't driving this poor cow I'd be now! Why, then, isn't it too bad tliat it should be there covered over with earth, and many a one besides me wanting? Well, if it's God's will, I'll have some money myself coming back."

So saying, he moved on after his beast; 't was a fine day, and the sun shone brightly on the walls of the old abbey as he passed under them; he then crossed an extensive mountain tract, and after six long miles he came to the top of that hill—Bottle Hill't is called now, but that was not the name of it then, and just there a man overtook him. " Good morrow," says he. " Good morrow," kindly, says Mick, looking at the stranger, who was a little man, you'd almost call him a dwarf, only he wasn't quite so little neither: he had a bit of an old, wrinkled, yellow face, for all the world like a dried cauliflower, only he had a sharp little nose, and red eyes, and white hair, and his lips were not red, but all his face was one colour, and his eyes never were quiet, but looking at every thing, and although they were red, they made Alick feel quite cold when he looked at them. In truth he did not much like the little man's company; and he couldn't see one bit of his legs, nor his body; for, though the day was warm, he was all wrapped up in a big great-coat.]\Iick drove his cow something faster, but the little man kept up with him. Mick didn't know how he walked, for he was almost afraid to look at him, and to cross himself, for fear the old man would be angry. Yet he thought his fellow-traveller did not seem to walk like other men, nor to put one foot before the other, but to glide over the rough 1)2

road, and rough enough it was, like a shadow, without noise and without effort. Mick's heart trembled within him, and he said a prayer to himself, wising he hadn't come out that day, or that he was on Fair-Hill, or that he hadn't the cow to mind, that he might run away from the bad thing —when, in the midst of his fears, he was again addressed by his companion.

" Where are you going with the cow, honest man?"

" To the fair of Cork then," says Mick, trembling at the shrill and piercing tones of the voice.

" Are you going to sell herl" said the stranger.

" Why, then, what else am I going for but to sell her?"

" Will you sell her to me ?"

Mick started—he was afraid to have any thing to do with the little man, and he was more afraid to say no.

" What'11 you give for her ?" at last says he.

" I '11 tell you what, I '11 give you this bottle," said the little one, pulling a bottle from under his coat.

Mick looked at him and the bottle, and, in spite of his terror, he could not help bursting into a loud fit of laughter.

" Laugh if you will," said the little man, " but I tell you this bottle is better for you than all the money you will get for the cow in Cork—ay, than ten thousand times as much."

Mick laughed again. " Why then," says he, " do you think I am such a fool as to give my good cow for a bottle—and an empty one, too ? indeed, then, I won't."

" You had better give me the cow, and take the bottle—you'll not be sorry for it."

" Why, then, and what would Molly say? I'd never hear the end of it; and how would I pay the rent ? and what would we all do without a penny of money ?"

" I tell you this bottle is better to you than money; take it, and give me the cow. I ask you for the last time, Mick Purcell."

Mick started.

" How does he know my name?" thought he.

The stranger proceeded: " Mick Purcell, I know you, and I have a regard for you ; therefore do as I warn you, or you may be soiTy for it. How do you know but your cow will die before you get to Cork ?"

Mick was going to say " God forbid!" but the little man went on (and he was too attentive to say any thing to stop him; for Mick was a very civil man, and he knew better than to interrupt a gentleman, and that's what many people, that hold their heads higher, don't mind now).

" And how do you know but there will be much cattle at the fair, and you will get a bad price, or may be you might be robbed when you are coming home? but what need I talk more to you, when you are determined to throw away your luck, Mick Purcell?"

" Oh ! no, I woiild not throw away my luck, sir," said Mick; " and if I was sure the bottle was as good as you say, though I never liked an empty bottle, although I had drank what was in it, I'd give you the cow in the name "

" Never mind names," said the stranger, " but

38 LEGEND OF BOTTLE HILL.

give me the cow; I would not tell you a lie. Here, take the bottle, and when you go home do what I direct exactly."

Mick hesitated.

" Well then, good bye, I can stay no longer: once more, take it, and be rich; refuse it, and beg for your life, and see your children in poverty, and your wife dying for want: that will happen to you, Mick Purcell! " said the little man with a malicious grin, which made him look ten times more ugly than ever.

" May be 'tis true," said Mick, still hesitating: he did not know what to do—he could hardly help believing the old man, and at length in a fit of desperation he seized the bottle—" Take the cow," said he, " and if you are telling a lie, the curse of the poor will be on you."

" I care neither for your curses nor your blessings, but I have spoken truth, Mick Purcell, and that you will find to-night, if you do what I tell you."

" And what's that ?" says Mick.

" "When you go home, never mind if your wife is angry, but be quiet yourself, and make her sweep the room clean, set the table out right, and spread a clean cloth over it; then put the bottle on the ground, saying these words: ' Bottle, do your duty,' and you will see the end of it."

" And is this all ?" says Mick.

" No more," said the stranger. " Good bye, Mick Purcell—^you are a rich man."

"God grant it!" said Mick, as the old man moved after the cow, and Mick retraced the road towards his cabin; but he could not help turning

LEGEND OP BOTTLE HILL. 39

back his head, to look after the purchaser of his cow, who was nowhere to be seen.

"Lord between us and harm!" said Mick: " He can't belong to this earth; but where is the cow ? " She too was gone, and Mick went homeward muttering prayers, and holding fast the bottle.

" And what would I do if it broke ?" thought he. " Oh ! but I'll take care of that;" so he put it into his bosom, and went on anxious to prove his bottle, and doubting of the reception he should meet from his wife; balancing his anxieties with his expectation, his fears with his hopes, he reached home in the evening, and surprised his wife, sitting over the turf fire in the big chimney.

" Oh ! Mick, are you come back ? Sure you weren't at Cork all the way I What has happened to you ? Where is the cow ? Did you sell her ? How much money did you get for her ? AVhat news have you ? Tell us everything about it."

" Why then, Molly, if you'll give me time, I'll tell you all about it. If you want to know where the cow is, 'tisn't Mick can tell you, for the never a know does he know where she is now."

" Oh! then, you sold her; and where's the money ? "

" Arrah ! stop awhile, Molly, and I'll tell you all about it."

" But what is that bottle under your waistcoat ? " said Molly, spying its neck sticking out.

" Why, then, be easy now, can't you,' says Mick, " till I tell it to you ?" and putting the bottle on the table, " That's all I got for the cow."

His poor wife was thunderstruck. " All you got I and what good is that, Mick ? Oh ! I never thought you were such a fool; and what 11 we do for the rent, and what "

" Now, Molly," says Mick, " can't you hearken to reason ? Didn't I tell you how the old man, or whatsomever he was, met me,—no, he did not meet me neither, but he was there with me—on the big hill, and how he made me sell him the cow, and told me the bottle was the only thing for me ?"

" Yes, indeed, the only thing for you, you fool!" said Molly, seizing the bottle to hurl it at lier poor husband's liead; but Mick caught it, and quietly (for he minded the old man's advice) loosened his wife's grasp, and placed the bottle again in his bosom. Poor Molly sat down crying, while Mick told her his story, with many a crossing and blessinsj between him and harm. His wife could not help believing him, particularly as she had as much faith in fairies as she had in the pi'iest, who indeed never discouraged her belief in the fairies; may be, he didn't know she believed in them, and may be, he believed in them himself. She got up, however, without saying one word, and began to sweep the earthen floor with a bunch of heath; then she tidied up everything, and put out the long table, and spread the clean cloth, for she had only one, upon it, and Mick, placing the bottle on the ground, looked at it and said, " Bottle, do your duty."

" Look there ! look there, mammy 1" said his chubby eldest son, a boy about five years old—

" look there! look there I" and he sprang to his mother's side, as two tiny little fellows rose like light from the bottle, and in an instant covered the table with dishes and plates of gold and silver, full of the finest victuals that ever were seen, and when all was done went into the bottle again. Mick and his wife looked at everything with astonishment; they had never seen such plates and dishes before, and didn't think they could ever admire them enoiigh; the very sight almost took away their appetites; but at length Molly said, " Come and sit down, Mick, and try and eat a bit: sure you ought to be himgry after such a good day's work."

" Why, then, the man told no lie about the bottle."

Mick sat dowu, after putting the children to the table; and they made a hearty meal, though they couldn't taste half the dishes.

" Now," says Molly, " I wonder will those two good little gentlemen carry away these fine things again?" They waited, but no one came; so Molly put up the dishes and plates very carefully, saying, " Why, then, Mick, that was no lie sure enough ; but you'll be a rich man yet, Mick Pur-cell."

Mick and his wife and children went to their bed, not to sleep, but to settle about selling the fine things they did not want, and to take more land. Mick went to Cork and sold his plate, and bought a horse and cart, and began to show that he was making money; and they did all they could to keep the bottle a secret; but for all that, their landlord found it out, for he came to Mick one day, and asked him where he got all his money—sure it was not by the farm; and he bothered him so much, that at last Mick told him of the bottle. His landlord offered him a deal of money for it; but Mick would not give it, till at last he offered to give him all his farm for ever: so Mick, who was very rich, thought he'd never want any more money, and gave him the bottle:

but Mick was mistaken—he and his family spent money as if there was no end of it; and, to make the story short, they became poorer and poorer, till at last they had nothing left but one cow; and Mick once more drove his cow before him to seJl her at Cork fair, hoping to meet the old man and get another bottle. It was hardly daybreak when he left home, and he walked on at a good pace till he reached the big hill: the mists were sleeping in the valleys and curling like smoke-wreaths upon the brown heath around him. The sun rose on his left, and just at his feet a lark sprang from its grassy couch and poured forth its joyous matin song, ascending into the clear blue sky,

" Till its form like a speck in the airiness blending And thrilling with music, was melting in light"

Mick crossed himself, listening as he advanced to the sweet song of the lark, but thinking, notwithstanding, all the time of the little old man; when, just as he reached the summit of the hiU, and cast his eyes over the extensive prospect before and around him, he was startled and rejoiced by the same well-knoN\Ta voice :—" Well, Mick Purcell, I told you, you would be a rich man."

" Indeed, then, sure enough I was, that's no lie for you, sir. Good morning to you, but it is not rich I am now—but have you another bottle, for I want it now as much as I did long ago ; so if you have it, sir, here is the cow for it."

" And here is the bottle," said the old man, smiling ; " you know what to do with it."

" Oh ! then, sure I do, as good right I have."

" Well, farewell for ever, Mick Purcell: I told you, you would be a rich man."

" And good bye to you, sir," said Mick, as he turned back ; " and good luck to you, and good luck to the big hill—it wants a name—Bottle Hill.—Good bye, sir, goodbye ;" so Mick walked back as fast as he could, never looking after the white-faced little gentleman and the cow, so anxious was he to bring home the bottle. Well, he an-ived with it safely enough, and called out, as soon as he saw Molly, " Oh! sure, I've another bottle !"

" Arrah! then have you ? why, then, you're a lucky man, Mick Purcell, that's what you are."

In an instant she put everything right; and Mick, looking at his bottle, exultingly cried out, " Bottle, do your duty." In a twinkling, two great stout men with big cudgels issued from the bottle (I do not know how they got room in it), and belaboured poor Mick and his wife and all his family, till they lay on the floor, when in they went again. Mick, as soon as he recovered, got up and looked about him; he thought and thought, and at last he took up his wife and his children; and, leaving them to recover as well as they could.

he took the bottle under his coat, and went to his landlord, who had a great company : he got a servant to tell him he wanted to speak to him, and at last he came out to Mick, " "Well, what do you want now ? " " Nothing, sir, only I have another bottle." " Oh ! ho ! is it as good as the first ?" " Yes, sir, and better; if you like, I will show it to you before all the ladies and gentlemen."

" Come along, then," So saying, Mick was brought into the great hall, where he saw his old bottle standing high up on a shelf: " Ah ! ha!" says he to himself, " may be I won't have you by and by."

" Now," says his landlord, " show us your bottle." Mick set it on the floor, and uttered the words ; in a moment the landlord was tumbled on the floor; ladies and gentlemen, servants and all, were running and roaring, and sprawling, and kicking, and shrieking. Wine cups and salvers were knocked about in every direction, until the landlord called out, " Stop those two devils,

Mick Purcell, or I'll have you hanged !"

" They never shall stop," said Mick, " till I get my own bottle that I see up there at top of that shelf."

" Give it down to him, give it down to him, before we are all killed !" says the landlord.

Mick put the bottle in his bosom; in jumped the two men into the new bottle, and he carried the bottles home. I need not lengthen my story by telling how he got richer than ever, how his son married his landlord's only daughter, how he and his wife died when they were very old, and how

LEGEND OF BOTTLE HILL.

45

some of the servants, fighting at their wake, broke the bottles; bi;t still the hill has the name upon it; ay, and so 't will be always Bottle Hill to the end of the world, and so it ought, for it is a strange story.

THE
CONFESSIONS OF TOM BOURKE.

Tom Bourke lives in a low long form-house, resembling in outward appearance a large bam, placed at the bottom of the hill, just where the new road strikes off from the old one, leading from the town of Kilworth to that of Lismore. He is of a class of persons who are a sort of black swans in Ireland ; he is a wealthy farmer. Tom's father had, in the good old times, when a hundred pounds were no inconsiderable treasure, either to lend or spend, accommodated his landlord with that sum, at interest; and obtained, as a return for the civility, a long lease, about half-a-dozen times more valuable than the loan which procured it. The old man died worth several hundred pounds, the greater part of which, with his farm, he bequeathed to his son Tom. But, besides all this, Tom received from his father, upon his deathbed, another gift, far more valuable than worldly riches, greatly as he prized, and is still known to prize them. He was invested with the privilege, enjoyed by few of the sons of men, of communicating with those mysteripus beings called " the good people."

Tom Bourke is a little, stout, healthy, active

man, about fifty-five years of age. His hair is perfectly white, short and bushy behind, but rising in front erect and thick above his forehead, like a new clothes-brush. His eyes are of that kind which I have often observed with persons of a quick but limited intellect—they are small, grey, and lively. The large and projecting eyebrows under, or rather within, which they twinkle, give them an expression of shrewdness and intelligence, if not of cunning. And this is very much the character of the man. If you want to make a bargain with Tom Bourke, you must act as if you were a general besieging a town, and make your advances a long time before you can hope to obtain possession; if you march up boldly, and tell him at once your object, you are for the most part sure to have the gates closed in your teeth. Tom does not wish to part with what you wish to obtain, or another person has been speaking to him for the whole of the last week. Or, it may be, your proposal seems to meet the most favourable reception. " Very well, sir;" " That's true, sir;" "I'm very thankful to your honour," and other expressions of kindness and confidence, greet you in reply to every sentctnce; and you part from him wondering how he can have obtained the character which he universally bears, of being a man whom no one can make anything of in a bargain. But when you next meet him, the flattering illusion is dissolved: you find you are a great deal farther from your object than you were when you thought you had almost succeeded : his eye and his tongue express a total forgetfulness of what the mind within never lost

sight of for an instant; and you have to begin operations afresh, with the disadvantage of having put your adversary completely upon his guard.

Yet, although Tom Bourke is, whetlier from supernatural revealings, or (as many will think more probable) from the tell-truth, experience, so distrustful of mankind, and so close in his dealings with them, he is no misanthrope. No man loves better the pleasures of the genial board. The love of money, indeed, which is with him (and who will blame him ?) a very ruling propensity, and the gratification which it has received from habits of industry, sustained throughout a pretty long and successful life, have taught him the value of sobriety, dviring those seasons, at least, when a man's business requires him to keep possession of his senses. He has therefore a general rule, never to get drunk but on Sundays. But, in order that it should be a general one to all intents and purposes, he takes a method which, according to better logicians than he is, always proves the rule. He has many exceptions : among these, of course, are the evenings of all the fair and market days that happen in his neighbourhood ; so also all the days on which funerals, marriages, and christenings, take place among his friends within many miles of him. As to this last class of exceptions, it may appear at first very singular, that he is much more punctual in his attendance at the funerals than at the baptisms or weddings of his friends. This may be construed as an instance of disinterested affection for departed worth, very uncommon in this selfish world. But I am afraid that the motives which lead Tom Bourke

to pay more court to the dead than the living are precisely those which lead to the opposite conduct in the generality of mankind—a hope of future benefit and a fear of future evil. For the good people, who are a race as powerful as they are capricious, have their favourites among those who inhabit this world; often show their affection, by easing the objects of it from the load of this burdensome life ; and frequently reward or punish the living, according to the degree of reverence paid to the obsequies and the memory of the elected dead.

It is not easy to prevail on Tom to speak of those good people, with whom he is said to hold frequent and intimate communications. To the faithful, who believe in their power, and their occasional delegation of it to him, he seldom refuses, if properly asked, to exercise his high prerogative, when any unfortunate being is struck"" in his neighbourhood. Still, he will not be won unsued : he is at first difficult of persuasion, and must be overcome by a little gentle violence. On these occasions he is unusually solemn and mysterious, and if one word of reward be mentioned, he at once abandons the unhappy patient, such a pro-

* The term " fairy struck " is applied to paralytic affections, which are supposed to proceed from a blow given by the invisible hand of an offended fairy ; this belief, of course, creates fairy doctors, who by means of charms and mysterious journeys profejs to cure the afflicted. It is only fair to add, that the term has also a convivial acceptation, the fairies being not

unfrequently marie to bear the blame of the effects arising from too copious a sacrifice to the jolly god.

The importance attached to the manner and place of burial by the peasantry is almost incredible ; it is always a matter of consideration and often of dispute whether the deceased shall be buried with his or her " own people."

E

position being a direct insult to his supernatural superiors. It is true, that as the labourer is worthy of his hire, most persons, gifted as he is, do not scruple to receive a token of gratitude from the patients or their friends after their recovery.

To do Tom Bourke justice, he is on these occasions, as I have heard from many competent authorities, perfectly disinterested. Not many months since, he recovered a young woman (the sister of a tradesman living near him), who had been struck speechless after returning from a funeral, and had continued so for several days. He stedfastly refused receiving any compensation; saying, that even if he had not as much as would buy him his supper, he could take nothing in this case, because the girl had offended at the funeral one of i\\e good p&yple belonging to his own family, and though he would do her a kindness, he could take none from her.

About the time this last remarkable affair took place, my friend Mr. Martin, who is a neighbour of Tom's, had some business to transact with him, which it was exceedingly difficult to bring to a conclusion. At last Mr. Martin, having tried all quiet means, had recourse to a legal process, which brought Tom to reason, and the matter was arranged to their mutual satisfaction, and with perfect good-humour between the parties. The accommodation took place after dinner at Mr. Martin's house, and he invited Tom to walk into the parlour and take a glass of punch, made of some excellent potteen, which was on the table: he had long wished to draw out liis highly-endowed neighbour on the subject of his super-

natural powers, and as Mrs. Martin, who was in

the room, was rather a favourite of Tom's, this seemed a good opportunity.

" Well, Tom," said Mr. Martin, " that was a curious business of Molly Dwyer's, who recovered her speech so suddenly the other day."

" You may say that, sir," replied Tom Bourke; " but I had to travel far for it: no matter for that, now. Your health, ma'am," said he, turning to Mrs. Martin.

" Thank you, Tom. But I am told you had some trouble once in that way in your own family," said Mrs. Martin.

" So I had, ma'am ; trouble enough ; but you were only a child at that time."

" Come, Tom," said the hospitable Mr. Martin, interrupting him, " take another tumbler;" and he then added, " I wish you would tell us something of the manner in which so many of your children died. I am told they dropped off, one after another, by the same disorder, and that your eldest son was cured in a most extraordinary way, when the physicians had given over."

" 'Tis true for you, sir," returned Tom ; " your father, the doctor (God be good to him, I won't belie him in his grave) told me, when my fourth little boy was a week sick, that himself and Doctor BaiTy did all that man could do for him; but they could not keep him from going after the rest. No more they could, if the people that took away the rest wished to take him too. But they left him; and sorry to the heart I am I did not know before why they were taking my boys

from me; if I did, I would not be left trusting to two of 'em now."

" And how did you find it out, Tom?" inquired Mr, Martin,

" Why, then, I'U tell you, sir," said Bourke. " When your father said what I told you, I did not know very well what to do. I walked down the little hohereen^ you know, sir, that goes to the river side near Dick Heafy's ground; for 'twas a lonesome place, and I wanted to think of myself. I was heavy, sir, and my heart got weak in me, when I thought I was to lose my little boy; and I did not know well how to face his mother with the news, for she doted down upon him. Beside, she never got the better of all she cried at his brother's berrin (burying) the week before. As I was going down the bohereen, I met an old bo-cough*, that used to come about the place once or twice a year, and used always sleep in our bam while he staid in the neighbourhood. So he asked me how I was. ' Bad enough, Shamous (James),' says I. ' I'm sorry for your trouble,' says he; ' but you're a foolish man, Mr. Bourke. Your son would be well enough if you would only do what you ought with him.' ' What more can I do with him, Shamous?' says I: 'the doctors give him over.' ' The doctors know no more what ails him than they do what ails a cow when she stops her milk,' says Shamous: ' but go to such a one,' says he, telling me his name, ' and try what he'll say to you.'"

" And who was that, Tom ?" asked Mr. Martin.

* A peculiar class of beggars resembling the Gaberlunzie man o' Scotland.

" I could not tell you that, sir," said Bourke, with a mysterious look : " howsoever, you often saw him, and he does not live far from this. But I had a trial of him before; and if I went to him at first, may be I'd have now some of them that's gone, and so Shamous often told me. Well, sir, I went to this man, and he came with me to the house. By course, I did everything as he bid me. According to his order, I took the little boy out of the dwelling-house immediately, sick as he was, and made a bed for him and myself in the cow-house. Well, sir, I lay down by his side, in the bed, between two of the cows, and he fell asleep. He got into a perspiration, saving your presence, as if he was drawn through the river, and breathed hard, with a great i?n-pression (oppression) on his chest, and was very bad—very bad entirely through the night. I thought about twelve o'clock he was going at last, and I was just getting up to go call the man I told you of; but there was no occasion. My friends were getting the better of them that wanted to take him away from me. There was nobody in the cow-house but the child and myself. There was only one half-penny candle lighting, and that was stuck in the wall at the far end of the house. I had just enough of light where we were laying to see a person walking or standing near us : and there was no more noise than if it was a churchyard, except the cows chewing the fodder in the stalls. Just as I was thinking of getting up, as I told you^—I won't belie my father, sir—be was a good father to me—I saw him standing at the bed-side, holding out his

right hand to me, and leaning his other hand on the stick he used to carry when he was alive, and looking pleasant and smiling at me, all as if he was telling me not to be afeard, for I would not lose the child. 'Is that you, father?' says I. He said nothing. ' If that's you,' says I again, ' for the love of them that's gone, let me catch your hand.' And so he did, sir; and his hand was as soft as a child's. He stayed about as long as you'd be going from this to the gate below at the end of the avenue, and then went away. In less than a week the child was as well as if nothing ever ailed him; and there isn't to-night a healthier boy of nineteen, from this blessed house to the towTi of Ballyporeen, across the Kilworth mountains."

"But I think, Tom," said Mr. Martin, "it appears as if you are more indebted to your father than to the man recommended to you by Shamous; or do you suppose it was he who made favour with your enemies among the good people, and that then your father "

" I beg your pardon, sir," said Bourke, interrupting him; " but don't call them my enemies. 'T would not be wishing to me for a good deal to sit by when they are called so. No oflFence to you, sir.—Here's wishing you a good health and long life."

" I assure you," returned Mr. Martin, " I meant no offence, Tom; but was it not as I say? "

" I can't tell you that, sir," said Bourke ; "I'm bound down, sir. Howsoever, you may be sure the man I spoke of, and my father, and thoso they know, settled it between them."

There was a pause, of which Mrs. Martin took advantage to inquire of Tom, whether soraetliing remarkable had not happened about a goat and a pair of pigeons, at the time of his son's illness— circumstances often mysteriously hinted at by Tom.

" See that now," said he, returning to Mr, Martin, " how well she remembers it! True for you, ma'am. The goat I gave the mistress, your mother, when the doctors ordered her goats' whey."

Mrs. Martin nodded assent, and Tom Bourke continued—" Why, then, I'll tell you how that was. The goat was as well as e'er a goat ever was, for a month after she was sent to Killaan to your father's. The morning after the night I just told you of, before the child woke, his mother was standing at the gap, leading out of the barnyard into the road, and she saw two pigeons flying from the town of Kilworth, off the church, down towards her. Well, they never stopped, you see, till they came to the house on the hill at the other side of the river, facing our farm. They pitched upon the chimney of that house, and after looking about them for a minute or two, they flow straight across the river, and stopped on the ridge of the cow-house where the child and I were lying. Do you think they came there for nothing, sir ? "

" Certainly not, Tom," returned Mr. Martin.

" Well, the woman came in to me, frightened, and told me. She began to cry.—' Whisht, you fool!' says I : ' 't is all for the better.' 'Twas true for me. What do you think, ma'am; the goat that I gave your mother, that was seen

feeding at sunrise that morning by Jack Cronin, as merry as a bee, dropped down dead, without anybody knowing why, before Jack's face ; and at that very moment he saw two pigeons fly from the top of the house out of the town, towards the Lismore road. 'Twas at the same time my woman saw them, as I just told you."

" 'Twas very strange, indeed, Tom," said ^Ir. Martin; " I wish you could give us some explanation of it."

" I wish I could, sir," was Tom Bourke's answer; "but I'm bound down. I can't tell but what I'm allowed to tell, any more than a sentry is let walk more than his rounds."

" I think you said something of having had some former knowledge of the man that assisted in the cure of your son,' said Mr. Martin.

*' So I had, sir," returned Bourke. " I had a trial of that man. But that's neither here nor there. I can't tell you anything about that, sir. But would you like to know how he got his skill?"

" Oh ! very much, indeed," said Mr. Martin.

" But you can tell us his Christian name, that we may know him the better through the story," added Mrs. Martin. Tom Bourke paused for a minute to consider this proposition.

" AVell, I believe I may tell you that, any how; his name is Patrick. He was always a smart, active, 'cute boy, and would be a great clerk if he stuck to it. The first time I knew him, sir, was at my mother's wake. I was in great trouble, for I did not know where to bury her. Pier people and my father s people—I mean their friends^

sir, among the good people^ had the greatest battle tliat was known for many a year, at Dunmanway-cross, to see to whose churchyard she'd be taken. They fought for three nights, one after another, without being able to settle it. The neighbours wondered how long I was before I buried ray mother; but I had my reasons, though I could not tell them at that time. Well, sir, to make my story short, Patrick came on the fourth morning and told me he settled the business, and that day we buried her in Kilcrumper churchyard, with my father's people."

" He was a valuable friend, Tom," said Mrs. Martin, with difficulty suppressing a smile." " But you were about to tell how he became so skilful."

" So I will, and welcome," replied Bourke. " Your health, ma'am. I am drinking too much of this punch, sir; but to tell the truth, I never tasted the like of it: it goes down one's throat like sweet oil. But what was I going to say ?— Yes—well—Patrick, many a long year ago, was coming home from a herrin late in the evening, and walking by the side of the river, opposite the big inch*, near Ballyhefaan fordt. He had taken a drop, to be sure ; but he was only a little merry, as you may say, and knew very well what he was doing. The moon was shining, for it was in the month of August, and the river was as smooth and as bright as a looking-glass. He heard nothing for a long time but the fall of the water at

* Inch—low meadow ground near u river.

t A ford of the river Fuiiclieon (the Fanchin of Spenser), on the road leading from Fermoy to Araglin.

the mill wier about a mile down the river, and now and then the crying of the lambs on the other side of tlie river. All at once, there was a noise of a great number of people, laughing as if they'd break their hearts, and of a piper playing among them. It came from the inch at the other side of the ford, and he saw, through the mist that hung over the river, a whole crowd of people dancing on the inch. Patrick was as fond of a dance as he was of a glass, and that's saying enough for him; so he whipped* off his shoes and stockings, and away with him across tlie ford. After putting on his shoes and stockings at the other side of the river, he walked over to the crowd, and mixed with tliem for some time without being minded. He thought, sir, that he'd show them better dancing than any of themselves, for he was proud of his feet, sir, and good right he had, for there was not a boy in the same parish could foot a double or treble with him. But pwah !— his dancing was no more to theirs than mine would be to the mistress there. They did not seem as if they had a bone in their bodies, and they kept it up as if nothing could tire them. Patrick was 'shamed within himself, for he thought he had not his fellow in all the country roiind; and was going away, when a little old man, that was looking at the company for some time bitterly, as if he did not like what was going on, came up to him. ' Patrick,' says he. Patrick started, for he did not think anybody there knew him. ' Patrick,' says he, ' you're discouraged, and no wonder for you. But you

* t. «. " in the time of the crack of a whip," he took off his shoet and stockings.

have a friend near you. I'm your friend, and your father's friend, and I think worse (more) of your little finger than I do of all that are here, though they think no one is as good as themselves. Go into the ring and call for a lilt. Don't be afeard. I tell you the best of them did not do as well as you shall, if you will do as I bid you.' Patrick felt something within him as if he ought not to gainsay the old man. He went into the ring, and called the piper to play up the best double he had. And, sure enough, all that the others were able for was nothing to him! He bounded like an eel, now here and now there, as light as a feather, although the people could hear the music answered by bis steps, that beat time to every turn of it, like the left foot of the piper. He first danced a hornpipe on the ground. Then they got a table, and he danced a treble on it that drew down shouts from the whole company. At last he called for a trencher; and when they saw him, all as if he was spinning on it like a top, they did not know what to make of him. Some praised him for the best dancer that ever entered a ring; others hated him because he was better than themselves; although they had good right to think themselves better than him or any other man that never went the long journey."

" And what was the cause of his great success ?" inquired Mr. Martin.

" He could not help it, sir," replied Tom Bourke. " They that could make him do more than that made him do it. Howsomever, when lie had done, they wanted him to dance again, but he was tired, and they could not persuade him.

At last he got angry, and swore a big oath, saving your presence, tliat he would not dance a step more; and the word was hardly out of his mouth, when he found himself all alone, with nothing but a white cow grazing by his side."

" Did he ever discover why he was gifted with these extraordinary powers in the dance, Tom ?" said Mr. Martin.

" I'll tell you that too, sir," answered Bourke, " when I come to it. When he went home, sir, he was taken with a shivering, and went to bed ; and the next day they found he got the fever, or something like it, for he raved like as if he was mad. But they couldn't make out what it was he was saying, though he talked constant. The doctors gave him over. But it's little they know what ailed him. When he was, as you may say, about ten days sick, and everybody thought he was going, one of the neighbours came in to him with a man, a friend of his, from Ballinlacken, that was keeping with him some time before. I can't tell you his name either, only it was Darby. The minute Darby saw Patrick, he took a little bottle, with the juice of herbs in it, out of his pocket, and gave Patrick a drink of it. He did the same every day for three weeks, and then Patrick was able to walk about, as stout and as hearty as ever he was in his life. But he was a long time before he came to himself; and he used to walk the whole day sometimes by the ditch side, talking to himself, like as if there was some one along with him. And so there was, surely, or he wouldn't be the man he is to-day."

" I suppose it was from some such companion he learned his skill," said Mr. Martin,

" You have it all now, sir," replied Bourke. " Darby told him his friends were satisfied with what he did the night of the dance ; and though they couldn't hinder the fever, they'd bring him over it, and teach him more than many knew beside him. And so they did. For you see all the people he met on the inch that night were friends of a different faction ; only the old man that spoke to him; he was a friend of Patrick's family, and it went again' his heart, you see, that the others were so light and active, and he was bitter in himself to hear 'em boasting how they'd dance with any set in the whole country round. So he gave Patrick the gift that night, and afterwards, gave him the skill that makes him the wonder of all that know him. And to be sure it was only learning he was that time when he was wandering in his mind after the fever."

" I have heard many strange stories about that inch near Ballyhefaan ford," said Mr. Martin. " 'Tis a great place for the good people, isn't it, Tom?"

" You may say that, sir," returned Bourke. " I could tell you a great deal about it. Many a time I sat for as good as two hours by moonlight, at th' other side of the river, looking at 'em playing goal as if they'd break their hearts over it; with their coats and waistcoats off, and white liandkerchiefs on the heads of one party, and red ones on th' other, just as you'd see on a Svmday in Mr. Simming's big field. I saw 'em one night play till the moon set, without one party being able to take the ball from th' other. I'm sure they were going to fight, only 'twas near morning. I'm told your grandfather, ma'am, used to see 'em there, too," said Bourke, turning to Mrs. Martin.

" So I have been told, Tom," replied Mrs. Martin. "But don't they say that the churchyard of Kilcrumper * is just as favourite a place with the good people, as Ballyhefaan inch."

" Why, then, may be, you never heard, ma'am, what happened to Davy Roche in that same churchyard," said Bourke; and turning to Mr. Martin, added, " 't was a long time before he went into your service, sir. He was walking home, of an evening, from the fair of Kilcummer, a little merry, to be sure, after the day, and he came up with a berrin. So he walked along with it, and thought it very queer, that he did not know a mother's soul in the crowd, but one man, and he was sure that man was dead many years afore. Howsomever, he went on with the berrin, till they came to Kilcrumper churchyard ; and faith he went in and staid with the rest, to see the corpse buried. As soon as the grave was covered, what should they do but gather about a piper that come along with 'em, and fall to dancing as if it was a wedding. Davy longed to be among 'em (for he hadn't a bad foot of his own, that time, whatever he may now) ; but he was loath to begin, because they all seemed strange to him, only the man I told you that he thought was dead. Well, at last this man saw what Davy wanted, and came

* About tno hundred yards off the Dublin mail-coach road, nearly mid-way between Kilworlb and Fermoy.

up to him. ' Davy,' says he,' take out a partner, and show what you can do, but take care and don't offer to kiss her,* ' That I won't,' says Davy, ' although her lips were made of honey.' And with that he made his bow to the purtiest girl in the ring, and he and she began to dance. 'Twas a jig they danced, and they did it to th' admiration, do you see, of all that were there. 'Twas all very well till the jig was over; but just as they had done, Davy, for he had a drop in, and was warm with the dancing, forgot himself, and kissed his partner, according to custom. The smack was no sooner off of his lips, you see, than he was left alone in the churchyard, without a creature near him, and all he could see was the tall tombstones. Davy said they seemed as if they were dancing too, but I suppose that was only the wonder that happened him, and he being a little in drink. Howsomever, he foimd it was a great many hours later than he thought it; 't was near morning when he came home; but they couldn't get a word out of him till the next day, when he 'woke out of a dead sleep about twelve o'clock."

When Tom had finished the account of Davy Roche and the berrin, it became quite evident that spirits of some sort were working too strong within him to admit of his telling many more tales of the good people. Tom seemed conscious of this.—He muttered for a few minutes broken sentences concerning churchyards, river-sides, leprechans, and dina magh, which were quite unintelligible, perhaps to himself, certainly to Mr. Martin and his lady. At length he made a slight motion of the head upwards, as if he would say,

" I can talk no more;" stretched his arm on the table, upon which he placed the empty tumbler slowly, and with the most knowing and cautious air ; and rising from his chair, walked, or rather rolled, to the parlour-door. Here he turned round to face his host and hostess ; but after various ineffectual attempts to bid them good night, the words, as they rose, being always choked by a violent hiccup, while the door, which he held by the handle, swung to and fro, carrpng his unyielding body along with it, he was obliged to depart in silence. The cow-boy, sent by Tom's wife, who knew well what sort of allure -ment detained him, when he remained out after a certain hour, was in attendance to conduct his master home. I have no doubt that he returned without meeting any material injury, as I know that within the last month, he was, to use his o\\ti words, " As stout and hearty a man as any of his age in the county Cork."

VIII.

John Mulligan was as fine an old fellow as ever threw a Carlow spur into the sides of a horse. He was, besides, as jolly a boon companion over a jug of punch as you would meet from Camsore Point to Bloody Farland. And a good horse he used to ride; and a stifter jug of punch than his was not in nineteen baronies. May be he stuck more to it than he ought to have done—^but that is nothing whatever to the story I am going to tell.

John believed devoutly in fairies ; and an angry man was he if you doubted them. He had more fairy stories than would make, if properly printed in a rivulet of print running down a meadow of margin, two thick quartos for Mr. Murray, of Albemarle-street; all of which he used to tell on all occasions that he could find listeners. Many believed his stories—many more did not believe them—but nobody, in process of time, used to contradict the old gentleman, for it was a pity to vex him. But he had a couple of young neighbours who were just come down from their first vacation in Trinity College to spend the summer months with an uncle of theirs, Mr. Whaley, an old Cromwellian, who lived at BallybegmuUina-hone, and they were too full of logic to let the old man have his own way undisputed.

F

Every story he told they laughed at, and said that it was impossible—that it was merely old woman's gabble, and other such things. When he would insist that all his stories were derived from the most credible sources—nay, that some of them had been told him by his own grandmother, a very respectable old lady, but slightly affected in her faculties, as things that came under her own knowledge—they cut the matter short by declaring that she was in her dotage, and at the best of times had a strong propensity to pulling a long bow.

" But," said they, " Jack Mulligan, did you ever see a fairy yourself?"

" Never," was the reply.—" Never, as I am a man of honour and credit."

" Well, then," they answered, " until you do, do not be bothering us with any more tales of my grandmother."

Jack was particularly nettled at this, and took up the cudgels for his grandmother; but the younkers were too sharp for him, and finally he got into a passion, as people generally do who have the worst of an argument. This evening— it was at their uncle's, an old crony of his, with whom he had dined—he had taken a large portion of his usual beverage, and was quite riotous. He at last got up in a passion, ordered his horse, and, in spite of his host's entreaties, galloped off, although he had intended to have slept there; declaring that he would not have anything more to do with a pair of jackanapes puppies, who, because they had learned how to read good-for-nothing books in cramp wi-iting, and were taught by a parcel of

wiggy, red-snouted, prating prigs, (" not," added he, " however, that I say a man may not be a good man and have a red nose,") they imagined they knew more than a man who had held buckle and tongue together facing the wind of the world for five dozen years.

He rode off in a fret, and galloped as hard as his horse Shaunbuie could powder away over the limestone. "Damn it!" hiccuped he, "Lord pardon me for swearing! the brats had me in one thing—I never did see a fairy; and I would give up five as good acres as ever grew apple-potatoes to get a glimpse of one—and by the powers ! what is that?"

He looked, and saw a gallant spectacle. His road lay by a noble demesne, gi'acefully sprinkled with trees, not thickly planted as in a dark forest, but disposed, now in clumps of five or six, now standing singly, towering over the plain of verdure around them as a beautiful promontory arising out of the sea. He had come right opposite the glory of the wood. It was an oak, which in the oldest title-deeds of the county, and they were at least five hundred years old, was called the old oak of Ballinghassig. Age had hollowed its centre, but its massy boughs still waved with their dark serrated foliage. The moon was shining on it bright. If I were a poet, like Mr. Wordsworth, I should tell you how the beautiful light was broken into a thousand different fragments—and how it filled the entii'e tree with a glorious flood, bathing every particular leaf, and showing forth every particular bough ; but, as I am not a poet, I shall go on with mv storv. By this light Jack saw a f2

brilliant company of lovely little forms dancing under the oak with an xinsteady and rolling motion. The company was large. Some spread out far beyond the farthest boundary of the shadow of the oak's branches—some were seen glancing through the flashes of liglit shining through its leaves—some were barely visible, nestling under the trunk—some no doubt were entirely concealed from his eyes. Never did man see anything more beautiful. They were not three inches in height, but they were white as the driven snow, and beyond number numberless. Jack threw the bridle over his horse's neck, and drew up to the low wall which bounded the demesne, and leaning over it, surveyed, with infinite delight, their diversified gambols. By looking long at them, he soon saw objects which had not struck him at first; in particular that in the middle was a chief of superior stature, round whom the group appeared to move. He gazed so long that he was quite overcome with joy, and could not help shouting out, " Bravo ! little fellow," said he, " well kicked and strong." But the instant he uttered the words the night was darkened, and the fairies vanished with the speed of lightning.

" I wish," said Jack, " I had held my tongue; but no matter now. I shall just turn bridle about and go back to BallybegmuUinahone Castle, and beat the young Master Whaleys, fine reasoners as they think themselves, out of the field clean."

No sooner said than done: and Jack was back again as if upon the wings of the wind. He rapped fiercely at the door, and called aloud for the two coUesrians.

• Halloo !" said he, " young Flatcaps, come down now, if you dare. Come down, if you dare, and I shall oive you oc-oc-ocular demonstration of the truth of what I was saying."

Old Whaley put his head out of the window, and said, " Jack Mulligan, what brings you back so soon?"

" The fairies," shouted Jack ; " the fairies!" " I am afraid," muttered the Lord of Ballybeg-mullinahone, " the last glass you took was too little watered; but, no matter—come in and cool yourself over a tumbler of punch."

He came in and sat down again at table. In great spirits he told his story;—how he had seen thousands and tens of thousands of fairies dancing about the old oak of Ballinghassig; he described their beautiful dresses of shining silver; their flat-crowned hats, glittering in the moonbeams; and the princely stature and demeanour of the central figure. He added, that he heard them singing and playing the most enchanting music ; but this was merely imagination.

The young men laughed, but Jack held his ground. " Suppose," said one of the lads, " we join company with you on the road, and ride along to the place, where you saw that fine company of fairies?"

" Done!" cried Jack; "but I will not promise that you will find them there, for I saw them scudding up in the sky like a flight of bees, and heard their wings whizzing through the air." This, you know, was a bounce, for Jack had heard no such thing.

Ofi" rode the three, and came to the demesne of Oakwood. They arrived at the wall flanking the

field where stood the great oak ; and the moon, by this time, having again emerged from the clouds, shone bright as when Jack had passed. " Look there," he cried, exultingly : for the same spectacle again caught his eyes, and he pointed to it with his horsewhip; " look, and deny if you can."

" Why," said one of the lads, pausing, " true it is that we do see a company of white creatures ; but were they fairies ten times over, I shall go among them;" and he dismounted to climb over the wall.

" Ah, Tom! Tom ;" cried Jack, " stop, man, stop! what are you doing ? The fairies—the good people, I mean—hate to be meddled with. You will be pinched or blinded; or your horse will cast its shoe; or—look ! a wilful man will have his way. Oh! oh ! he is almost at the oak — God help him ! for he is past the help of man."

By this time Tom was under the tree and burst out laughing. " Jack," said he, " keep your prayers to yourself. Your fairies are not bad at all. I believe they will make tolerably good catsup."

" Catsup," said Jack, who, when he found that the two lads (for the second had followed his brother) were both laughing in the middle of the fairies, had dismounted and advanced slowly—. " What do you mean by catsup ?"

" Nothing," replied Tom, " but that they are mushrooms (as indeed they were) ; and youc Oberon is merely this overgrown pufF-ball."

Poor Mulligan gave a long whistle of amazement, staggered back to his horse without saying

a word, and rode home in a hard gallop, never looking behind him. Many a long day was it before he ventured to face the laughers at Bally-begmuUinahone; and to the day of his death the people of the parish, aye, and five parishes round, called him nothing but musharoon Jack, such being their pronunciation of mushroom.

I should be sorry if all my fairy stories ended with so little dignity; but—

" These our actors, ^ . As I foretold you, were all spirits, and
Are melted into air—into thin air."

The name Shefro (variously written S)A bftUo, SjcBiiOa, Si5bno5, 81056(105, SjoJbftuS, &c.) by which the foregoing section is distinguished, literally signifies a fairy house or mansion, and is adopted as a general name for the Elres who are supposed to live in troops or communities, and were popularly supposed to have castles or mansions of their own—See Stewart's Popular Superstitions cf the Highlands, 1823. pp. 90, 91,&c.

Sia, sigh, tighe, sigheann, liabkra, sxachaire, tiogidh, are Irish words, evidently springing from a common Celtic root, used to express a fairy or goblin, and even a hag or witch. Thus we have the compounds Leannan-sighe, a familiar, from Leannan, a pet, and Siogh-dhraoidheachd, enchantment with or by spirits.

Sigh gdoithe or siaheann-gdoithe, a whirlwind, is so termed because it is said to b« raised by the fairies. The close of day is called Sia, because twilight,

" That sweet hour, when day is almost closing,"

is the time when the fairies are most frequently seen. Again, Sigh is a hill or hillock, because the fairies are believed to dwell within. Sidhe, tidheadh, and sigh, are names for a blast or blight, because it is supposed to proceed from the fairies.

The term Shoges, i. e. Sigh ages (young or little Spirits), Fairies, is used in a curious poem printed under the name of " The Irish Hudi-bras," 1689, pp. 23, and 81; a copy of which, entitled " The Fingal-lian Travesty," is among the Sloane MSS. No. 900. In the Third Part of O'Flaherty's Ogygia, it is related that St. Patriclc and some of his followers, who were chanting matins beside a fotmtain, were taken for " Sidhe, or fairies," by some pagan ladies.

" The Irish," according to the Rev. James Hely's translation of O'Flaherty, " call these Sidhe, atrial spirits or phantoms, because they are seen to come out of pleasant hills, where the common people imagine they reside, which fictitious habitations are called by us Sidhe or Siodha."

For a similar extended use of the German word Alp, Elf, &c., see Introductory Essay to the Grimms' Irische ElfenmUrchen, pp. 55—63.

FAIRY LEGENDS.
THE CLURICAUNE.

That sottish elf
■Who quaffs with swollen lips the ruby wine.
Draining the cellar with as free a hand
As if it were his purse which ne'er lacked coin;—
And then, with feign'd contrition ruminates
Upon his wasteful pranks, and revelry,
In some secluded dell or lonely grove
Tinsel'd by Twilight"—

A.

LEGENDS OF THE CLURICAUNE.

THE HAUNTED CELLAR.

IX.

There are few people who have not heard of the Mac Carthies—one of the real old Irish families, with the true Milesian blood running in their veins, as thick as buttermilk. Many were the clans of this family in the south; as the Mac Carthy-more—and the Mac Carthy-reagh—and the Alac Carthy of Mviskerry; and all of them were noted for their hospitality to strangers, gentle and simple.

But not one of that name, or of any other, exceeded Justin Mac Carthy, of Ballinacarthy, at putting plenty to eat and drink upon his table; and there was a right hearty welcome for every one who would share it with him. Many a wine-cellar would be ashamed of the name if that at Ballinacarthy was the proper pattern for one; large as that cellar was, it was crowded with bins of wine, and long rows of pipes, and hogsheads, and casks, that it would take more time to count than any sober man could spare in such a place, with plenty to drink about him, and a hearty welcome to do so.

There are many, no doubt, who will think that the butler would have little to complam of in such a house; and the whole country round would have agreed with them, if a man could be found to remain as Mr. Mac Carthy's butler for any length of time worth speaking of; yet not one who had been in his service gave him a bad word,

" We have no fault," they would say, " to find with the master; and if he could but get any one to fetch his wine from the cellar, we might every one of us have grown gray in the house, and have lived quiet and contented enough in his service imtil the end of our days."

"'Tis a queer thing that, surely," thought young Jack Leary, a lad who had been brought up from a mere child in the stables of Ballina-carthy to assist in taking care of the horses, and had occasionally lent a hand in the butler's pantry :—" 'tis a mighty queer thing, surely, that one man after another cannot content himself with the best place in the house of a good master, but that every one of them must quit, all through the means, as they say, of the wine-cellar. If the master, long life to him! would but make me his butler, I warrant never the word more would be heard of grumbling at his bidding to go to the wine-cellar."

Young Leary accordingly watched for what he conceived to be a favourable opportunity of presenting himself to the notice of his master.

A few mornings after, Mr. Mac Carthy went into his stable-yard rather earlier than usual, and called loudly for the groom to saddle his horse, as he intended going out with the hounds. But there was no groom to answer, and young Jack Leary led Rainbow out of the stable.

" Where is William ?" enquired Mr. Mac Carthy.

"Sir?" said Jack; and Mr. Mac Carthy repeated the question.

" Is it William, please your honour ?" returned Jack ; " why, then, to tell the truth, he had just one drop too much last night."

" Where did he get it ?" said Mr. Mac Carthy; " for since Thomas went away, the key of the wine-cellar has been in my pocket, and I have been obliged to fetch what was drank myself."

" Sorrow a know I know," said Leary, " unless the cook might have given him the least taste in life of whiskey. But," continued he, performing a low bow by seizing with his right hand a lock of hair, and pulling down his head by it, whilst his left leg, which had been put forward, was scraped back against the ground, "may I make so bold as just to ask your honour one question ?"

" Speak out. Jack," said Mr. Mac Carthy.

" Why, then, does your honour want a butler ?"

" Can you recommend roe one," returned his master, with the smile of good humour upon his countenance, " and one who will not be afraid of going to my wine-cellar ? "

"Is the wine-cellar all the matter?" said young Leary ; " devil a doubt I have of myself then for that."

" So you mean to offer me your services in the capacity of butler ? " said Mr. Mac Carthy, with some surprise.

" Exactly so," answered Leary, now for the first time looking up from the ground.

" Well, I believe you to be a good lad, and have no objection to give you a trial."

" Long may your honour reign over us, and the Lord spare you to us!" ejaculated Leary, •with another national bow, as his master rode off; and he continued for some time to gaze after him with a vacant stare, which slowly and gradually assumed a look of importance.

*•' Jack Leary," said he at length, " Jack—is it Jack ?" in a tone of wonder; " faith, 'tis not Jack now, but Mr. John, the butler;" and with an air of becoming consequence he strided out of the stable-yard towards the kitchen.

It is of little purport to my story, although it may afford an instructive lesson to the reader, to depict the sudden transition of nobody into somebody. Jack's former stable companion, a poor superannuated hound named Bran, who had been accustomed to receive many an affectionate pat on the head, was spurned from him with a kick and an " Out of the way, sirrah." Indeed, poor Jack's memory seemed sadly affected by this sudden change of situation. What established the point beyond all doubt was his almost forgetting the pretty face of Peggj', the kitchen wencli, whose heart he had assailed but the preceding week by the offer of purchasing a gold ring for the fourth finger of her right hand, and a lusty imprint of good-will upon her lips.

When INIr. Mac Carthy returned from hunting, he sent for Jack Leary—so he still continued to call his new butler. " Jack," said he, " I believe you are a trustworthy lad, and here are the keys of my cellar. I have asked the gentlemen with

whom I bunted to-day to dine with me, and I hope they may be satisfied at the way in which you will wait on them at table; but above all, let there be no want of wine after dinner."

Mr. John having a tolerably quick eye for such things, and being naturally a handy lad, spread his cloth accordingly, laid his plates and knives and forks in the same manner he had seen his predecessors in office perform these mysteries, and really, for the first time, got through attendance on dinner very well.

It must not be forgotten, however, that it was at the house of an Irish country squire, who was entertaining a company of booted and spurred fox-hunters, not very particular about what are considered matters of infinite importance under other circumstances and in other societies.

For instance, few of Mr. Mac Cartliy's guests, (though all excellent and worthy men in their way,) cared much whether the punch produced after soup was made of Jamaica or Antigua rum ; some even would not have been inclined to question the con'ectness of good old Irish whiskey; and, with the exception of their liberal host himself, every one in company preferred the port which Mr. Mac Carthy put on his table to the less ardent flavour of claret,—a choice rather at variance with modem sentiment.

It was waxing near midnight, when ^Ir. Mac Carthy rang the bell three times. This was a signal for more wine; and Jack proceeded to the cellar to procure a fresh supply, but it must be confessed not without some little hesitation.

The luxury of ice was then unknown in the

south of Ireland ; but the superiority of cool wine had been acknowledged by all men of sound judgment and true taste.

The grandfather of Mr. Mac Carthy, who had built the mansion of Ballinacarthy upon the site of an old castle which had belonged to his ancestors, was fully aware of this important fact; and in the construction of his magnificent wine-cellar had availed himself of a deep vault, excavated out of the solid rock in former times as a place of retreat and security. The descent to this vault was by a flight of steep stone stairs, and here and there in the wall were narrow passages—I ought rather to call them crevices ; and also certain projections which cast deep shadows, and looked very frightful when any one went down the cellar stairs with a single light: indeed, two lights did not much improve the matter, for though the breadth of the shadows became less, the narrow crevices remained as dark and darker than ever.

Summoning up all his resolution, down went the new butler, bearing in his right hand a lantern and the key of the cellar, and in his left a basket, which he considered sufficiently capacious to contain an adequate stock for the remainder of the evening: he arrived at the door without any interruption whatever; but when he put the key, which was of an ancient and clumsy kind—for it was before the days of Bramah's patent,—and turned it in the lock, he thought he heard a strange kind of laughing within the cellar, to which some empty bottles that stood upon the floor outside vibrated so violently, that they struck against each other: in this he could not be mistaken, al-

though he may have been deceived in the laugh, for the bottles were just at his feet, and he saw them in motion.

Leary paused for a moment, and looked about him with becoming caution. He then boldly seized·the handle of the key, and turned it with all his strenofth in the lock, as if he doubted his own power of doing so; and the door flew open with a most tremendous crash, that, if the house had not been built upon the solid rock, would have shook it from the foundation.

To recount what the poor fellow saw would be impossible, for he seems not to know very clearly himself: but what he told the cook the next morning was, that he heard a roaring and bellowing like a mad bull, and that all the pipes and hogsheads and casks in the cellar went rocking backwards and forwards with so much force, that he thought every one would have been staved in, and that he should have been drowned or smothered in wine.

"When Leary recovered, he made his way back as well as he could to the dining-room, where he found his master and the company very impatient for his return.

" What kept you ?" said Mr. Mac Carthy in an angry voice; " and where is the wine ? I rung for it half an hour since."

"The wine is in the cellar, I hope, sir," said Jack, trembling violently; "I hope 'tis not all lost."

"What do you mean, fool?" exclaimed Mr. Mac Carthy in a still more angry tone: " why did you not fetch some with you ?" a

Jack looked wildly about him, and only uttered a deep groan.

"Gentlemen," said Mr. Mac Carthy to his guests, "this is too much. When I next see you" to dinner, I hope it will be in another house, for it is impossible I can remain longer in this, where a man has no command over his own wine-cellar, and cannot get a butler to do his duty, I have long thought of moving from Ballinacarthy ; and I am now determined, with the blessing of God, to leave it to-morrow. But wine shall you have, were I to go myself to the cellar for it." So saying, he rose from the table, took the key and lantern from his half-stupified servant, who regarded him with a look of vacancy, and descended the narrow stairs, already described, which led to his cellar.

When he arrived at the door, which he found open, he thought he heard a noise, as if of rats or mice scrambling over the casks, and on advancing perceived a little figure, about six inches in height, seated astride upon the pipe of the oldest port in the place, and bearing a spigot upoij his shoulder. Raising the lantern, ^Ir. Mac Carthy contemplated the little fellow with wonder: he wore a red nightcap on his head; before him was a short leather apron, which now, ft'om his attitude, fell rather on one side; and he had stockings of a light blue colour, so long as nearly to cover the entire of his legs ; with shoes, having huge silver buckles in them, and with high heels (perhaps out of vanity to make him appear taller). His face was like a withered winter apple; and his nose, which was of a bright crimson colour,

about the tip wore a delicate purple bloom, like that of a plum : yet his eyes twinkled
" like those mites Of candied dew in moony nights—
and his mouth twitched up at one side with an arch gi-in.

" Ha, scoundrel!" exclaimed Mr. Mac Carthy, " have I found you at last ? disturber of my cellar —what are you doing there ?"

" Sure, and master," returned the little fellow, looking up at him with one eye, and with the other throwing a sly glance towards the spigot on his shoulder, " a'n't we going to move tomorrow ? and sure you would not leave your own little Cluricaune Naggeneen behind you ?"

" Oh !" thought Mr. Mac Carthy, " if you are to follow me. Master Naggeneen, I don't see much use in quitting Ballinacarthy." So filling with wine the basket which young Leary in his fright had left behind him, and locking the cellar door, he rejoined his guests.

For some years after, Mr. Mac Carthy had always to fetch the wine for his table himself, as the little Cluricaune Naggeneen seemed to feel a personal respect towards him. Notwithstanding the labour of these journeys, the worthy lord of Ballinacarthy lived in his paternal mansion to a good roxuid age, and was famous to the last for the excellence of his wine, and the conviviality of his company ; but at the time of his death, that same conviviality had nearly emptied his wine-cellar; and as it was never so well filled again, nor so often visited, the revels of master Naggeneen be-g2

came less celebrated, and are now only spoken of amongst the legendary lore of the country. It is even said that the poor little fellow took the declension of the cellar so to heart, that he became negligent and careless of himself, and that he has been sometimes seen going about with hardly a skreed to cover him.

Some, however, believe that he turned brogue-maker, and assert that they have seen him at his work, and heard him whistling as merry as a blackbird on a May morning, under the shadow of a brown jug of foaming ale, bigger—ay bigger than himself ; decently dressed enough, they say ; —only looking mighty old. But still 't is clear he has his wits about him, since no one ever ha4 the luck to catch him, or to get hold of the purse he has with him, yfhichthey caX\spre-na-skillina</h, and 't is said is never without a shilling: in it.

^^rv«^>«^

MASTER AND MAN.

Billy Mac Daniel was once as likely a young man as ever shook his brogue at a patron, emptied a quart, or handled a shillelagh: fearing for nothing but the want of drink; caring for nothing but who should pay for it; and thinking of nothing but how to make fun over it: drunk or sober, a word and a blow was ever the way with Billy Mac Daniel; and a mighty easy way it is of either getting into or ending a dispute. More is the jiity that, through the means of his drinking, and fearing and caring for nothing, this same Billy Mac Daniel fell into bad company ; for surely the good people are the worst of all company any one could come across.

It so happened that Billy was going home one clear frosty night not long after Christmas; the moon was round and bright; but although it was as fine a night as heart could wish for, he felt jnnched with the cold. *' By my word," chattered Billy, " a drop of good liquor would be no bad thing to keep a man's soul from freezing in him; and I wish I had a full measure of the best."

" Never wish it twice, Billy," said a little man in a three-cornered hat, bound all aboiit with gold lace, and with great silver buckles in his shoes, so big that it was a wonder how he could

carry them, and he held out a glass as big as himself, filled with as good liquor as ever eye looked on or lip tasted.

" Success, my little fellow," said Billy Mac Daniel, nothing daunted, though well he knew the little man to belong to the good people; " here's your health, any way, and thank you kindly; no matter who pays for the drink ;" and he took the glass and drained it to the very bottom, without ever taking a second breath to it.

" Success," said the little man; " and you're heartily welcome, Billy; but don't think to cheat me as you have done others,—out with your purse and pay me like a gentleman."

" Is it I pay you ?" said Billy : " could I not just take you up and put you in ray pocket as easily as a blackberry ?"

" Billy Mac Daniel," said the little man, getting very angry, " you shall be my servant for seven years and a day, and that is the way I will be paid; so make ready to follow me."

When Billy heard this, he began to be very sorry for having used such bold words towards the little man ; and he felt himself, yet could not tell how, obliged to follow the little man the livelong night about the country, up and down, and over hedge and ditch, and through bog and brake, without any rest.

When morning began to dawn, the little man turned round to him and said, " You may now go home, Billy, but on your peril don't fail to meet me in the Fort-field to-night; or if you do, it may be the worse for you in the long run. If I find you a good servant, you will find me an indulgent master,"

Home went Billy Mac Daniel; and though he was tired and weary enough, never a wink of sleep could he get for thinking of the little man; but he was afraid not to do his bidding, so up he got in the evening, and away he went to the Fort-field. He was not long there before the little man came towards him and said, " Billy, I want to go a long journey to-night; so saddle one of my horses, and you may saddle another for yourself, as you are to go along with me, and may be tired after your walk last night."

Billy thought this very considerate of his master, and thanked him accordingly: " But," said he, " if I may be so bold, sir, I would ask which is the way to your stable, for never a thing do I see but the fort here, and the old thorn-tree in the corner of the field, and the stream running at the bottom of the hill, with the bit of bog over against us."

" Ask no questions, Billy," said the little man, " but go over to that bit of bog, and bring me two of the strongest nishes you can find."

Billy did accordingly, wondering what the little man would be at; and he picked out two of the stoutest nishes he could find, with a little bunch of brown blossom stuck at the side of each, and brought them back to his master.

" Get up, Billy," said the little man, taking one of the rushes from him and striding across it.

" Where will I get up, please your honour?" said Billy.

" Why, upon horseback, like me, to be sure," said the little man.

" Is it after making a fool of me you 'd be,"

said Billy, " bidding me get a horse-back upon that bit of a rush ? May be you want to persuade me that the rush I pulled but while ago out of the bog over there is a horse ?"

" Up ! up ! and no words," said the little man, looking very vexed; " the best horse you ever r(Me was but a fool to it." So Billy, thinking all this was in joke, and fearing to vex his master, straddled across the rush : " Borram ! Borram ! Borram !" cried the little man three times (which, in English, means to become great), and Billy did the same after him: presently the rushes swelled up into fine horses, and away they went full speed; but Billy, who had put the rush between his legs, without much minding how he did it, found himself sitting on horseback the wrong way, which was rather awkward, with his face to the horse's tail; and so quickly had his steed started off with him, that he had no power to turn round, and there was therefore nothing for it but to hold on by the tail.

At last they came to their journey's end, and stopped at the gate of a fine house : " Now, Billy," said the little man, " do as you see me do, and follow me close; but as you did not know your horse's head from his tail, mind that your o"wti head does not spin round until you can't tell whether you are standing on it or on your heels : for remember that old liquor, though able to make a cat speak, can make a man dumb."

The little man then s.aid some queer kind of words, out of which Billy could make no meaning ; but he contrived to say them after him for all that; and in they both went through the key-hole of the door, and through one key-hole after another, until they got into the wine-cellar, which was well stored with all kinds of wine.

Tlie little man fell to drinking as hard as he could, and Billy, noway disliking the example, did the same. " The best of masters are you surely," said Billy to him ; " no matter who is the next; and well pleased will I be with your service if you continvie to give me plenty to drink."

" I have made no bargain with you," said the little man, " and will make none; but up and follow me." Away they went, through key-hole after key-hole; and each mounting upon the rush wliich he had left at the hall-dooi", scampered off, kicking the clouds before them like snow-balls, as soon as the words, " Borram, Borram, Borram," had passed their lips.

When they came back to the Fort-field, the little man dismissed Billy, bidding him to be there the next night at the same hour. Thus did they go on, night after night, shaping their course one night here, and another night there—sometimes north, and sometimes east, and sometimes south, until there was not a gentleman's wine-cellar in all Ireland they had not visited, and could tell the flavour of every wine in it as well—aye, better than the butler himself.

One night, when Billy Mac Daniel met the little man as usual in the Fort-field, and was going to the bog to fetch the horses for their journey, his master said to him, " Billy, I shall want another horse to-night, for may be we may bring back more company with us than we take."

So Billy, who now knew better than to question any order given to him by his master, brought a third rush, much wondering who it might be that would travel back in their company, and whether he was about to have a fellow-servant. " If I have," thought Billy, " he shall go and fetch the horses from the bog every night; for I don't see why I am not, every inch of me, as good a gentleman as my master."

Well, away they went, Billy leading the third horse, and never stopped until they came to a snug farmer's house in the coimty Limerick, close under the old castle of Carrigogunniel, that was built, they say, by the great Brian Boru. Within the house there was great carousing going forward, and the little man stopped outside for some time to listen; then turning round all of a sudden, said, " Billyy I will be a thousand years old tomorrow !"

" God bless us, sir," said Billy, " will you !"

" Don't say these words again, Billy," said the little man, " or you vnll be my ruin for ever. Now, Billy, as I will be a thousand years in the world to-morrow, I think it is full time for me to get married."

" I think so too, without any kind of doubt at all," said Billy, " if ever you mean to marry."

" And to that purpose," said the little man, " have I come all the way to Carrigogunniel; for in this house, this very night, is young Darby Riley going to be married to Bridget Rooney; and as she is a tall and comely girl, and has come of decent people, I think of marrying her myself, and taking her off with me."

" And what will Darby Riley say to that ?" said Billy.

" Silence!" said the little man, putting on a mighty severe look : " I did not bring you here with me to ask questions ;" and without holding further argument, he began saying the qiieer words, wliich liad the power of passing him through the key-hole as free as air, and which Billy thought himself mighty clever to be able to say after him.

In they both went; and for the better viewing the company, the little man perched himself up as nimbly as a cock-sparrow upon one of the big beams which went across the house over all their heads, and Billy did the same upon another facing him; but not being much accustomed to roosting in such a place, his legs hung down as untidy as may be, and it was quite clear he had not taken pattern after the way in which the little man had bundled himself up together. If the little man had been a tailor all his life, he could not have sat more contentedly upon his haunches.

There they were, both master and man, looking down upon the fun that was going forward—and under them were the priest and piper—and the father of Darby Riley, with Darby's two brothers and his imcle's son—and there were both the father and the mother of Bridget Rooney, and proud enough the old couple were that night of their daughter, as good right they had—and her four sisters with bran new ribands in their caps, and her three brothers all looking as clean and as clever as any three boys in Munster—and there were uncles and aunts, and gossips and

cousins enough besides to make a full house of it —and plenty was there to eat and drink on the table for every one of them, if they had been double the number.

Now it happened, just as Mrs. Rooney had helped his reverence to the first cut of the pig's head which was placed before her, beautifully bolstered up with white savoys, that the bride gave a sneeze which made every one at table start, but not a soul said " God bless us." All thinking that the priest would have done so, as he ought if he had done his duty, no one wished to take the word out of his mouth, which unfortunately was pre-occupied with pig's head and greens. And after a moment's pause, the fun and merriment of the bridal feast went on without the pious benediction.

Of this circumstance both Billy and his master were no inattentive spectators from tlieir exalted stations. " Ha!" exclaimed the little man, throwing one leg from under him witli a joyous flourish, and his eye twinkled with a strange light, whilst his eyebrows became elevated into the curvature of Gothic arches—" Ha !" said he, leering down at the bride, and then up at Billy, " I have half of her now, surely. Let her sneeze but twice more, and she is mine, in spite of priest, mass-book, and Darby Riley."

Again the fair Bridget sneezed; but it was so gently, and she blushed so much, that few except the little man took, or seemed to take, any notice : and no one thought of saying " God bless us."

Billy all tliis time regarded the poor girl with

a most nieful expression of countenance; for he could not help thinking what a terrible thing it was for a nice young girl of nineteen, with large blue eyes, transparent skin, and dimpled cheeks, suffused with health and joy, to be obliged to marry an "ugly little bit of a man who was a thousand years old, barring a day.

At this critical moment the bride gave a third sneeze, and Billy roared out with all his might, " God save us !" Whether this exclamation resulted from his soliloquy, or from the mere force of habit, he never could tell exactly himself; but no sooner was it uttered, than the little man, his face glowing with rage and disappointment, spning from the beam on which he had perched himself, and shrieking out in the shrill voice of a cracked bagpipe, " I discharge you my service, Billy Mac Daniel—take that for your wages," gave poor Billy a most furious kick in the back, which sent his unfortunate servant sprawling upon his face and hands right in the middle of the supper table.

If Billy was astonished, how much more so was every one of the company into which he was thrown with so little ceremony; but when they heard his story. Father Cooney laid down his knife and fork, and married the young couple out of hand with all speed; and I3illy Mac Daniel danced the Rinka at their wedding, and plenty did he drink at it too, which was what he thought more of than dancing.

THE LITTLE SHOE.

XI.

" Now tell me, Molly," said Mr. Coote to Molly Cogan, as he met her on the road one day, close to one of the old gateways of Kilmallock*, " did you ever hear of the Cluricaune ?"

" Is it the Cluricaune ? why, then, sure I did, often and often; many's the time I heard my father, rest his soul! tell about 'em."

" But did you ever see one,]\Iolly, yourself?" " Och ! no, I never see one in my life; but my grandfather, that's my father's father, you know, he see one, one time, and caught him too." " Caught him ! Oh ! Molly, tell me how ?" *' Why, then, I'll tell you. My grandfather, you see, was out there above in the bog, drawing home turf, and the poor old mare was tired after her day's work, and the old man went out to the stable to look after her, and to see if she was eating her hay; and when he came to the stable door there, my dear, he heard something hammering, hammering, hammering, just for all the world like a shoemaker making a shoe, and whistling all the time the prettiest tune he ever heard in his whole life before. Well, my grandfather, he thought it was the Cluricaune, and he said to himself, says he, ' I'll catch you, if I can,

* " Kilmallock seemed to me like the court of the Queen of Silence."— O'Kefff's Recolleclions,

and then I '11 have money enough always.' So lie opened the door very quietly, and did n't make a bit of noise in the world that ever was heard; and looked all about, but the never a bit of the little man he could see anywhere, but he heard him hammering and whistling, and so he looked and looked, till at last he see the little fellow; and where was he, do you think, but in the girth under the mare ; and there he was with his little bit of an apron on him, and hammer in his hand, and a little red nightcap on his head, and he making a shoe; and he was so busy with his work, and he was hammering and whistling so loud, that he never minded my grandfather till he caught him fast in his hand. ' Faith, I have you now,' says he, ' and I '11 never let you go till I get your purse—that's what I won't; so give it here to me at once, now.'—' Stop, stop,' says the Cluricaune, ' stop, stop,' says he, ' till I get it for you.' So my gi-andfather, like a fool, you see, opened his hand a little, and the little fellow jumped away laughing, and he never saw him any more, and the never the bit of the purse did he get, only the Cluricaune left his little shoe that he was making; and my grandfather was mad enough angry with himself for letting him go ; but he had the shoe all his life, and my own mother told me she often see it, and had it in her hand, and 't was the prettiest little shoe she ever saw." " And did you see it yourself, Molly ?" " Oh ! no, my dear, it was lost long afore I was born ; but my mother told me about it often and often enough."

The main point of distinction between the Cluricaune and the Shefro, arises from the sottish and solitary habits of the former, who are rarely found in troops or communities.

The Cluricaune of the county of Cork, the Luricaune of Kerry, and the Lurigadauoe of TIpperary, appear to be the same as the Lepre-chan or Leprochaune of Leinster, and the Logherrv-man of Ulster ; and these words are probably all provincialisms of liiAC^jtrQAl) the Irish for a pigmy.

U is possible, and is in some measure borne out by the text of one of the preceding stories [IX.], that the word luacharman is merely an Anglo-Irish induction, compounded of lUACA]tt (a rush), and the

English word, man A rushy man,—that may be, a man of the height of a rush, or a being who dwelt among rushes, i. e. unfrequented or boggy places.

The following dialogue is said to have taken place in an Irish court of justice, upon the witness having used the word Leprochaune:—

Cowl. —Pray what is a leprochaune ? the law knows no such character or designation.

Wilneit. —My Lord, it is a little counsellor man in the fairies, or an attorney that robs them all, and he always carries a purse that is full of money, and if you see him and keep your eyes on him, and that you never turn them aside, he cannot get away, and if you catch him he gives you the purse to let him go, and then you 're as rich as a Jew.

Court. —Did you ever know of any one that caught a Leprochaune ? I wish I could catch one.

Witnett Yes, my lord, there was one

Court.—That will do.

With respect to " money matters," there appears to be a strong resemblance between the ancient Roman Incubus and the Irish Cluricaune.—" Sed quomodo dicunt, ego nihil scio, sed audivi, quomodo incuboni pileum rapuisset et the»aurum invenit," are the words of Petronius.—See, for further arguments in support of identity of the two spirits, the Brothers Grimm's Essay on the Nature of the Elves, prefixed to their translation of this work, under the head of " .Ancient Testimonies."

" Old German and Northern poems contain numerous accounts of the skill of the dwarfs in curious smiih's-work."—" The Irish Cluricaune is heard hammering; he is particularly fond of making shoes, but these were in ancient times made of metal (in the old Northern language a shoe-maker is called a shoe-smilh) ; and, singularly enough, the wights in a German tradition manifest the same propensity ; for, whatever work the shoe maker has been able to cut out in the day, they finish with incredible quickness during the night."

Tub Brothers Grimm.

FAIRY LEGENDS.

THE BANSHEE.

' Wlio sits upon the heath forlorn, With robe so free and tresses torn ? Anon she pours a harrowing strain, -And then—she sits all mute again ! Now peals the wild funereal er3'— And now—it sinks into a sigh."

LEGENDS Of THE BANSHEE.

XII.

The Reverend Charles Bunworth was rector of Buttevant, in the county of Cork, about the middle of the last century. He was a man of unaffected piety, and of sound learning; pure in heart, and benevolent in intention. By the rich he was respected, and by the poor beloved; nor did a difference of creed prevent their looking up to " the minister" (so was Mr. Bunworth called by them) in matters of difficulty and in seasons of distress, confident of receiving from him the advice and assistance that a father would afford to his children. He was the friend and the benefactor of the surrounding country—to him, from the neighbouring town of Newmarket, came both Curran and Yelverton for advice and instruction, previous to their entrance at Dublin College. Young, indigent and inexperienced, these afterwards eminent men received from him, in addition to the advice they sought, pecuniary aid; and the brilliant career which was theirs, justified the discrimination of the giver.

But what extended the fame of Mr, Bunworth,
far beyond the limits of the parishes adjacent to
his own, was his performance on the Irish harp,
and his hospitable reception and entertainment of

n 2

the poor harpers who travelled from house to house about the country. Grateful to their patron, these itinerant minstrels sang his praises to the tingling accompaniment of their harps, invoking in return for his bounty abundant blessings on his white head, and celebrating in their rude verses the blooming charms of his daughters, Elizabeth and Mary. It was all these poor fellows could do; but who can doubt that tlieir gratitude was sincere, when, at the time of Mr. Bunworth's death, no less than fifteen harps were deposited on the loft of his granary, bequeathed to him by the last members of a race which has now ceased to exist. Trifling, no doubt, in intrinsic value were these relics, yet there is something in gifts of the heart that merits preservation; and it is to be regretted that, when he died, these harps were broken up one after the other, and used as fire-wood by an ignorant follower of the family, who, on their removal to Cork for a temporary change of scene, was left in charge of the house.

The circumstances attending the death of Mr. Bunworth may be doubted by some; but there are still living credible witnesses who declare their authenticity, and who can be produced to attest most, if not all of the following particulars.

About a week previous to his dissolution, and early in the evening, a noise was heard at the haU-door resembling the shearing of sheep; but at the time no particular attention was paid to it. It was nearly eleven o'clock the same night, when Kavanagh, the herdsman, returned from Mallow, whither he had been sent in the afternoon for

some medicine, and was observed by Miss Bun-worth, to whom he delivered the parcel, to be much agitated. At this time, it must be observed, her father was by no means considered in danger.

" AVhat is the matter, Kavanagh ?" asked Miss Bunworth: but the poor fellow, with a bewildered look, only uttered, " The master, Miss — the master—he is going from us;" and, overcome with real grief, he burst into a flood of tears.

Miss Bunworth, who was a woman of strong nerve, inquired if any thing he had learned in Mallow induced him to suppose that her father was worse.

" No, Miss," said Kavanagh; " it was not in Mallow "

" Kavanagh," said Miss Bunworth, with that stateliness of manner for which she is said to have been remarkable, " I fear you have been drinking, which, I must say, I did not expect at such a time as the present, when it was your duty to have kept yourself sober;—I thought you might have been trusted:—what should we have done if you had broken the medicine bottle, or lost it ? for the doctor said it was of the greatest consequence that your master should take the medicine to-night. But I will speak to you in the morning, when you are in a fitter state to understand what I say."

Kavanagh looked up with a stupidity of aspect which did not serve to remove the impression of his being drunk, as his eyes appeared heavy and dull after the flood of tears;—but his voice was not that of an intoxicated person.

*' Miss," said he, " as I hope to receive mercy hereafter, neither bit nor sup has passed my lips since I left this house : but the master "

" Speak softly," said Miss Bunworth ; " he sleeps, and is going on as well as we could expect."

" Praise be to God for that, any way," replied Kavanagh ; " but oh ! Miss, he is going from us surely—we will lose him — the master—we will lose him, we will lose him!" and he wrung his hands together.

" What is it you mean, Kavanagh ?" asked Miss Bunworth.

"Is it mean?" said Kavanagh : " the Banshee has come for him. Miss; and 'tis not I alone who have heard her."

"'Tis an idle superstition," said Miss Brai-'worth.

*' May be so," replied Kavanagh, as if the words ' idle superstition' only sounded upon his ear without reaching his mind—" May be so," he continued; " but as I came through the glen of Ballybeg, she was along with me keening, and screeching, and clapping her hands, by my side, every step of the way, with her long white hair falling about her shoulders, and I could hear her repeat the master's name every now and then, as plain as ever I heard it. When I came to the old abbey, she parted from me there, and turned into the pigeon-field next the herrin ground, and folding her cloak about her, down she sat under the tree that was struck by the lightning, and began keening so bitterly, that it went through one's heart to hear it."

" Kavanagh," said Miss Bunworth, who had, however, listened attentively to this remarkable relation, " ray father is, I believe, better; and I hope will himself soon be up and able to convince you that all this is but your own fancy; nevertheless, I charge you not to mention what you have told me, for there is no occasion to frighten your fellow-servants with the story."

Mr. Bunworth gradually declined; but nothing particular occurred until the night previous to his death: that night both his daughters, exhausted with continued attendance and watching, were prevailed upon to seek some repose; and an elderly lady, a near relative and friend of the family, remained by the bedside of their father. The old gentleman then lay in the parlour, where he had been in the morning removed at his own request, fancying the change would aflFord him relief; and the head of his bed was placed close-to the window. In a room adjoining sat some male friends, and, as usual on like occasions of illness, in the kitchen many of the followers of the family had assembled.

The night was serene and moonlit—^the sick man slept—and nothing broke the stillness of their melancholy watch, when the little party in the room adjoining the parlour, the door of which stood open, was suddeiJy roused by a sound at the window near the bed: a rose-tree grew outside the window, so close as to touch the glass; this was forced aside with some noise, and a low moaning was heard, accompanied by clapping of hands, as if of a female in deep affliction. It seemed as if the sound proceeded from a person

holding her mouth close to the window. Tlie lady who sat by the bedside of Mr. Bunworth went into the adjoining room, and in a tone of alam), inquired of the gentlemen there, if they had heard the Banshee? Sceptical of supernatural appearances, two of them rose hastily and went out to discover the cause of these sounds, which they also had distinctly heard. They walked all round the house, examining every spot of ground, particularly near the window from whence the voice had proceeded; the bed of earth beneath, in which the rose-tree was planted, had been recently dug, and the print of a footstep —if the tree had been forced aside by mortal hand — would have inevitably remained; but they could perceive no such impression; and an unbroken stillness reigned without. Hoping to dispel the mystery, they continued their search anxiously along the road, from the straightness of which and the lightness of the night, they were enabled to see some distance around them; but all was silent and deserted, and they returned surprised and disappointed. How much more then were they astonished at learning that the whole time of their absence, those who remained within the house had heard the moaning and clapping of hands even louder and more distinct than before they had gone out; and no sooner was the door of the room closed on them, than they again heard the same mournful sounds! Every succeeding hour the sick man became worse, and as the first glimpse of the morning appeared, Mr. Bunworth expired.

LEGENDS OF THE BANSHEE.

XIII.

The family of Mac Carthy have for some generations possessed a small estate in the county of Tipperary. They are the descendants of a race, once numerous and powerful in the south of Ireland ; and though it is probable that the property they at present hold is no part of the large possessions of their ancestors, yet the district in which they live is so connected with the name of Mac Carthy by those associations which are never forgotten in Ireland, that they have preserved with all ranks a sort of influence much greater than that which their fortune or connections could otherwise give them. They are, like most of this class, of the Roman Catholic persuasion, to which they adhere with somewhat of the pride of ancestry, blended with a something, call it what you will, whether bigotry, or a sense of wrong, arising out of repeated diminutions of their family possessions, during the more rigorous periods of the penal laws. Being an old family, and especially being an old Catholic family, they have of course their Banshee; and the circumstances under which the appearance, which I shall relate, of this mysterious harbinger of death, took place, were told me by an old lady, a near connexion of theirs, who knew many of the parties concerned, and who, though not deficient in

understanding or education, cannot to this day be brought to give a decisive opinion as to the truth or authenticity of the story. The plain inference to be drawn from this is, that she believes it, though she does not own it; and as she was a contemporary of the persons concerned—as she heard the account from many persons about the same period, all concurring in the important particulars—as some of her authorities were themselves actors in the scene—and as none of the parties were interested in speaking what was false; I think we have about as good evidence that the whole is undeniably true as we have of many narratives of modem history, which I could name, and which many grave and sober-minded people would deem it very great pyrrhonism to question. This, however, is a point which it is not my province to determine. People who deal out stories of this sort must be content to act like certain young politicians, who tell very freely to their friends what they hear at a great man's table; not guilty of the impertinence of weighing the doctrines, and leaving it to their hearers to understand them in any sense, or in no sense, just as they may please.

Charles Mac Carthy was, in the year 1749, the only surviving son of a very numerous family. His father died when he was little more than twenty, leaving him the Mac Carthy estate, not much encumbered, considering that it was an Irish one. Charles was gay, handsome, unfettered either by poverty, a father, or guardians, and therefore was not, at the age of one-and-twenty, a pattern of regularity and virtue. In plain

terms, he was an exceedingly dissipated—I fear I may say debauched young man. His companions were, as may be supposed, of the higher classes of the youth in his neighbourhood, and, in

feneral, of those whose fortunes were larger than is own, whose dispositions to pleasure were therefore under still less restrictions, and in whose example he found at once an incentive and an apology for his irregularities. Besides, Ireland, a place to this day not very remarkable for the coolness and steadiness of its youth, was then one of the cheapest countries in the world in most of those articles which money supplies for the indulgence of the passions. The odious exciseman, with his portentous book in one hand, his unrelenting pen held in the other, or stuck beneath his hat-band, and the ink-bottle (' black emblem of the informer') dangling from his waistcoat-button—went not then from ale-house to ale-house, denouncing all those patriotic dealers in spirit, who preferred selling whiskey, which had nothing to do with English laws (but to elude them), to retailing that poisonous liquor, which derived its name from the British " Parliament," that compelled its circulation among a reluctant people. Or if the gauger—recording angel of the law—wrote down the peccadillo of a publican, he dropped a tear upon the word, and blotted it out for ever ! For, welcome to the tables of their hospitable neighbours, the guardians of the excise, where they existed at all, scrupled to abridge those luxuries which they freely shared; and thus the competition in the market between the smuggler, who incurred little hazard, and the personage ycleped fair trader, who enjoyed little protection, made Ireland a land flowing, not merely with milk and honey, but with whiskey and wine. In the enjoyments supplied by these, and in the many kindred pleasures to which frail youth is but too prone, Charles Mac Carthy indulged to such a degree, that just about the time when he had completed his four-and-twentieth year, after a week of great excesses, he was seized with a violent fever, which, from its malignity, and the weakness of his frame, left scarcely a hope of his recovery. His mother, who had at first made many efforts to check his vices, and at last had been obliged to look on at his rapid progress to ruin in silent despair, watched day and night at his pillow. The anguish of parental feeling wap blended with that still deeper misery which those only know who have striven hard to rear in virtue and piety a beloved and favourite child; have foimd him grow up all that their hearts could desire, until he reached manhood; and then, when their pride was highest, and their hopes almost ended in the fulfilment of their fondest expectations, have seen this idol of their affections plunge headlong into a course of reckless profligacy, and, after a rapid career of vice, hang upon the verge of eternity, without the leisure for, or the power of, repentance. Fervently she prayed that, if his life could not be spared, at least the delirium, which continued with increasing violence from the first few hours of his disorder, might vanish before death, and leave enough of light and of calm for making his peace with offended Heaven. After several days, however,

nature seemed quite exhausted, and he sunk into a state too like death to be mistaken for the repose of sleep. His face had that pale, glossy, marble look, which is in general so sure a symptom that life has left its tenement of clay. His eyes were closed and sunk ; the lids having that compressed and stiflfened appearance which seemed to indicate that some friendly hand had done its last office. The lips, half-closed and perfectly ashy, discovered just so much of the teeth as to give to the features of death their most ghastly, but most impressive look. He lay upon his back, with his hands stretched beside him, quite motionless; and his distracted mother, after repeated trials, could discover not the least symptom of animation. The medical man who attended, liaving tried the usual modes for ascertaining the presence of life, declared at last his opinion that it was flown, and prepared to depart from the house of mourning. His horse was seen to come to the door. A crowd of people who were collected before the windows, or scattered in groups on the lawn in front, gathered round when the door opened. These were tenants, fosterers, and poor relations of the family, with others attracted by affection, or by that interest which partakes of curiosity, but is something more, and which collects the lower ranks round a house where a human being is in his passage to another world. They saw the professional man come out from the hall door and approach his horse, and while slowly, and with a melancholy air, he prepared to mount, they clustered round him with inquiring and wishful looks. Not a word was spoken ; but

their meaning could not be misunderstood; and the physician, when he had got into his saddle, and while the servant was still holding the bridle, as if to delay him, and was looking anxiously at his face, as if expecting that he would relieve the general suspense, shook his head, and said in a low voice, "It's all over, James;" and moved slowly away. The moment he had spoken, the women present, who were very numerous, uttered a shrill cry, which, having been sustained for about half a minute, fell suddenly into a full, loud, continued and discordant but plaintive wailing, above which occasionally were heard the deep sounds of a man's voice, sometimes in broken sobs, sometimes in more distinct exclamations of sorrow. This was Charles's foster-brother, who moved about in the crowd, now clapping his hands, now rubbing them together in an agony of grief. The poor fellow had been Charles's playmate and companion when a boy, and afterwards his servant; had always been distinguished by his peculiar regard, and loved his young master, as much, at least, as he did his own life.

When Mrs. Mac Carthy became convinced that the blow was indeed struck, and that her beloved son was sent to his last account, even in the blossoms of his sin, she remained for some time gazing with fixedness upon liis cold features; then, as if something had suddenly touched the string of her tenderest affections, tear after tear trickled down her cheeks, pale with anxiety and watching. Still she continued looking at her son, apparently unconscious that she was weeping, without once lifting her handkerchief to her

eyes, until reminded of the sad duties which the custom of the country imposed upon her, by the crowd of females belonging to the better class of the peasantry, who now, crying audibly, nearly filled the apartment. She then withdrew, to give directions for the ceremony of waking, and for supplying the numerous visitors of all ranks with the refreshments usual on these melancholy occasions. Though her voice was scarcely heard, and though no one saw her but the servants and one or two old followers of the family, who assisted her in the necessary arrangements, everything was conducted with the greatest regularity ; and though she made no effort to check her sorrows, they never once suspended her attention, now more than ever required to preserve order in her household, which, in this season of calamity, but for her would have been all confusion.

The night was pretty far advanced ; the boisterous lamentations which had prevailed during part of the day in and about the house had given place to a solemn and mournful stillness; and Mrs. Mac Carthy, whose heart, notwithstanding her long fatigue and watching, was yet too sore for sleep, was kneeling in fervent prayer in a chamber adjoining that of her son:—suddenly her devotions were disturbed by an unusual noise, proceeding from the persons who were watching round the body. First, there was a low murmur—then all was silent, as if the movements of those in the chamber were checked by a sudden panic—and then a loud cry of terror burst from all within:—the door of the chamber was thrown open, and all who were not overturned in

the press rushed wildly into the passage wiiich led to the stairs, and into which Mrs. JVIac Carthy's room opened. Mrs. Mac Carthy made her way through the crowd into her son's chamber, where she found him sitting up in the bed, and looking vacantly around like one risen from the grave. The glare tlirown upon his sunk features and thin lathy frame gave an unearthly horror to his whole aspect. Mrs. Mac Carthy was a woman of some firmness; but she was a woman, and not quite free from the superstitions of her country. She di'opped on her knees, and, clasping her hands, began to pray aloud. The form before her moved only its lips and barely uttered, "Mother;"—^but though the pale lips moved, as if there was a design to finish the sentence, the tongue refused its oflBce. Mrs. ^Jac Carthy sprung forward, and catching the arm of her son, exclaimed, " Speak ! in the name of God and his saints, speak ! are you alive ?"

He turned to her slowly, and said, speaking still with apparent difficulty, " Yes, my mother,

alive, and ^But sit down and collect yourself;

I have that to tell, which will astonish you still more than what you have seen." He leaned back upon his pillow, and while his mother remained kneeling by the bedside, holding one of his hands clasped in hers, and gazing on him with the look of one who distrusted all her senses, he proceeded :—" Do not interrupt me until I have done. I wish to speak while the excitement of returning life is upon me, as I know I shall soon need much repose. Of the commencement of my illness I have only a confused recollection;

but within the last twelve hours, I have been before the judgment-seat of God. Do not stare incredulously on me—'tis as true as have been my crimes, and, as I trust, shall be my repentance. I saw the awful Judge arrayed in all the terrors which invest him when mercy gives place to justice. The dreadful pomp of offended omnipotence, I saw,—I remember. It is fixed here; printed on my brain in characters indelible; but it passeth human language. What I can describe I will —I may speak it briefly. It is enough to say, I was weighed in the balance and found wanting. The irrevocable sentence was upon the point of being pronounced; the eye of my Almighty Judge, which had already glanced upon me, half spoke my doom ; when I observed the guardian saint, to whom you so often directed my prayers when I was a child, looking at me with an expression of benevolence and compassion. I stretched forth my hands to him, and besought his intercession; I implored that one year, one month might be given to me on earth, to do penance and atonement for my transgressions, lie threw himself at the feet of my Judge, and supplicated for mercy. Oh ! never— not if I should pass through ten thousand successive states of being—never, for eternity, shall I forget the horrors of that moment, when my fate hung suspended—when an instant was to decide whether torments unutterable were to be my portion for endless ages? But Justice suspended its decree, and Mercy spoke in accents of firmness, but mildness, ' Return to that world in which thou hast lived but to outrage the laws 1

of Him who made that world and thee. Three years are given thee for repentance; when these are ended, thou shalt again stand here, to be saved or lost for ever.'—I heard no more; I saw no more, until I awoke to life, the moment before you entered."

Charles's strength continued just long enough to finish these last words, and on uttering them he closed his eyes, and lay quite exhausted. His mother, though, as was before said, somewhat disposed to give credit to supernatural visitations, yet hesitated whether or not she should believe that, although awakened from a swoon, which might have been the crisis of his disease, he was still under the influence of delirium. Repose, however, was at all events necessary, and she took immediate measures that he should enjoy it undisturbed. After some hours' sleep, he awoke refreshed, and thenceforward gradually but steadily recovered.

Still he persisted in his account of the vision, as he had at first related it; and his persuasion of its reality had an obvious and decided influence on his habits and conduct. He did not altogether abandon the society of his former associates, for his temper was not soured by his reformation; but he never joined in their excesses, and often endeavoured to reclaim them. How his pious exertions succeeded, I have never learnt; but of himself it is recorded, that he was religious without ostentation, and temperate without austerity; giving a practical proof that vice may be exchanged for virtue, without a loss of respectability, popularity, or happiness.

Time rolled on, and long before the three years were ended, the story of his vision was forgotten, or, when spoken of, was usually mentioned as an instance proving the folly of believing in such things. Charles's health, from the temperance and regularity of his habits, became more robust than ever. His friends, indeed, had often occasion to rally him upon a seriousness and abstractedness of demeanour, which grew upon him as he approached the completion of his seven-and-twentieth year, but for the most part his manner exhibited the same animation and cheerfulness for wliich he had always been remarkable. In company, he evaded every endeavour to draw from him a distinct opinion on the subject of the supposed prediction; but among his own family it was well known that he still firmly believed it. However, when the day had nearly arrived on which the prophecy was, if at all, to be fulfilled, his whole appearance gave such promise of a long and healthy life, that he was persuaded by his friends to ask a large party to an entertainment at Spring House, to celebrate his birth-day. But the occasion of this party, and the circumstances which attended it, will be best learned from a perusal of the following letters, which have been carefully preserved by some relations of his family. The first is from Mrs. Mac Carthy to a lady, a very near connection and valued friend of hers, who lived in the county of Cork, at about fifty miles' distance from Spring House.

" To Mrs. Barrj/y Castle Barry.

" Spring House, Tuesday mominjr, October IStb, 1753.

" MY DEAREST MARY,

" I am afraid I am going to put your affection for your old friend and kinswoman to a severe trial. A two days'journey at this season, over bad roads and through a troubled country, it will indeed require friendship such as yours to persuade a sober woman to encounter. But the truth is, I have, or fancy I have, more than usual cause for wishing you near me. You know my son's story. I can't tell how it is, but as next Sunday approaches, when the prediction of his dream or his vision will be proved false or true, I feel a sickening of the heart, which I cannot suppress, but which your presence, my dear Mary, will soften, as it has done so many of my sorrows. My nephew, James Ryan, is to be married to Jane Osborne (who, you know, is my son's ward), and the bridal entertainment will take place here on Sunday next, though Charles pleaded hard to have it postponed a day or two longer. Would to God—^but no more of this till we meet. Do prevail upon yourself to leave your good man for one week, if his farming concerns will not admit of his accompanying you; and come to us, with the girls, as soon before Sunday as you can.

"Ever my dear Mary's attached cousin and friend,

" Ann Mac Carthy."

LtGENDS OP THE BANSHEE. 117

Although this letter reached Castle Barry early on Wednesday, the messenger having travelled on foot, over bog and moor, by paths impassable to horse or carriage, Mrs. Barry, who at once determined on going, had so many arrangements to make for the regulation of her domestic affairs (which, in Ireland, among the middle orders of the gentry, fall soon into confusion when the mistress of the family is away), that she and her two younger daughters were unable to leave home until late on the morning of Friday. The eldest daughter remained, to keep her father company, and superintend the concerns of the household. As the travellers were to journey in an open one-horse vehicle, called a jaunting-car (still used in Ireland), and as the roads, bad at all times, were rendered still worse by the heavy rains, it was their design to make two easy stages; to stop about mid-way the first night, and reach Spring House early on Saturday evening. This arrangement was now altered, as they found that, from the lateness of their departure, they could proceed, at the utmost, no further than twenty miles on the first day; and they therefore purposed sleeping at the house of a Mr. Bourke, a friend of theirs, who lived at somewhat less than that distance from Castle Barry. They reached Mr. Bourke's in safety, after rather a disagreeable drive. What befel them on their journey the next day to Spring House, and after their arrival there, is fully related in a letter from the second Miss Barry to her eldest sister.

" Spring House, Sunday ereniog, 20th October, 1752. " DEAR ELLEN,

" As my mother's letter, which encloses this^ will announce to you briefly the sad intelligence which I shall here relate more fully, I think it better to go regularly through the recital of the extraordinary events of the last two days.

" The Bourkes kept us up so late on Friday night, that yesterday was pretty far advanced before we could begin our journey, and the day closed when we were nearly fifteen miles distant from this place. The roads were excessively deep, from the heavy rains of the last week, and we proceeded so slowly, that at last my mother resolved on passing the night at the house of Mr. Bourke's brother (who lives about a quarter of a mile off the road), and coming here to breakfast in the morning. The day had been windy and showery, and the sky looked fitful, gloomy, and uncertain. The moon was full, and at times shone clear and bright; at others, it was wholly concealed behind the thick, black, and rugged masses of clouds, that rolled rapidly along, and were every moment becoming larger, and collecting together, as if gathering strength for a coming storm. The wind, which blew in our faces, whistled bleakly along the low hedges of the narrow road, on which we proceeded with difficulty from the number of deep sloughs, and which afforded not the least shelter, no plantation being within some miles of us. My mother, therefore, asked Leary, who drove the jaunting-car, how far

we were from Mr. Bourke's. ' 'Tis about ten spades from this to the cross, and we have then only to turn to the left into the avenue, ma'am.' ' Very well, Leary : turn up to Mr. Bourke's as soon as you reach the cross roads.' My mother liad scarcely spoken these words, when a shriek that made us thrill as if our very hearts were pierced by it, burst from the hedge to the right of our way. If it resembled anything earthly, it seemed the cry of a female, struck by a sudden and mortal blow, and giving out her life in one long deep pang of expiring agony. ' Heaven defend us!' exclaimed my mother. ' Go you over the hedge, Leary, and save that woman, if she is not yet dead, while we rvm back to the hut we just passed, and alarm the village near it.' * Woman !' said Leary, beating the horse violently, while his voice trembled—' that's no woman : the sooner we get on, ma'am, the better;' and he continued his efforts to qixicken the horse's pace. We saw nothing. The moon was hid. It was quite dark, and we had been for some time expecting a heavy fall of rain. But just as Leary had spoken, and had succeeded in making the horse trot briskly forward, we distinctly heard a loud clapping of hands, followed by a succession of screams, that seemed to denote the last excess of despair and anguish, and to issue from a person running forward inside the hedge, to keep pace with our progress. Still we saw nothing ; until, when we were within about ten yards of the place where an avenue branched off to Mr. Bourke's to the left, and the road turned to Spring House on the right, the moon started suddenly from behind

a cloud, and enabled us to see, as plainly as I now see this paper, the figure of a tall thin woman, with uncovered head, and long hair that floated round her shoulders, attired in something which seemed either a loose white cloak, or a sheet thrown hastily about her. She stood on the comer hedge, where the road on which we were met that which leads to Spring House, with her face towards us, her left hand pointing to this place, and her right arm waving rapidly and violently, as if to draw us on in that direction. The horse had stopped, apparently frightened at the sudden presence of the figure, which stood in the manner I have described, still uttering the same piercing cries, for about half a minute. It then leaped upon the road, disappeared from our view for one instant, and the next was seen standing upon a high wall a little way up the avenue, on which we purposed going, still pointmg towards the road to Spring House, but in an attitude of defiance and command, as if prepared to oppose our passage up the avenue. The figure was now quite silent, and its garments, which had before flown loosely in the wind, were closely wrapped around it. ' Go on, Leary, to Spring House, in God's name,' said my mother ; ' whatever world it belongs to, we will provoke it no longer.' ' 'Tis the Banshee, ma'am,' said Leary ; ' and I would not, for Avhat my life is worth, go any where this blessed night but to Spring House. But I'm afraid there's something bad going forward, or the would not send us there.' So saying, he drove forward; and as we turned on the road to the right, the moon suddenly withdrew its light, and

we saw the apparition no more; but we heard plainly a prolonged clapping of hands, gradually-dying away, as if it issued from a person rapidly retreating. We proceeded as quickly as the badness of the roads and the fatigue of the poor animal that drew us would allow, and arrived here about eleven'o'clock last night. The scene which awaited us you have learned from my mother's letter. To explain it fully, I must recount to you some of the transactions which took place here during the last week.

" You are aware that Jane Osborne was to have been maiTied this day to James Ryan, and that they and their friends have been here for the last week. On Tuesday last, the very day on the morning of which cousin Mac Carthy despatched the letter inviting us here, the whole of the company were walking about the grounds a little before dinner. It seems that an unfortunate creature, who had been seduced by James Ryan, was seen prowling in the neighbourhood in a moody melancholy state for some days previous. He had separated from her for several months, and, they say, had provided for her rather handsomely ; but she had been seduced by the promise of his marrying her; and the shame of her unhappy condition, uniting with disappointment and jealousy, had disordered her intellects. During the whole forenoon of this Tuesday, she had been walking in the plantations near Spring House, with her cloak folded tight round her, the hood nearly covering her face; and she had avoided conversing with or even meeting any of the family.

" Charles Mac Carthy, at the time I mentioned, was walking between James Ryan and another, at a little distance from the rest, on a gravel path, skirting a shnibber\'7d'-. The whole party were thrown into the utmost consternation by tlie report of a pistol, fired from a thickly planted part of the shrubbery, which Charles and his companions had just passed. He fell instantly, and it was found that lie had been wounded in the leg. One of the party was a medical man; his assistance was immediately given, and, on examining, he declared that the injury was very slight, that no bone was broken, that it was merely a flesh wound, and that it would certainly be well in a few days. ' We shall know more by Sunday,' said Charles, as he was carried to his chamber. His wound was immediately dressed, and so slight was the inconvenience which it gave, that several of his friends spent a portion of the evening in his apartment.

" On inquiry, it was found that the imlucky shot was fired by the poor girl I just mentioned. It was also manifest that she had aimed, not at Charles, but at the destroyer of her innocence and happiness, who was walking beside him. After a fruitless search for her through the groimds, she walked into the house of her own accord, laughing, and dancing and singing wildly, and every moment exclaiming that she had at last killed Mr. Ryan. When she heard that it was Charles, and not Mr. Ryan, who was shot, she fell into a violent fit, out of which, after working convulsively for some time, she sprung to the door, escaped from the crowd that pursued her, and could never

be taken until last night, when she was brought here, perfectly frantic, a little before our arrival.

" Charles's wound was thought of such little consequence, that the preparations went forward, as usual, for the wedding entertainment on Sunday. But on Friday night he grew restless and feverish, and on Saturday (yesterday) morning felt so ill, that it was deemed necessary to obtain additional medical advice. Two physicians and a surgeon met in consultation about twelve o'clock in the day, and the dreadful intelligence was announced, that unless a change, hardly hoped for, took place before night, death must happen within twenty-four hours after. The wound, it seems, had been too tightly bandaged, and otherwise injudiciously treated. The physicians were right in their anticipations. No favourable symptom appeared, and long before we reached Spring House every ray of hope had vanished. The scene we witnessed on our arrival would have wrung the heart of a demon. We heard briefly at the gate that 3Ir. Charles was upon his death-bed. When we reached the house, the information was confirmed by the servant who opened the door. But just as we entered, we were horrified by the most appalling screams issuing from the staircase. My mother thought she heard the voice of poor Mrs. Mac Carthy, and sprung forward. We followed, and on ascending a few steps of the stairs, we found a young woman, in a state of frantic passion, struggling furiously with two men-servants, whose united strength was hardly sufficient to prevent her rushing up stairs over the body of Mrs. Mac Carthy, who was lying in strong hysterics upon

the steps. This, I afterwards discovered, was the unhappy girl I before described, who was attempting to gain access to Charles's room, to ' get his forgiveness,' as she said, ' before he went away to accuse her for having killed him.' This wild idea was mingled with another, which seemed to dispute with the former possession of her mind. In one sentence she called on Charles to forgive her, in the next she would denounce James Ryan as the murderer both of Charles and her. At length she was torn away ; and the last words I heard her scream were, ' James Ryan, 'twas you killed him, and not I—'twas you killed him, and not I.'

" Mrs. Mac Carthy, on recovering, fell into the arms of my mother, whose presence seemed a great relief to her. She wept—^the first tears, I was told, that she had shed since the fatal accident. She conducted us to Charles's room, who, she said, had desired to see us the moment of our arrival, as he found his end approaching, and wished to devote the last hours of his existence to uninterrupted prayer and meditation. We found him perfectly calm, resigned, and even cheerful. He spoke of the awful event which was at hand with courage and confidence, and treated it as a doom for which he had been preparing ever since his former remarkable illness, and which he never once doubted was truly foretold to him. He bade us farewell with the air of one who was about to travel a short and easy journey; and we left him with impressions which, notwithstanding all their anguish, will, I trust, never entirely forsake us.

" Poor Mrs. Mac Carthy but I am just

called away. There seems a slight stir in the family; perhaps "

The above letter was never finished. The enclosure to which it more than once alludes, told the sequel briefly, and it is all that I have farther learned of this branch of the Mac Carthy family. Before the sun had gone down upon Charles's seven-and-twentieth birthday, his soul had gone to render its last account to its Creator.

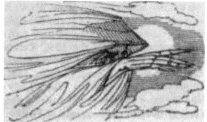

" Banshee, correctly written IjeAOriae, plural iDtjΛ-nSe. ste-fairies or women fairies, credulously supposed, by the common people, to be so affected to certain families, that they are heard to sing mournful lamentations about their houses at ni^ht, whenever any of the family labours under a sickness which is to end in death. But no families which are not of an ancient and noble stock are believed to be honoured with this fairy privilege."— O'Brien's Irish Dictionary.

For accounts of the appearance of the Irish Banshee, see " Personal Sketches, &c. by Sir Jonah Barrington ; " Miss Lefanu's Memoirs of her Grandmother, Mrs. Frances Sheridan (1824), p. 32; "The Memoirs of Lady Fanshaw" (quoted by Sir Walter Scott in a note on " the Lady of tlie Lake,") &c.

Sir Walter Scott terms the belief in the appearance of the Banshee " one of the most beautiful" of the leading superstitions of Europe. In his " Letters on Demonology," he says that "several families of the Highlands of Scotland anciently laid claim to the distinction of an attendant spirit, who performed the office of the Irish Banshee," and particularly refers to the supernatural cries and lamentations which foreboded the death of the gallant Mac Lean of Lochbuy.

" The Welsh Gwrach y Rhibyn (or the hag of the Dribble) bears some resemblance to the Irish Banshee, being regarded as an omen of death. She is said to come after dusk and flap her leathern wings against the window where she warns of death, and in a broken, howling tone, to call on the one who is to quit mortality by his or her name several times, as Ihas, A-a-a-n-nii-i-i! Anni." — MS. Communica-tion/rom Dr. Owen Pcjghe. For some further particulars, see, in "A Relation of Apparitions, &c. by the Rev. Edmund Jones," his account of the Kyhirraeth, " a doleful foreboding noise before death;" and Howell's " Cambrian Superstitions," (Tipton, 1831), p. 31.

The reader will probably remember the White Lady of the House of Brandenburgh, and the fairy Melusine, who usually prognosticated the recurrence of mortality in some noble family of Poitou. Prince, in his " Worthies of Devon," records the appearance of a white bird performing the same office for the worshipful lineage of Oxenham.

" In the Tyrol, too, they believe in a spirit which looks in at the window of the house in which a person is to die (Deutsche Sagen, No. 260 ; the white woman with a veil over her head (267), answers to the Banshee; but the tradition of the Klage-tceib (mourning woman), in the Lilneburger Heath \'7bSpiels Archiv. ii. 297), resembles it still more closely. On stormy nights, when the moon shines faintly through the fleeting clouds, she stalks, of gigantic stature, with deathlike aspect, and black hollow eyes, wrapt in grave-clothes which float in the wind, and stretches her immense arm over the solitary hut, uttering lamentable cries in the tempestuous darkness. Beneath the roof over which the Klage-weib has leaned, one of the inmates must die in the course of the month."— The Brothers Grimm, and MS, Communication from Dk. William Grimm.

FAIRY LEGENDS.
THE PHOOKA.

' Ne let house-fires, nor lightnings helpless harms, Ne let the Pouke, nor other evil spright, Ne let mischievous witches with their charms, Ne let hobgoblins, names whose sense we see not, Fray us with things that be not."

Spbnsbr.

LEGENDS OF THE PHOOKA.

THE SPIRIT HORSE.

XIV.

The history of Morty Sullivan ought to be a warning to all young men to stay at home, and to live decently and soberly if they can, and not to go roving about the world. Morty, when he had just turned of fourteen, ran away from his father and mother, who were a mighty respectable old couple, and many and many a tear they shed on his account. It is said they both died heartbroken for his loss: all they ever learned about him was that he went on board of a ship bound to America.

Thirty years after the old couple had been laid peacefully in their graves, there came a stranger to Beer haven inquiring after them—it was their son Morty; and, to speak the truth of him, his heart did seem full of sorrow when he heard that his parents were dead and gone;—but what else could he expect to hear ? Repentance generally comes when it is too late.

Morty Sullivan, however, as an atonement for his' sins, was recommended to perform a pilgrim-

K

age to the blessed chapel of Saint Gobnate, which is in a wild place called Ballyvoumey.

This he readily undertook ; and willing to lose no time, commenced his journey the same afternoon. He had not proceeded many miles before the evening came on: there was no moon, and the starlight was obscured by a thick fog, which ascended from the valleys. His way was through a mountainous country, with many cross-paths and by-ways, so that it was difficult for a stranger like Morty to travel without a guide. He was anxious to reach his destination, and exerted himself to do so; but the fog grew thicker and thicker, and at last he became doubtful if the track he was in led to the blessed chapel of Saint Gobnate. But seeing a light which he imagined not to be far off, he went towards it, and when he thought himself close to it, the light suddenly seemed at a great distance, twinkling dimly through the fog. Though Morty felt some surprise at this, he was not disheartened, for he thought that it was a light sent by the holy Saint Gobnate to guide his feet through the mountains to her chapel.

And thus did he travel for many a mile, continually, as he believed, approaching the light, which would suddenly start off to a great distance. At length he came so close as to perceive tliat the light came from ^ tire : seated beside which he plainly saw an old woman;—then, indeed, his faith was a little shaken, and much did he wonder that both the fire and the old woman should travel before liim, so many weary miles, and over such uneven roads.

" In the holy names of the pious Gobnate, and of her preceptor Saint Abban," said Morty, " how can that burning fire move on so fast before me, and who can that old woman be sitting beside the moving fire ?"

These words had no sooner passed Morty's lips than he found himself, without taking another step, close to this wonderful fire, beside which the old woman was sitting munching her supper. AYith every wag of the old woman's jaw her eyes would roll fiercely upon Morty, as if she was angry at being disturbed; and he saw with more astonishment than ever that her eyes were neither black, nor blue, nor gray, nor hazel, like the human eye, but of a wild red colour, like the eye of a ferret. If before he wondered at the fire, much greater was his wonder at the old woman's appearance ; and stout-hearted as he was, he could not but look upon her with fear— judging, and judging rightly, that it was for no good purpose her supping in so unfrequented a place, and at so late an hour, for it was near midnight. She said not one word, but munched and munched away, while Morty looked at her in silence.—" What's your name?" at last demanded the old hag, a sulphureous puff coming out of her mouth, her nostrils distending, and her eyes growing redder than ever, when she had finished her question.

Plucking up all his courage, " Morty Sullivan," replied he, " at your service;" meaning the latter words only in civility.

" Uhhubho ! " said the old woman, " we'll soon see that;" and the red fire of lier eyes turned into a pale green colour. Bold and fearless as

K'2

Morty was, yet much did he tremble at hearing this dreadful exclamation: he would have fallen down on his knees and prayed to Saint Gobnate, or any other saint, for he was not particular ; but he was so petrified with horror, that he could not move in the slightest way, much less go down on his knees.

" Take hold of my hand, Morty," said the old woman : " I'll give you a horse to ride that will soon carry you to your journey's end." So saying, she led the way, the fire going before them ;—it is beyond mortal knowledge to say how, but on it went, shooting out bright tongues of flame, and flickering fiercely.

Presently they came to a natural cavern in the side of the mountain, and the old hag called aloud in a most discordant voice for her horse! In a moment a jet-black steed started from its gloomy stable, the rocky floor whereof rung with a sepulchral echo to the clanging hoofs.

" Mount, Morty, mount!" cried she" seizing him with supernatural streng-th, and forcing him upon the back of the horse. 5lorty finding human power of no avail, muttered, " 0 that I had spurs !" and tried to gi*asp the horse's mane; but he caught at a shadow; it nevertheless bore him up and bounded forward with him, now springing down a fearful precipice, now clearing the rugged bed of a torrent, and rushing like the dark midnight storm through the mountains.

The following morning Morty Sullivan was discovered by some pilgrims (who came that way after taking their rounds at Gougane Barra) lying on the flat of his back, under a steep cliff, down

which he had been flung by the Phooka. Morty was severely bruised by the fall, and he is said to have sworn on the spot, by the hand of O'SuUivan (and that is no sntiall oath),* never again to take a full quart bottle of whiskey with him on a pil-grintiage.

* " Nulla manus, Tam liberalis Atque generalis Atque universalis Quam Sullivanis."

DANIEL OTtOURKE,

XV.

People may have heard of the renowned adventures of Daniel O'Rourke, but how few are there who know that the cause of all his perils, above and below, was neither more nor less than his having slept under the walls of the Phooka's tower ! I knew the man well; he lived at the bottom of Hungry HiU, just at the right hand side of the road as you go towards Bantry. An old man was he at the time that he told me the story, with gray hair, and a red nose; and it was on the 25th of June, 1813, that I heard it from his own lips, as he sat smoking his pipe under the old poplar tree, on as fine an evening as ever shone from the sky. I was going to visit the caves in Dursey Island, having spent the morning at GlengarifF.

" I am often axed to tell it, sir," said he, " so that this is not the first time. The master's son, you see, had come from beyond foreign parts in France and Spain, as young gentlemen used to go, before Buonaparte or any such was heard of; and sure enough there was a dinner given to all the people on the ground, gentle and simple, high and low, rich and poor. The ould gentlemen were the gentlemen, after all, saving your honour's presence. They'd swear at a body a little, to be sure, and, may be, give one a cut of a whip now and then, but we were no losers by it in the end;

-—and they were so easy and civil, and kept such rattling houses, and thousands of welcomes;— and there was no grinding for rent, and few agents; and there was hardly a tenant on the estate that did not taste of his landlord's bounty often and often in the year;—but now it's another thing: no matter for that, sir, for I'd better be telling you my story.

" Well, we had every thing of the best, and plenty of it; and we ate, and we drank, and we danced, and the young master by the same token danced with Peggy Barry, from the Bohereen— a lovely young couple they were, though they are both low enough now. To make a long story short, I got, as a body may say, the same thing as tipsy almost, for I can't I'emember ever at all, no ways, liow it was I left the place : only I did leave it, that's certain. Well, I thought, for all that, in myself, I'd just step to Molly Cronohan's, the fairy woman, to speak a word about the bracket heifer that was bewitched; and so as I was crossing the stepping-stones of the ford of Ballyasheenough, and was looking up at tlie stars and blessing myself—for why ? it was Lady-day —I missed my foot, and souse I fell into the water. ' Death alive 1' thought I, ' I'll be drowned now !' However, I began swimming, swimming, swimming away for the dear life, till at last I got ashore, somehow or other, but never the one of me can tell how, upon a dissolute island.

" I wandered and wandered about there, without knowing where I wandered, until at last I got into a big bog. The moon was shining as

bright as day, or your fair lady's eyes, sir (with your pardon for mentioning her), and I looked east and west, and north and south, and every way, and nothing did I see but bog, bog, bog;— I could never find out how I got into it; and my heart grew cold with fear, for sure and certain I was that it would be my berrin place. So I sat down upon a stone w-hich, as good luck would have it, was close by me, and I began to scratch my head and sing the Ullagone —when all of a sudden the moon grew black, and I looked up, and saw something for all the world as if it was moving dowTi between me and it, and I could not tell what it was. Down it came with a pounce, and looked at me full in the face ; and what was it but an eagle ? as fine a one as ever flew from the kingdom of Kerry. So he looked at me in the face, and says he to me, ' Daniel O'Rourke,' says he, ' how do you do V 'Very well, I thank you, sir,' says I : ' I hope you're well;' wondering out of my senses all the time how an eagle came to speak like a Cliristian. ' What brings you here, Dan ?' says he. ' Nothing at all, sir,' says I: 'only I wish I was safe home again.' 'Is it out of the island you want to go, Dan ?' says he. ' 'Tis, sir,' says I : so I up and told him how I had taken a drop too much, and fell into the water; how I swam to the island; and how I got into the bog and did not know my way out of it. ' Dan,' says he, after a minute's thought, ' though it is very improper for you to get drunk on Lady-day, yet as you are a decent sober man, who 'tends mass well, and never flings stones at me nor mine, nor cries out after us in the fields—

my life for yours,' says be; 'so get up on my back, and grip me well for fear you'd fall off, and I'll fly you out of the bog.' ' I am afraid,' says I, ' your honour's making game of me ; for who ever heard of riding a horseback on an eagle before ? ' ' 'Pon the honour of a gentleman,' says he, putting liis right foot on his breast, ' I am quite in earnest; and so now either take my offer or starve in the bog—besides, I see that your weight is sinking the stone.'

" It was true enough as he said, for I found the stone eveiy minute going from under me. I had no choice; so thinks I to myself, faint heart never won fair lady, and this is fair per-suadance :—' I thank your honour,' says I, ' for the loan of your civility; and I'll take your kind offer.' I therefore mounted upon the back of the eagle, and held him tight enough by the throat, and up he flew in the air like a lark. Little I knew the trick he was going to serve me. Up—up—up—God knows how far up he flew. ' Wliy, then,' said I to him,—thinking he did not know tlie right road home—very civilly, because wliy ?—I was in his power entirely ;—' sir,' says I, ' please your honour's glory, and with humble submission to your better judgment, if you'd fly down a bit, you're now just over my cabin, and I could be i)ut down there, and many thanks to your worship.'

" '• Arrah, Dan,' said he, ' do you think me a fool ? Look do^^^l in the next field, and don't you see two men and a gim ? By my word it would be no joke to be shot this way, to oblige a dnmken blackguard that I picked up off of a could stone

in a bog.' ' Bother you,' said I to myself, but I did not speak out, for where was the use? Well, sir, up he kept, flying, flying, and I asking him every minute to fly down, and all to no use. ' Where in the world are you going, sir ?' says I to him. ' Hold your tongue, Dan,' says he: ' mind your own business, and don't be interfering with the business of other people.' ' Faith, this is my business, I think,' says I. 'Be quiet, Dan,' says he: so I said no more.

" At last, where should we come to, but to the moon itself. Now you can't see it from this, but there is, or there was in my time, a reaping-hook sticking out of the side of the moon, this way, (drawing the figure thus (^~\. on the ground

with the end of his stick).

" ' Dan,' said the eagle, ' I'm tired with this long fly; I had no notion 'twas so far.' ' And my lord, sir,' said I, ' who in the world aj;ed you to fly so far—was it I ? did not I beg, and pray, and beseech you to stop half an hour ago ?' ' There's no use talking, Dan,' said he; ' I'm tired bad enough, so you must get ofl^, and sit down on the moon until I rest myself.' ' Is it sit down on the moon ?' said I; ' is it upon that little round thing, then ? why, then, sure I'd fall ofl'in a minute, and be kilt and split, and smashed all to bits : you are a vile deceiver,—so you are.' ' Not at all, Dan,' said he : ' you can catch fast hold of the reaping-hook that's sticking out of the side of the moon, and 'twill keep you up.' ' I won't, then,' said I. ' May be not,' said he, quite quiet. ' If you don't, my man, I shall just give you a shake, and one slap of my wing, and send

you down to the ground, where every bone in your body will be smashed as small as a drop of dew on a cabbage-leaf in the morning.' ' Why, then, I'm in a fine way,' said I to myself, ' ever to have come along with the likes of you;' and so giving him a hearty curse in Irish, for fear he'd know what I said, I got oif his back with a heavy heart, took a hold of the reaping-hook, and sat down upon the moon; and a mighty cold seat it was, I can tell you that.

" When he had me there fairly landed, he turned about on me, and said, ' Good morning to you, Daniel O'Rourke,' said he : 'I think I've nicked you fairly now. You robbed my nest last year,' ('twas true enough for him, but how he found it out is hard to say,) ' and in return you are freely welcome to cool your heels dangling upon the moon like a cockthrow.'

" ' Is that all, and is this the way you leave me, you brute, you ?' says I. ' You ugly unnatural haste, and is this the way you serve me at last ? Bad luck to yourself,lwith your hook'd nose, and to all your breed, you blackguard.' 'Twas all to no manner of use : he spread out his great big wings, burst out a laughing, and flew away like lightning. I bawled after him to stop ; but I might have called and bawled for ever, without his minding me. Away he went, and I never saw him from that day to this—sorrow fly away with him! You may be sure I was in a disconsolate condition, and kept roaring out for the bare grief, when all at once a door opened right in the middle of the moon, creaking on its hinges as if it had not been opened for a month

before, I suppose they never thought of greasing 'em, and out there walks—wiio do you think but the man in the moon himself ? I knew him by his bush.

" ' Good morrow to you, Daniel O'Rourke,' said he : ' How do you do ?' ' Very well, thank your honour,' said I. ' I hope your honour's well,' ' What brought you here, Dan ? ' said he. So I told him how I was a little overtaken in liquor at the master s, and how I was cast on a dissolute island, and how I lost my way in the bog, and how the thief of an eagle promised to fly me out of it, and how instead of that he had fled me up to the moon.

" ■ ' Dan,' said the man in the moon, taking a pinch of snuff when I was done, ' you must not stay here.' ' Indeed, sir,' says I, ' 'tis much against my will I'm here at all; but how am I to go back ? ' ' That's your business,' said he, ' Dan : mine is to tell you that here you must not stay, so be off in less than no time.' ' I'm doing no harm,' says I, ' only holding on hard by the reaping-hook, lest I fall off.' 'That's what you must not do, Dan,' says he. * Pray, sir,' says I, ' may I ask how many you are in family, that you would not give a poor traveller lodging: I'm sure 'tis not so often you're troubled with strangers coming to see you, for 'tis a long way.' ' I'm by myself, Dan,' says he; ' but you'd better let go the reaping-hook.' ' Faith, and with your leave,' says I, ' I'll not let go the grip, and the more you bids me, the more I won't let go;—so I will,' ' You had better, Dan,' says he again, ' Why, then, my little fel-

low,' says I, taking the whole weight of him with my eye from head to foot, ' there are two words to that bargain; and I'll not hudge, but you may if you like.' ' We'll see how that is to be,' says lie; and back he went, giving the door sucli a great bang after him (for it was plain he was huffed), that I thought the moon and all would fall down with it.

" Well, I was preparing myself to try strength with liim, when back again he comes, with the kitchen cleaver in his hand, and v^thout saying a word, he gives two bangs to the handle of the reaping-hook that was keeping me up, and ichap ! it came in two. ' Good morning to you, Dan,' says the spiteful little old blackguard, when he saw me cleanly falling down with a bit of the handle in my hand: ' I thank you for your visit, and fair weather after you, Daniel.' I had not time to make any answer to him, for I was tumbling over and over, and rolling and rolling at the rate of a fox-lumt. ' God help me,' says I, ' but this is a pretty pickle for a decent man to be seen in at this time of night; I am now sold fairly.' The word was not out of my mouth, wlien whiz ! what should fly by close to my ear but a flock of wild geese; all the way from my own bog of Ballyasheenough, else how should they know me ? The ould gander, who was their general, turning about his head, cried out to me,' Is that you, Dan ?' ' The same,' said I, not a bit daunted now at what he said, for I was by this time used to all kinds of bedevilment, and, besides, I knew him of ould. ' Good morrow to you,' says he, ' Daniel O'Rourke: how are you in health this

morning ?' ' Very well, sir,' says I, ' I thank you kindly,' drawing my breath, for I was mightily in want of some, ' I hope your honour's the same.' * I think 'tis falling you are, Daniel,' says he, ' You may say that, sir,' says I. ' And where are you going all the way so fast ?' said the gander. So I told him how I had taken the drop, and how I came on the island, and how I lost my way in the bog, and how the thief of an eagle flew me up to the moon, and how the man in the. moon turned me out. ' Dan,' said he, ' I'll save you : put out your hand and catch me by the leg, and I'll fly you home.' ' Sweet is your hand in a pitcher of honey, my jewel,' says I, though all the time I thought in myself that I don't much trust you; but there was no help, so I caught the gander by the leg, and away I and the other geese flew after him as fast as hops.

" We flew, and we flew, and we flew, until we came right over the wide ocean. I knew it well, for I saw Cape Clear to my right hand, sticking up out of the water. ' Ah ! my lord,' said I to the goose, for I thought it best to keep a civil tongue m my head any way,' fly to land, if you please.' ' It is impossible, you see, Dan,' said he, ' for a while, because you see we are going to Arabia.' ' To Arabia !' said I; ' that's surely some place in foreign parts, far away. Oh ! Mr. Goose: why then, to be sure, I'm a man to be pitied among you.' ' Whist, whist, you fool,' said he, ' hold your tongue; I tell you Arabia is a very decent sort of place, as like West Carbery as one egg is like another, only there is a little more sand there.'

" Just as we were talking, a ship hove in sight, scudding so beautiful before the wind: ' Ah! then, sir,' said I, ' will you drop me on the ship, if you please V ' We are not fair over it,' said he. ' We are,' said I, ' We are not,' said he: ' If I dropped you now, you would go splash into the sea.' ' I would not,' says I: ' I know better than that, for it's just clean under us, so let me drop now at once.'

" ' If you must, you must,' said he. ' There, take your own way ;' and he opened his claw, and faith he was right—sure enough I came down plump into the very bottom of the salt sea! Down to the very bottom I went, and I gave myself up then for ever, when a whale walked up to me, scratching himself after his night's sleep, and looked me full in the face, and never the word did he say, but lifting up his tail, he splashed me all over again with the cold salt water, till there wasn't a dry stitch upon my whole carcass; and I heard somebody saying— 'twas a voice I knew too—' Get up, you drunken brute, off of that;' and with that I woke up, and there was Judy with a tub full of water, which she was splashing all over me;—for, rest her soul! though she was a good wife, she never could bear to see me in drink, and had a bitter hand of her own.

" ' Get up,' said she again: ' and of all places in the parish, would no place sarve your turn to lie down upon but under the ould walls of Carrig-aphooka ? an uneasy resting I am sure you had of it.' And sure enough I had ; for I was fairly bothered out of my senses with eagles, and men

DANIEL OROURKE.

of the moon, and flying ganders, and whales, driving me through hogs, and up to the moon, and down to the bottom of the green ocean. If I was in drink ten times over, long wonld it be before I'd lie down in the same spot again, I know that."

THE CEOOKENED BACK.
XVI.

Peggy Barrett was once tall, well-shaped, and comely. She was in her youth remarkable for two qualities, not often found together, of being the most thrifty housewife, and the best dancer in her native village of Ballyhooley. But she is now upwards of sixty years old; and during the last ten years of her life, she has never been able to stand upright. Her back is bent nearly to a level; yet she has the freest use of all her limbs that can be enjoyed in such a posture ; her health is good, and her mind vigorous ; and, in the family of her eldest son, with whom she has lived since the death of her husband, she performs all the domestic services which her age, and the infirmity just mentioned, allow. She washes the potatoes, makes the fire, sweeps the house (labours in which she good-humouredly says " she finds her crooked back mighty convenient"), plays with the children, and tells stories to the family and their neighbouring friends, who often collect round her sou's fireside to hear them during the long winter evenings. Her powers of conversation are highly extolled, both for humour and in narration; and anecdotes of droll or awkward incidents, connected with the posture in which she has been so long fixed, as well as the history of the occurrence to which she owes that misfortune, are favourite topics of her discourse.

L

Among other matters, she is fond of relating how, on a certain day, at the close of a bad harvest, when several tenants of the estate on which she lived concerted in a field a petition for an abatement of rent, they placed the paper on which they wrote upon her back, which was found no very inconvenient substitute for a table.

Peggy, like all experienced story-tellers, suited her tales, both in length and subject, to the audience and the occasion. She knew that, in broad daylight, when the sun shines brightly, and the trees are budding, and the birds singing around us, when men and women, like ourselves, are moving and speaking, employed variously in business or amusement; she knew, in short (though certainly without knowing or much caring wherefore), that when we are engaged about the realities of life and nature, we want that spirit of credulity, without which tales of the deepest interest will lose their power. At such times Peggy was brief, very particular as to facts, and never dealt in the marvellous. But round tlie blazing hearth of a Christmas evening, when infidelity is banished from all companies, at least in low and simple life, as a quality, to say the least of it, out of season; when the winds of " dark December" whistled bleakly round the walls, and almost through the doors of the little mansion, reminding its inmates, that as the world is vexed by elements superior to human power, so it may be visited by beings of a superior nature:—at such times would Peggy Barrett give full scope to her memory, or her imagination, or both; and upon one of these occasions, she gave the follow-

ing circumstantial account of the " crookening of her back."

" It was, of all days in the year, the day before May-day, that I went out to the garden to weed the potatoes. I would not have gone out that day, but I was dull in myself, and sorrowful, and wanted to be alone; all the boys and girls were laughing and joking in the house, making goaling-balls and dressing out ribands for the mummers next day. I couldn't bear it. 'Twas only at the Easter that was then past (and that's ten years last Easter—I won't forget the time), that I buried my poor man; and I thought how gay and joyful I was, many a long year before that, at the May-eve before our wedding, when with Robin by my side, I sat cutting and sewing the ribands for the goaling-ball I was to give the boys on the next day, proud to be preferred above all the other girls of the banks of the Black water, by the handsomest boy and the best hurler in the village; so I left the house and went to the garden. I staid there all the day, and didn't come home to dinner. I don't know how it was, but somehow I continued on, weeding, and thinking sorrowfully enough, and singing over some of the old songs that I sung many and many a time in the days that are gone, and for them that never will come back to me to hear them. The truth is, I hated to go and sit silent and mournful among the people in the house, that were merry and young, and had the best of their days before them. 'Twas late before I thought of returning home, and I did not leave the garden till some 12

time after sunset. The moon was up; but though there wasn't a cloud to be seen, and though a star was winking here and there in the sky, the day wasn't long enough gone to have it clear moonlight; still it shone enough to make everything on one side of the heavens look pale and silvery-like; and the thin white mist was just beginning to creep along the fields. On the other side, near where the sun was set, there was more of daylight, and the sky looked angry, red, and fiery through the trees, like as if it was lighted up by a great town burning below. Every thing was as silent as a churchyard, only now and then one covdd hear far off a dog barking, or a cow lowing after being milked. There wasn't a creature to be seen on the road or in the fields. I wondered at this first, but then I remembered it was May-eve, and that many a thing, both good and bad, would be wandering about that night, and that I ought to shun danger as well as others. So I walked on as quick as I could, and soon came to the end of the demesne wall, where the trees rise high and thick at each side of the road, and almost meet at the top. My heart misgave me when I got under the shade. There was so much light let down fi'om the opening above, that I could see about a stone-throw before me. All of a sudden I heard a rustling among the branches, on the right side of the road, and saw something like a small black goat, only with long wide horns turned out instead of being bent backwards, standing upon its hind legs upon the top of the wall, and looking down on me.

My breath was stopped, and I couldn't move for near a minute. I couldn't help, somehow, keeping my eyes fixed on it; and it never stirred, but kept looking in the same fixed way down at me. At last I made a rush, and went on ; but I didn't go ten steps, when I saw the very same sight, on the wall to the left of me, standing in exactly the same manner, but three or four times as high, and almost as tall as the tallest man. The horns looked frightful; it gazed upon me as before; my legs shook, and my teeth chattered, and I thought I would drop down dead every moment. At last I felt as if I was obliged to go on—and on I went; but it was without feeling how I moved, or whether my legs carried me. Just as I passed the spot where this frightful thing was standing, I heard a noise as if something sprung from the wall, and felt like as if a heavy animal plumped down upon me, and held with the fore feet clinging to my shoulder, and the hind ones fixed in my gown, that was folded and pinned up behind me. 'Tis the wonder of my life ever since how I bore the shock; but so it was, I neither fell, nor even staggered with the weight, but walked on as if I had the strength of ten men, though I felt as if I couldn't help moving, and couldn't stand still if I wished it. Though I gasped with fear, I knew as well as I do now what I was doing. I tried to cry out, but couldn't; I tried to nm, but wasn't able; I tried to look back, but my head and neck were as if they were screwed in a vice. I could barely roll my eyes on each side, and then I could see, as clearly and plainly as if it was in

the broad light of the blessed sun, a black and cloven foot planted upon each of my shoulders. I heard a low breathing in my ear; I felt, at every step I took, my leg strike back against the feet of the creature that was on my back. Still I could do nothing but walk straight on. At last I came within sight of the house, and a welcome sight it was to me, for I thought I would be released when I reached it. I soon came close to the door, but it was shut; I looked at the little window, but it was shut too, for they were more cautious about May-eve than I was; I saw the light inside, through the chinks of the door; I heard 'em talking and laughing within; I felt myself at three yards' distance from them that .would die to save me;—and may the Lord save me fi'om ever again feeling what I did that night, when I found myself held by what couldn't be good uor friendly, but without the power to help myself, or to call my friends, or to put out my hand to knock, or even to lift my leg to strike the door, and let them know that I was outside it! 'Twas as if my hands grew to my sides, and my feet were glued to the ground, or had the weight of a rock fixed to them. At last I thought of blessing myself; and my right hand, that would do nothing else, did that for me. Still the weight remained on my back, and all was as before. I blessed' myself again: 'twas still all the same. I then gave myself up for lost: but I blessed myself a third time, and my hand no sooner finished the sign, than all at once I feh the burthen spring off of my back ; the door flew

open as if a clap of thunder burst it, and I was pitched forward on my forehead, in upon the middle of the floor. When I got up my back was crookened, and I never stood straight from that night to this blessed hour."

There was a pause when Peggy Barrett finished. Those who had heard the story before had listened with a look of half-satisfied interest, blended, however, with an expression of that serious and solemn feeling, which always attends a tale of supernatural wonders, how often soever told. They moved upon their seats out of the posture in which they had remained fixed during the narrative, and sat in an attitude which denoted that their curiosity as to the cause of this strange occurrence had been long since allayed. Those to whom it was before unknown still retained their look and posture of strained attention, and anxious but solemn expectation. A grandson of Peggy's, about nine years old (not the child of the son with whom she lived), had never before heard the story. As it grew in interest, he was observed to cling closer and closer to the old woman's side; and at the close he was gazing stedfastly at her, with his body bent back across her knees, and his face turned up to hers, with a look, through which a disposition to weep seemed contending with curiosity. After a moment's pause, he could no longer restrain his impatience, and catching her gray locks in one hand, while the tear of dread and wonder was just dropping from his eye-lash, he cried, " Granny, what was it ? •"

The old woman smiled first at the elder part of her audience, and then at her grandson, and patting him on the forehead, she said, " It was the Pliooka."

The Pmike or Phooka, as the word is pronounced, means, in plain terms, the Evil One. " Playing the puck," a common Anglo-Irish phrase, is equivalent to " playing the devil." Much learning has been displayed in tracing this word through various languages, vide Quarterly Review [vol. xxii.] &c. The commentators on .Shakspeare derive the beautiful and frolicksome Puck of the Midsummer Night's Dream from the mischievous Pouke—Vide Drayton's Xympbidia.

" This Puck seems but a dreaming dolt. Still walking like a ragged colt," &c.

In Golding'a tranUtion of Ovid's Metamorphoses (ISft?) we find,

•' and the countrie where Chymaera, that same Pooke,
Hath goatish bodie," &c.

The Irish Phooka, in its nature, perfectly resembles the Mahr ; and we have only to observe, that there is a particular German tradition of a spirit, which sits among reeds and alder bushes ; and which, like the Phooka, leaps upon the back of those who pass by in the night, and does not leave them till they faint and fall to the earth.

Thb Brothers Grium.

FAIRY LEGENDS.
THIERXA NA OGE.

' On Lough-Neagh'9 bank, as the fisherman strays. When the clear cold eve's declining, He sees the round towers of other days In the wave beneath him shining."

MOORB.

THIERNA NA OGE.

FIOR USGA.

A LITTLE way beyond the Gallows Green of Cork, and just outside the town, there is a great lough of water, where people in the winter go and skate for the sake of diversion; but the sport above the water is nothing to what is under it, for at the very bottom of this lough there are buildings and gardens, far more beautiful than any now to be seen, and how they came there was in this manner.

Long before Saxon foot pressed Irish ground, there was a great king called Core, whose palace stood where the lough now is, in a round green valley, that was just a mile about. In the middle of the court-yard was a spring of fair water, so pure, and so clear, that it was the wonder of all the world. Much did the king rejoice at having so great a curiosity within his palace; but as people came in crowds from far and near to draw the precious water of this spring, he was sorely afraid that in time it might become dry; so he caused a high wall to be bixilt up round it, and would allow nobody to have the water, which was

a very great loss to the poor people living about the palace. Whenever he wanted any for himself, he would send his daughter to get it, not liking to trust his servants with the key of the well-door, fearing that they might give some away.

One night the king gave a grand entertainment, and there were many great princes present, and lords and nobles without end; and there were wonderful doings throughout the palace: there were bonfires, whose blaze reached up to the very sky ; and dancing was there, to such sweet music, that it ought to have waked up the dead out of their graves; and feasting was there in the greatest of plenty for all who came; nor was any one turned away from the palace gates— but " you're welcome—you're welcome, heartily," was the porter's salute for all.

Now it happened at this grand entertainment there was one young prince above all the rest mighty comely to behold, and as tall and as straight as ever eye would wish to look on. Right merrily did he dance that night with the old king's daughter, wheeling here, and wheeling there, as light as a feather, and footing it away to the admiration of every one. The musicians played the better for seeing their dancing; and they danced as if their lives depended upon it. After all this dancing came the supper ; and the young prince was seated at table by the side of his beautiful partner, who smiled upon him as often as he spoke to her; and that was by no means so often as he wished, for he Iiad constantly to turn to the company and thank them for the many compliments passed upon his fair partner and himself.

In the midst of this banquet, one of the great lords said to King Core, " May it please your majesty, here is everything in abundance that heart can wish for, both to eat and drink, except water."

" Water!" said the king, mightily pleased at some one calling for that of which purposely there was a want: " water shall you have, my lord, speedily, and that of such a delicious kind, that I challenge all the world to equal it. Daughter," said he, " go fetch some in the golden vessel which I caused to be made for the purpose."

The king's daughter, who was called Fior Usga, (which signifies, in English, Spring Water,) did not much like to be told to perform so menial a service before so many people, and though she did not venture to refuse the commands of her father, yet hesitated to obey him, and looked down upon the ground. The king, who loved his daughter very much, seeing this, was sorry for what he had desired her to do, but having said the word, he was never known to recall it; he therefore thought of a way to make his daughter go speedily and fetch the water, and it was by proposing that the young prince her partner should go along with her. Accordingly, with a loud voice, he said, " Daughter, I wonder not at your fearing to go alone so late at night; but I doubt not the young prince at your side will go with you." The prince was not displeased at hearing this; and taking the golden vessel in one liand, with the other led the king's daughter out of the hall so gracefully that all present gazed after them with delight.

When they came to the spring of water, in the court-yard of the palace, the fair Usga unlocked the door with the greatest care, and stooping down with the golden vessel to take some of the water out of the well, found the vessel so heavy that she lost her balance and fell in. The young prince tried in vain to save her, for the water rose and rose so fast, that the entire court-yard was speedily covered with it, and he hastened back almost in a state of distraction to the king.

The door of the well being left open, the water, which had been so long confined, rejoiced at obtaining its liberty, rushed forth incessantly, every moment rising higher and higher, and was in the hall of the entertainment sooner than the young prince himself, so that when he attempted to speak to the king he was up to his neck in water. At length the water rose to such a height, that it filled the entire of the green valley in which the king's palace stood, and so the present lough of Cork was formed.

Yet the king and his guests were not drowned, as would now happen, if such an awful inundation were to take place ; neither was his daughter, the fair Usga, who returned to the banquet-hall the very next night after this dreadful event; and every night since the same entertainment and dancing goes on in the palace at the bottom of the lough, and will last until some one has the luck to bring up out of it the golden vessel which was the cause of all this mischief.

Nobody can doubt that it was a judgment upon the king for his shutting up the well in the courtyard from the poor people: and if there are any

who do not credit my story, they may go and see the lough of Cork, for there it is to be seen to this day ; the road to Kinsale passes at one side of it; and wlien its waters are low and clear, the tops of towers and stately buildings may be plainly viewed in the bottom by those who have good eyesight, without the help of spectacles.

CORMAC AND MARY.

XVIII.

" She is not dead—she has no grave-She lives beneath Lough Corrib's water * ;
And in the murmur of each wave
Methinks I catch the songs I taught her."
Thus many an evening on the shore Sat Cormac raving wild and lowly;
Still idly muttering o'er and o'er,
" She lives, detain'd by spells unholy.
*' Death claims her not, too fair for earth. Her spirit lives—'alien of heaven ;
Nor will it know a second birth When sinful mortals are forgiven!
" Cold is this rock—the wind comes chill, And mists the gloomy waters cover;
But oh! her soul is colder still—
To lose her God—to leave her lover!"
The lake was in profound repose.
Yet one white wave came gently curling.
And as it reach'd the shore, arose
Dim figures—banners gay unfurling.
• In the county of Galway.
Onward they move, an airy crowd :
Through each thin form a moonlight ray shone ; While spear and helm, in pageant proud.
Appear in liquid undulation.

Bright barbed steeds curvetting tread Their trackless way with antic capers;
And curtain clouds hang overhead,
Festoon'd by rainbow-colour d vapours.
And when a breath of air would stir
That drapery of Heaven's own wreathing,
Light wings of prismy gossamer
Just moved and sparkled to the breathing.
Nor wanting was the choral song.
Swelling in silvery chimes of sweetness ;
To sound of which this subtile throng Advanced in playful grace and fleetness.
With music's strain, all came and went Upon poor Cormac's doubting vision ;
Now rising in wild merriment, Now softly fading in derision.
" Christ, save her soul," he boldly cried ;
And when that blessed name was spoken, Fierce yells and fiendish shrieks replied,
And vanished all,'—the spell was broken.
M

CORMAC AND MARY.

And now on Coirib's lonely shore,
Freed by his word from power of faery,
To life, to love, restored once more,
Yoimg Cormac welcomes back his Mary.

THE LEGEND OF LOUGH GUR.

Larry Cotter had a farm on one side of Lougli Gur*, and was thriving in it, for lie was an industrious proper sort of man, who would have lived quietly and soberly to the end of his days, but for the misfortune that came upon him, and you shall hear how that was. He had as nice a bit of meadow-land, dowTi by the water-side, as ever a man would wish for; but its grovvi;h was spoiled entirely on him, and no one could tell how.

One year after the other it was all ruined just in the same way : the bounds were well made up, and not a stone of them was disturbed; neither could his neighbours' cattle have been guilty of the trespass, for they were spancelledf ; but however it was done, the grass of the meadow was destroyed, which was a great loss to Larry.

" What in the wide world wiU I do ?" said Larry Cotter to his neighbour, Tom Welsh, who was a very decent sort of man himself: " that bit of meadow-land, which I am paying the great rent for, is doing nothing at all to make it for me; and the times are bitter bad, without the help of that to make them worse."

" 'T is true for you, Larry," replied Welsh: "the times are bitter bad—no doubt of that; but may be if you were to watch by night, you

» In the county of Limerick. t Spancelled—fettereJ. M 2

might make out all about it: sure there's Mick and Terry, my two boys, will watch with you ; for 't is a thousand pities any honest man like you should be ruined in such a scheming way."

Accordingly, the following night, Larry Cotter, with Welsh's two sons, took their station in a comer of the meadow. It was just at the full of the moon, which was shining beautifully down upon the lake, that was as calm all over as the sky itself; not a cloud was there to be seen any where, nor a sound to be heard, but the crj' of the comcreaks answering one another across the water.

" Boys! boys !" said Larry, " look there ! look there! but for your lives don't make a bit of noise, nor stir a step till I say the word."

They looked, and saw a great fat cow, followed by seven milk-white heifers, moving on the smooth surface of the lake towards the meadow.

"'T is not Tim Dwyer the piper's cow, any way, that danced all the flesh off her bones," whispered Mick to his brother.

" Now boys!" said Larry Cotter, when he saw the fine cow and her seven white heifers fairly in the meadow, "get between them and the lake if you can, and, no matter who they belong to, we '11 just put them into the pound."

But the cow must have overheard Larry speaking, for dowTi she went in a great hurrj' to the shore of the lake, and into it with her, before all their eyes : away made the seven heifers after her, but the boys got down to the bank before them, and work enough they had to drive them up from the lake to Larry Cotter.

Larry drove the seven heifers, and beautiful heasts they were, to the pound : but after he had them there for three days, and could hear of no owner, he took them out, and put them up in a field of his own. There he kept them, and they were thriving mighty well with him, until one night the gate of the field was left open, and in the morning the seven heifers were gone. Larry coiild not get any account of them after; and, beyond all doubt, it was back into the lake they went. Wherever they came from, or to what-eveiv world they belonged, Larry Cotter never had a crop of grass off the meadow through their means. So he took to drink, fairly out of the grief; and it was the drink that killed him, they say.

THE ENCHANTED LAKE.
XX.

In the west of Ireland there was a lake, and no doubt it is there still, in which many young men had been at various times drowned. What made the circumstance remarkable was, that the bodies of the drowned persons were never found. People naturally wondered at this: and at length the lake came to have a bad repute. Many dreadful stories were told about that lake; some would affirm, that on a dark night its waters appeared like fire—others would speak of horrid forms which were seen to glide over it; and every one agreed that a strange sulphureous smell issued from out of it.

There lived, not far distant from this lake, a young farmer, named Roderick Keating, who was about to be married to one of the prettiest girls in that part of the country. On his return from Limerick, where he had been to purchase the wedding-ring, he came up with two or three of his acquaintance, who were standing on the shore, and they began to joke with him about Peggy Honan. One said that young Delaney, his rival, had in his absence contrived to win the affection of his mistress;—but Roderick's confidence in his intended bride was too great to be disturbed at this tale, and putting his hand in his pocket, he produced and held up with a significant look the wedding-ring. As he was turning it between

his fore-finger and thumb, in token of triumph, siomehow or other the ring fell from his hand, and rolled into the lake : Roderick looked after it with the greatest sorrow ; it was not so much for its value, though it had cost him half-a-guinea, as for the ill-luck of the thing; and the water was so deep, that there was little chance of recovering it. His companions laughed at him, and he in vain endeavoured to tempt any of them by the oflfer of a handsome reward to dive after the ring: they were all as little inclined to venture as Roderick Keating himself; for the tales which they had heard when children were strongly impressed on their memories, and a superstitious dread filled the mind of each.

" Must I then go back to Limerick to buy another ring ?" exclauned the young farmer. " Will not ten times what the ring cost tempt any one of you to venture after it ?"

There was within hearing a man who was considered to be a poor, crazy, half-witted fellow, but he was as harmless as a child, and used to go wandering up and down through the country from one place to another. When lie heard of so great a reward, Paddeen, for that was his name, spoke out, and said, that if Roderick Keating would give him encouragement equal to what he had offered to others, he was ready to venturp after the ring into the lake; and Paddeen, all the while he spoke, looked as covetous after the sport as the money.

" I'll take you at your word," said Keating. So Paddeen pulled off his coat, and without a single syllable more, down he plunged, head fore-

most, into the lake: what depth he went to, no one can tell exactly; but he was going, going,-going down through the water, uutil the water parted from him, and he came upon the dry land ; the sky, and the light, and every thing, was there just as it is here; and he saw fine pleasure-grounds, with an elegant avenue through them, and a grand house, with a power of steps going up to the door. When he had recovered from his wonder at finding the land so dry and comfortable under the water, he looked about him, and what should he see but all the young men that were drowned working away in the pleasure-grounds as if nothing had ever happened to tliem ! ISome of them were mowing down the grass, and more were settling out the gravel walks, and doing all manner of nice work, as neat and as clever as if they had never been drowned; and they were singing away with high glee:—

" She is fair as Cappoquin ; Have you courage her to win ? And her wealth it far outshines CuUen's bog and Silvermines. She exceeds all heart can wish ; Not brawling like the Foherish, But as the brightly flowing Lee, Graceful, mild, and pure is she !"

Well, Paddeen could not but look at the young men, for he knew some of them before they were lost in the lake ; but he said nothing, though he thought a great deal more for all that, like an oyster:—no, not the wind of a word passed his lips; so on he went towards the big house, bold enough, as if he had seen nothing to speak of; yet all the time mightily wishing to know

who
the young woman could be that the young men were singing the song about.

Wlien he had nearly reached the door of the great house, out walks from the kitchen a powerful fat woman, moving along like a beer-barrel on two legs, with teeth as big as horses' teeth, and up she made towards him.

" Good morrow, Paddeen," said she.

" Good morrow, Ma'am," said he.

" What brought you here ?" said she,

" 'Tis after Rory Keating's gold ring," said he, " I'm come."

" Here it is for you," said Paddeen's fat friend; with a smile on her face that moved like boihng stirabout Cgruel.]]

" Thank you, Ma'am," replied Paddeen, taking it from her :—" I need not say the Lord increase you, for you're fat enough already. Will you tell me, if you please, am I to go back the same way I came ?"

" Then you did not come to marry me ?" cried the corpulent woman in a desperate fury.

" Just wait till I come back again, my darling," said Paddeen: " I 'm to be paid for my message, and I must return with the answer, or else they'll wonder what has become of me."

" Never mind the money," said the fat woman : " if you marry me, you shall live for ever and a day in that house, and want for nothing."

Paddeen saw clearly that, having got possession of the ring, the fat woman had no power to detain him ; so without minding any thing she said, he kept moving and moving down the avenue, quite quietly, and looking about him ; for, to tell

THE ENCHANTED LAKE.

the truth, he had no particular inclination to marry a fat faiiy. When he came to the gate, without ever saying good b'ye, out he bolted, and he found the water coming all about him again. Up he plunged tlirough it, and wonder enough there was, when Paddeen was seen swimming away at the opposite side of the lake; but he soon made the shore, and told Roderick Keating, and the other boys that were standing there looking out for him, all that had happened. Roderick paid him the five guineas for the ring on the spot; and Paddeen thought himself so rich with such a sum of money in his pocket, that he did not go back to marry the fat lady with the fine house at the bottom of the lake, knowing she had plenty of young men to choose a husband from, if she pleased to be married.

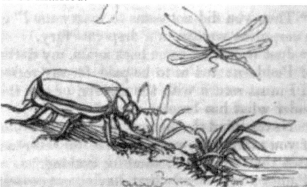

171 -THE LEGEND OF O'DONOGHUE.

XXI.

In an age so distant that the precise period is unknown, a chieftain named O'Donoghue ruled over the country which surrounds the romantic Lough Lean, now called the lake of

Killarney. Wisdom, beneficence, and justice, distinguished his reign, and the prosperity and happiness of his subjects were their natural results. He is said to have been as renowned for his warlike exploits as for his pacific virtues ; and as a proof that his domestic administration was not the less rigorous because it was mild, a rocky island is pointed out to strangers, called " O'Donoghue's Prison," in which this prince once confined his own son for some act of disorder and disobedience.

His end—for it cannot correctly be called his death—was singular and mysterious. At one of those splendid feasts for which his court was celebrated, surrounded by the most distinguished of his subjects, he was engaged in a prophetic relation of the events which were to happen in ages yet to come. His auditors listened, now wrapt in wonder, now fired with indignation, burning with shame, or melted into sorrow, as he faithfully detailed the heroism, the injuries, the crimes, and the miseries of their descendants. In the midst of his predictions he rose slowly from his seat, advanced with a solemn, measured, and

majestic tread to the shore of the lake, and walked forward composedly upon its unyielding surface. When he had nearly reached the centi-e, he paused for a moment, then turning slowly round, looked towards his friends, and waving his arms to them with the cheerful air of one taking a short fare-fell, disappeared from their view.

The memory of the good O'Donoghue has been cherished by successive generations with affectionate reverence : and it is believed tliat at sunrise, on every May-dew morning, the anniversary of his departure, he revisits his ancient domains : a favoured few only are in general permitted to see him, and this distinction is always an omen of good fortune to the beholders: when it is granted to many, it is a sure token of an abundant harvest,—a blessing, the want of which during this prince's reign was never felt by his people.

Some years have elapsed sinc« the last appearance of O'Donoghue. The April of that year had been remarkably wild and stormy ; but on May-morning the fury of the elements had altogether subsided. The air was hushed and still; and the sky, which was reflected in the serene lake, resembled a beautiful but deceitful countenance, whose smiles, after the most tempestuous emotions, tempt the stranger to believe that it belongs to a soul which no passion has ever ruffled.

The first beams of the rising sun were just gilding the lofty summit of Glenaa, when the waters near the eastern shores of the lake became suddenly and violently agitated, though all the rest of its surface lay smooth and still as a tomb

of polished marble; the next moment a foaming wave darted forward, and, like a proud high-crested war-horse, exulting in his strength, rushed across the lake towards Toomies mountain. Behind this wave appeared a stately warrior fully-armed, mounted upon a milk-white steed; his snowy plume waved gracefully from a helmet of polished steel, and at his back fluttered a light blue scarf. The horse, apparently exulting in his noble burden, sprang after the wave along the water, which bore him up like firm earth, whUe showers of spray that glittered brightly in the morning sun were dashed up at every bound.

The waiTior was O'Donoghue; he was followed by numberless youths and maidens who moved lightly and unconstrained over the watery plain, as the moonlight fairies glide through the fields of air : they were linked together by garlands of delicious spring flowers, and they timed their movements to strains of enchanting melody. When O'Donoghue had nearly reached the west-eni side of the lake, he suddenly turned his steed, and directed his course along the wood-fringed shore of Glenaa, preceded by the huge wave that curle<l and foamed up as high as the horse's neck, whose fiery nostrils snorted above it. The long train of attendants followed with

playful deviations the track of their leader, and moved on with unabated fleetness to their celestial music, till gradually, as they entered the narrow strait between Glenaa and Dinis, they became involved in the mists which still partially floated over the lakes, and faded from the view of the wondering

beholders: but the sound of their music still fell upon the ear, and echo, catching up the harmonious strains, fondly repeated and prolonged them in soft and softer tones, till the last faint repetition died away, and the hearers awoke as from a dream of bliss.

Thierna na Oge, or the Country of Youth, is the name given to the foregoing section, from the belief that those who dwell in regions of enchantment beneath the water are not affected by the movements of time.

FAIRY LEGENDS.
THE MERROW.

' The mysterious depths
And wild and u ondrous forms of ocean old.'
Mattima's Coiichuloyist.
. LEGENDS OF THE MERROW.
THE LADY OF GOLLERUS.
XXII.

On the shore of Smerwick harbour, one fine summer's morning, just at day-break, stood Dick Fitzgerald " shoghing the dudeen," which may be translated, smoking his pipe. The sun was gradually rising behind the lofty Brandon, the dark sea was getting green in the light, and the mists, clearing away out of the valleys, went rolling and curling like the smoke from the comer of Dick's mouth.

" 'Tis just the pattern of a pretty morning," said Dick, taking the pipe from between his lips, and looking towards the distant ocean, which lay as still and tranquil as a tomb of polished marble. " Well, to be sure." continued he, after a pause, " 'tis mighty lonesuuij to be talking to one's self by way of company, and not to have another soul to answer one—nothing but the child of one's own voice, the echo! I know this, that if I had the luck, or may be the misfortune," said Dick with a melancholy smile, " to have the woman, it

N

would not be this .way with me!—and what in the wide world is a man without a wife ? He's no more surely than a bottle without a drop of drink in it, or dancing without music, or the left leg of a scissars, or a fishing line without a hook, or any other matter tliat is no ways complete.— Is it not so?" said Dick Fitzgerald, casting his eyes towards a rock upon the strand, which, though it could not speak, stood up as firm and looked as bold as ever Kerry witness did.

But what was his astonishment at beholding, just at the foot of that rock a beautiful young creature combing her hair, which was of a sea-green colour; and now the salt water shining on it, appeared, in the morning light, like melted butter upon cabbage.

Dick guessed at once that she was a Merrow, although he had never seen one before, for he sjjied the cohuleen driuth, or little enchanted cap, which the sea people use for diving down into the ocean, lying upon the strand, near her; and he had heard, that if once he could possess himself of the cap, she would lose the power of going away into the water : so he seized it with all speed, and she, hearing the noise, turned her head about as natural as any Christian.

When the Merrow saw that her little diving-cap was gone, the salt tears—doubly salt, no doubt, from her—came trickling down her cheeks, and she began a low mournful cry with just the tender voice of a new-bom infant. Dick, although lie knew well enough what she was crying for, determined to keep the cohuleen driuth, let her cry never so much, to see what luck would come

out of it. Yet he could not help pitying her, and when the dumb thing looked up in his face, and her cheeks all nioist with tears, 'twas enough to make any one feel, let alone Dick, who had ever and always, like most of his countrymen, a mighty tender heart of his own.

" Don't cry, my darling," said Dick Fitzgerald; but the Merrow, like any bold child, only cried the more for that.

Dick sat himself down by her side, and took hold of her hand, by way of comforting her. 'Twas in no particular an ugly hand, only there was a small web between the fingers, as there is in a duck's foot; but 'twas as thin and as white as the skin between egg and shell.

" What's your name, my darling?" says Dick, thinking to make her conversant with him; but he got no answer; and he was certain sure now, either that she could not speak, or did not understand him: he therefore squeezed her hand in his, as the only way he had of talking to her. It's the universal language ; and there 's not a woman in the world, be she fish or lady, that does not understand it.

The Merrow did not seem much displeased at this mode of conversation; and, making an end of her whining all at once—" Man," says she, looking up in Dick Fitzgerald's face, " Man, will you eat me?"

" By all the red petticoats and check aprons between Dingle and Tralee," cried Dick, jumping up in amazement, " I'd as soon eat myself, my jewel! Is it I eat you, my pet ?—Now 'twas some ugly iU-looking thief of a fish put that notion n2

into your own pretty head, with the nice green hair down upon it, that is so cleanly combed out this morning!"

" Man," said the Merrow, " what will you do with me, if you won't eat me ?"

Dick's thoufflits were running on a wife : he saw, at the first glimpse, that she was handsome ; but since she spoke, and spoke too like any real woman, he was fairly in love with her. 'Twas the neat way she called him man, that settled the matter entirely.

" Fish," says Dick, trying to speak to her after her own short fashion; " fish," says he, " here's my word, fresh and fasting, for you this blessed morning, that I'll make you mistress Fitzgerald before all the world, and that's what I'll do."

" Never say the word twice," says she; " I'm ready and willing to be yours, mister Fitzgerald; but stop, if you please, 'till I twist up my hair."

It was some time before she had settltd it entirely to her liking; for she guessed, I suppose, that she was going among strangers, where she would be looked at. When that was done, the Merrow put the comb in her pocket, and then bent down her head and whispered some words to the water that was close to the foot of the rock.

Dick saw the murmur of the words upon the top of the sea, going out towards the ^vide ocean, just like a breath of wind rippling along, and says he in the greatest wonder, "Is it speaking you are, my darling, to the salt water ?"

'• It's nothing else," says she, quite carelessly, "■ I'm just sending word home to my fatlier, not

to be waiting breakfast for me; just to keep him from being uneasy in his mind."

"And who's your father, my duck?" says Dick.

" "What!" said the Merrow, "did you never hear of my father ? he's the king of the waves, to be sure!"

" And yourself, then, is a real king's daughter ?" >5aid Dick, opening his two eyes to take a full and true survey of his wife that was to be.

" Oh, I'm nothing else but a made man with you, and a king your father;—to be siire he has all tlie money that's down in the bottom of the sea!"

" Money," repeated the Merrow, " what's money ? "

"'Tis no bad thing to have when one wants it;" replied Dick ; " and may be now the fishes have the imderstanding to bring up whatever you bid them ?"

" Oh ! yes," said the Merrow, " they bring me what I want."

" To speak the truth, then," said Dick, " 't is a straw bed I have at home before you, and that, I 'm thinking, is no ways fitting for a king's daughter : so, if 'twould not be displeasing to you, just to mention, a nice feather-bed, with a pair of new blankets — but what am I talking about ? may be you have not such things as beds down imder the water ?"

" By all means," said she, " Mr. Fitzgerald— plenty of beds at your service. I've fourteen oyster-beds of my own, not to mention one just planting for the rearing of young ones."

■ *' You have ?" says Dick, scratching his head and looking a little puzzled. " 'Tis a featherbed I was speaking of — but clearly, yours is the very cut of a decent plan, to have bed and supper so handy to each other, that a person when they'd have the one, need never ask for the other."

However, bed or no bed, money or no money, Dick Fitzgerald determined to marrA* the Mer-row, and the Merrow had given her consent. Away they went, therefore, across the strand, from Gollerus to Ballinrunnig, where FathCT Fitzgibbon happened to be that morning.

" There are two words to this bargain, Dick Fitzgerald," said his Reverence, looking mighty glum. " And is it a fishy woman you'd marry ?— the Lord preserve us ! — Send the scaly creature home to her own people, that's my advice to you, wherever she came from."

Dick had the cokuleen driuth in his hand, and was about to give it back to the Merrow, who looked covetously at it, but he thouglit for a moment, and then, says he—

" Please your Reverence, she's a king's daughter."

" If she was the daughter of fifty kings," said Father Fitzgibbon, " I tell you, you can't marry her, she being a fish."

"Please your Reverence," said Dick again, in an under tone, " she is as mild and as beautiful as the moon."

" If she was as mild and as beautiful as the sun, moon, and stars, all put together, I tell you, Dick Fitzgerald," said the Priest, stamping his

right foot, " you can't marry her, she being a fish!"

"But she has all the gold that's down in the sea only for the asking, and I'm a made man if I marry her ; and," said Dick, looking up slily, " I can make it worth any one's while to do the job."

" Oh! that alters the case entirely," replied the Priest; " why there's some reason now in what you say : why didn't you tell me this before ? —marry her by all means if she was ten times a fish. Money, you know, is not to be refused in these bad times, and I may as well have the hansel of it as another, that may be would not take half the pains in counselling you as I have done."

So Father Fitzgibbon married Dick Fitzgerald to the Merrow, and like any loving couple, they returned to GoUerus well pleased with each other. Everything prospered with Dick—he was at the sunny side of the world; the Merrow made the best of wives, and they lived together in the greatest contentment.

It was wonderful to see, considering where she had been brought up, how she would busy herself about the house, and how well she nursed the children; for, at the end of three years, there were as many young Fitzgeralds—two boys and a girl.

In short, Dick was a happy man, and so he might have continued to the end of his days, if he had only the sense to take proper care of what he had got; many another man, however, beside Dick, has not had wit enough to do that.

One day when Dick was obliged to go to Tralee, he left his wife, minding the children at home after him, and thinking she had plenty to do without disturbing his fishing tackle.

Dick Avas no sooner gone than Mrs. Fitzgerald set about cleaning up the house, and chancing to pull down a fishing-net, what shoiild she find behind it in a hole in the wall but her own cohuleen driuth.

She took it out and looked at it, and then she thought of her father the king, and her mother the queen, and her brothers and sisters, and she felt a longing to go back to them.

She sat down on a little stool and thought over the happy days she had spent under the sea ; then she looked at her children, and thought on the love and affection of poor Dick, and how it would break his heart to lose her. " But," says she, " he won't lose me entirely, for I'll come back to him again ; and who can blame me for going to • see my father and my mother, after being so long away from them."

She got up and went towards the door, but came back again to look once more at the child that was sleeping in the cradle. She kissed it gently, and as she kissed it, a tear trembled for an instant in her eye and then fell on its rosy cheek. She wiped away the tear, and turning to the eldest little girl, told her to take good care of her brothers, and to be a good child herself, until she came back. The Merrow then went down to the strand.—The sea was lying calm and smooth, just heaving and glittering in the sun, and she thought she heard a faint sweet singing, inviting

her to come down. All her old ideas and feelings came flooding over her mind, Dick and her children were at the instant forgotten, and placing the cohuleen driuth on her head, she plunged in.

Dick came home in the evening, and missing his wife, he asked Kathelin, his little girl, what had become of her mother, but she could not tell him. He then inquired of the neighbours, and he learned that she was seen going towards the strand with a strange looking thing like a cocked hat in her hand. He returned to his cabin to search for the cohuleen drmth. It was gone, and the truth now flashed upon him.

Year after year did Dick Fitzgerald wait, expecting the return of his wife, but he never saw her more. Dick never married again, always thinking that the Merrow would sooner or later return to him, and nothing could ever persuade him but that her father the king kept her below by main force ; " For," said Dick, " she surely would not of herself give up her husband and her children."

While she was with him, she was so good a wife in every respect, that to this day she is spoken of in the tradition of the country as the pattern for one, under the name of the Lady op GoLLERUS.

?£?-

FLORY CANTILLON'S FUNERAL.

XXIIT.

The ancient burial-place of the Cantillon family was on an island in Ballyheigh Bay. This island was situated at no great distance from the shore, and at a remote period was overflowed in one of the encroachments which the Atlantic has made on that part of the coast of Kerry. The fishermen declare they have often seen the ruined walls of an old chapel beneath them in the water, as they sailed over the clear green sea, of a sunny afternoon *. However this may be, it is well known that the Cantillons were, like most other Irish families, strongly attached to their ancient burial-place; and this attachment led to the custom, when any of the family died, of carrying the corpse to the sea-side, where the coffin was left on the shore within reach of the tide. In the morning it had disappeared, being, as was traditionally believed, conveyed away by the ancestors of the deceased to their family tomb.

• "The neigbbourin? inhabitants," sayi Dr. Smith, in his History of Kerry, speaking of Ballyheigh, " shovr some roclcs visible in this bay only at low tides, which, they say, are the remains of an island, that was formerly the burial-place of the family of Cantillon, the ancient proprietors of Ballyheigh." p. 210.

Connor Crowe, a county Clare man, was related to the Cantillons by marriage. " Connor Mac in Cruagh, of the seven quarters of Brein-tragh," as he was commonly called, and a proud man he was of the name. Connor, be it known, would drink a quart of salt water, for its medicinal virtues, before breakfast; and for the same reason, I suppose, double that quantity of raw whiskey between breakfast and night, which last he did with as little inconvenience to himself as any man in the barony of Moyferta; and were I to add Clanderalaw and Ibrickan, I don't think I should say WTong.

On the death of Florence Cantillon, Connor Crowe was determined to satisfy himself about the truth of this story of the old church under the sea: so when he heard the news of the old fellow's death, away with him to Ardfert, where Flory was laid out in high style, and a beautiful corpse he made.

Flory had been as jolly and as roUocking a boy in his day as ever was stretched, and his wake was in every respect worthy of him. There was all kind of entertainment and all sort of diversion at it, and no less than three girls gf)t husbands there—more luck to them. Every thing was as it sliould be: all that side of the country, from Dingle to Tarbert, was at the funeral. The Keen was sung long and bitterly; and, according to the family custom, the coffin was carried to Ballyheigh strand, where it was laid upon the shore with a prayer for the repose of the dead.

The mourners departed, one group after another, and at last Connor Crowe was left alone :

he then pulled out his whiskey bottle, his drop of comfort as he called it, which he required, being in grief; and down he sat upon a big stone that was sheltered by a projecting rock, and partly concealed from view, to await with patience the appearance of the ghostly undertakers.

The evening came on mild and beautiful; he whistled an old air which he had heard in his childhood, hoping to keep idle fears out of his head; but the wild strain of that melody brought a thousand recollections with it, which only made the twilight appear mor e pensive.

" If 'twas near the gloomy tower of Dunmore, in my own sweet county, I was," said Connor Crowe, with a sigh, " one might well believe that the prisoners, who were murdered long ago, there in the vaults under the castle, would be the hands to carry off the cofl5n out of enxj, for never a one of them was buried decently, nor had as much as a coffin amongst them all. 'Tis often, sure enough, I have heard lamentations and great mourning coming fi-om the vaults of Dunmore Castle ; but," continued he, after fondly pressing his lips to the mouth of his companion and silent comforter, the whiskey bottle, " didn't I know all the time well enough, 'twas the dismal sounding waves working through the cliffs and hollows of the rocks, and fretting themselves to foam. Oh then, Dunmore Castle, it is you that are the gloomy-looking tower on a gloomy day, with the gloomy hills behind you; when one lias gloomy thoughts on their heart, and sees you like a ghost rising out of the smoke made by the kelp-burners on the strand, there is, the Lord save us! as tkai-

fill a look about yoxi as about the Blue Man's Lake at midnight. Well then, any how," said Connor, after a pause, " is it not a blessed night, though surely the moon looks mighty pale in the face ? St. Senan himself between us and all kinds of harm !"

It was, in truth a lovely moonlight night; nothing was to be seen around but the dark rocks, and the white pebbly beach, upon which the sea broke with a hoarse and melancholy murmur. Connor, notwithstanding his frequent draughts, felt rather queerish, and almost began to repent his curiosity. It was certainly a solenm sight to behold the black coffin resting upon the white strand. His imagination gradually converted the deep moaning of old ocean into a mournful wail for the dead, and from the shadowy recesses of the rocks he imaged forth strange and visionary forms.

As the night advanced, Connor became weary with watching; he caught himself more than once in the fact of nodding, when suddenly giving his head a shake, he would look towards the black coffin. But the narrow house of death remained unmoved before him.

It was long past midnight, and the moon was sinking into the sea, when he heard the soimd of many voices, which gradually became stronger, above the heavy and monotonous roll of the sea: he listened, and presently could distinguish a Keen, of exquisite sweetness, the notes of which rose and fell with the heaving of the waves, whose deep murmur mingled with and supported the strain!

190 FLORV caxtillon's funeral.

Tlie Keen grew louder and louder, and seeme^ to approach the beach, and then fell into a low plaintive wail. As it ended, Connor beheld a number of strange, and in the dim light, mysterious-looking figures, emerge from the sea, and surround the coffin, which they prepared to launch into the water.

" This comes of marrying with the creatures of earth," said one of the figures, in a clear, yet hollow tone.

" True," replied another, with a voice still more fearful, " our king would never have commanded his gnawing white-toothed waves to devour the rocky roots of the island cemetery, had not his daughter, DurfuUa, been buried there by her mortal husband!"

" But the time will come," said a third, bending over the coffin,

" When mortal eye—our work shall spy. And mortal ear—our dirge shall hear."

" Then," said a fourth, " our burial of the Cantillons is at an end for ever!"

As this was spoken, the coffin was borne from the beach by a retiring wave, and the company of sea people prepared to follow it; but at the moment, one chanced to discover Connor Crowe, as fixed with wonder and as motionless with fear as the stone on which he sat.

" The time is come," cried the unearthly being, " the time is come: a human eye looks on the forms of ocean, a human ear has heard their voices ; farewell to the Cantillons; the sons of the sea are no longer doomed to bury the dust of the earth!"

One after the other turned slowly round, and regarded Connor Crowe, who still remained as if bound by a spell. Again arose their funeral song; and on the next wave they followed the coffin. The sound of the lamentation died away, and at length nothing was heard but tlie rusli of waters. The coffin and the train of sea people sank over the old church-yard, and never, since the funeral of old Flory Cantillon, have any of the family been carried to the strand of Bally-heigh, for conveyance to their rightful burial-place, beneath the waves of the Atlantic.

THE LORD OF DUXKERRON.

XXIV.

The lord of Dunkerron*—O'Sullivan More, Why seeks he at midnight the sea-beaten shore ? His bark lies in haven, his hounds are asleep ; No foes are abroad on the land or the deep.

Yet nightly the lord of Dunkerron is known On the wild shore to watch and to wander alone ; For a beautiful spirit of ocean, 'tis said, The lord of Dunkerron would wdn to his bed.

When, by moonlight, the waters were hush'd to

repose, That beautiful spirit of ocean arose ; Her hair, full of lustre, just floated and fell O'er her bosom, that heaved with a billowy swell.

Long, long had he loved her—^long vainly essay'd To lure from her dwelling the coy ocean maid; And long had he wander d and watch'd by the tide. To claim the fair spirit

O'SuUivan's bride !

* The remains of Dunkerron Castle are distant about a mile from the Tillage of Kenmare, in the county of Kerry. It is recorded to have been built in 1596, by Owen O'Sullivan More.— [3Iorg, is merely an epithet signifying the Great.]

The maiden she gazed on the creature of earth, Whose voice in her breast to a feeling gave birth ; Then smiled; and, abashed as a maiden might be, Looking down, gently sank to her home in the sea.

Though gentle that smile, as the moonlight above, O'SuUivan felt 'twas the dawning of love, And hope came on hope, spreading over his mind, Like the eddy of circles her wake left behind.

The lord of Dunkerron he plunged in the waves, And sought through the fierce rush of waters,

their caves; The gloom of whose depth studded over with

spars, Had the glitter of midnight when lit up by stars.

Who can tell or can fancy the treasures that sleep, Intombed in the wonderful womb of the deep ? The pearls and the gems, as if valueless, thrown To lie 'mid the sea-wrack concealed and unknown,

Down, down went the maid,—still the chieftain

pursued; Who flies miist be followed ere she can be wooed. Untempted by treasures, unawed by alarms. The maiden at length he has clasped in his arms !

They rose from the deep by a smooth-spreading

strand, Whence beauty and verdure stretch'd over the

land.

'Twas an isle of enchantment I and lightly the

breeze, With a musical munnur, just crept through the

trees.

The haze-woven shroud of that newly bom isle, Softly faded away, from a magical pile, A palace of crystal, whose bright-beaming sheen Had the tints of the rainbow—red, yellow, and green.

And grottoes, fantastic in hue and in form. Were there, as flung up—the wild sport of the 'storm; Yet all was so cloudless, so lovely, and calm. It seemed but a region of sunshine and balm.

" Here, here shall we dwell in a dream of delight, Where the glories of earth and of ocean unite ! Yet, loved son of earth 1 I must from thee away ; There are laws which e'en spirits are bound to obey I

" Once more must I visit the chief of my race, His sanction to gain ere I meet thy embrace. In a moment I dive to the chambers beneath : One cause can detain me — one only — 'tis death!"

They parted in sorrow, with vows true and fond; Tlie language of promise had nothing beyond. His soul all on fire, with anxiety bums: The moment is gone—but no maiden returns.

What sounds from the deep meet his terrified ear— What accents of rage and of grief does he hear ? Wliat sees he ? what change has come over the

flood— What tinges its green with a jetty of blood ?

Can he doubt what the gush of warm blood would

explain ? That she sought the consent of her monarch in

vain! For see all around him, in white foam and froth, The waves of the ocean boil up in their wroth !

The palace of crystal has melted in air, And the dyes of the rainbow no longer are there; The grottoes with vapour and clouds are o'ercast, The sunshine is darkness—^the vision has past!

Loud, loud was the call of his serfs for their chief; They sought him with accents of wailing and grief: He heard, and he struggled—a wave to the shore, Exhausted and faint, bears O'Sullivan More!

o2

THE WONDERFUL TUNE.

XXV.

*

Maurice Connor was the king, and that's no small word, of all the pipers in Munster. He could play jig and planxty without end, and Ollis-trum's March, and the Eagle's Whistle, and the Hen's Concert, and odd tunes of every sort and kind. But he knew one, far more surprising than the rest, which had in it the power to set every thing dead or alive dancing.

In what way he learned it is beyond my knowledge, for he was mighty cajitious about telling how he came by so wonderful a tune. At the very first note of that tune, the brogues began shaking upon the feet of all who heard it — old or young, it mattered not — just as if their brogues had the ague ; then the feet began going — going — going from under them, and at last up and away with them, dancing like mad ! — whisking here, there, and everywhere, like a straw in a storm—there was no halting while the music lasted! ,

Not a fair, nor a wedding, nor a patron in the seven parishes round, was counted worth the speaking of without " blind Maurice and his pipes." His mother, poor woman, used to lead him about from one place to another, just like a dog.

Down through Iveragh—a place that ought to be proud of itself, for 'tis Daniel O'Connell's country—Maurice Connor and his mother were taking their rounds. Beyond all other places Iveragh is the place for stonny coast and steep mountains : as proper a spot it is as any in Ireland to get yourself drowned, or your neck broken on the land, should you prefer that. But, notwithstanding, in Ballinskellig bay there is a neat bit of ground, well fitted for diversion, and down from it, towards the water, is a clean smooth piece of strand —the dead image of a calm summer s sea on a moonlight night, with just the curl of the small waves upon it.

Here it was that Maurice's music had brought from all parts a great gathering of the young men and the young women— 0 the darlints ! — for 'twas not every day the strand of Trafraska was stirred up by the voice of a bagpipe. The dance began ; and as pretty a rinkafadda it was as ever was danced. " Brave music," said every body, " and well done," when Maurice stopped.

" More power to your elbow, Maurice, and a fair wind in the bellows," cried Paddy Donnan, a hump-backed dancing-master, who was there to keep order. " ' Tis a pity," said he, " if we'd let the piper run dry after such music ; 'twould be a disgrace to Iveragh, that didn't come on it since the week of the three Sundays." So, as well became him, for he was always a decent man, says he : " Did you drink, piper ?"

" I will, sir," says Maurice, answering the question on the safe side, for you never yet knew piper or schoolmaster who refused his dnnk.

" What will you drink, Maurice ?" says Paddy.

" I'm no ways particular," says Maurice ; " I drink any thing, and give God thanks, barring raw water ; but if 'tis all the same to you, mister Dorman, may be you wouldn't lend me the loan of a glass of whiskey."

" I've no glass, Maurice," said Paddy; " I've only the bottle."

" Let that be no hindrance," answered Maurice ; " my mouth just holds a glass to the drop; often I've tried it, sure."

So Paddy Dorman trusted him with the bottle — more fool was he; and, to his cost, he found that though Maurice's mouth might not hold more than the glass at one time, yet, owing to the hole in his throat, it took many a filling.

" That was no bad whiskey neither," says Maurice, handing back the empty bottle.

" By the holy frost, then!" says Paddy, " 'tis but could comfort there's in that bottle now ; and 'tis your word we must take for the strength of the whiskey, for you've left us no sample to judge by:" and to be sure Maurice had not.

Now I need not tell any gentleman or lady with common understanding, that if he or she was to drink an honest bottle of whiskey at one pull, it is not at all the same thing as drinking a bottle of water; and in the whole course of my life, I never knew more than five men who could do so without being overtaken by the liquor. Of these Maurice Connor was not one, though he had a stiff head enough of his own—he was fairly tipsy.

Don't think I blame him for it; 'tis often a good man's case ; but true is the word that says, " when liquor's in, sense is out;" and puflf", at a breath, before you could say " Lord save us !" out he blasted his wonderful tune.

'Twas really then beyond all belief or telling the dancing. Maurice himself could not keep quiet; staggering now on one leg, now on the other, and rolling about like a ship in a cross sea, trying to humour the tune. There was his mother too, moving her old bones as light as the youngest girl of them all; but her dancing, no, nor the dancing of all the rest, is not worthy the speaking about to the work that was going on down on the strand. Every inch of it covered with all manner of fish jumping and plunging about to the music, and every moment more and more would tumble in out of the water, charmed by the wonderful tune. Crabs of monstrous size spun round and round on one claw with the nimbleness of a dancing-master, and twirled and tossed their other claws about like limbs that did not belong to them. It was a sight surprising to behold. But perhaps you may have heard of father Florence Conry, a Franciscan Friar, and a great Irish poet; bolg an dana^ as they used to call him — a wallet of poems. If you have not, he was as pleasant a man as one would wish to drink with of a hot summer's day; and he has rhymed out all abovit the dancing fishes so neatly, that it would be a thousand pities not to give you his verses ; so here's my hand at an upset of them into English :

The big seals in motion. Like waves of the ocean,
Or gouty feet prancing, Came heading the gay fish, Crabs, lobsters, and cray fish.
Determined on dancing.

The 8weet somids they follow'd. The gasping cod swallow'd ; • Twas wonderful, really!
And turbot and flounder, 'Mid fish that were rounder. Just caper'd as gaily.

John-dories came tripping; Dull hake, by their skipping
To frisk it seem'd given; Bright mackerel went springing, Like small rainbows winging
Their flight up to heaven.

The whiting and haddock Left salt-water paddock.

This dance to be put in : Where skate with flat faces Edged out some odd plaices;

But soles kept their footing.

Sprats and herrings in powers Of silvery showers

AU number out-number'd; And great ling so lengthy Were there in such plenty,

The shore was encumber'd.

The scollop and oyster Their two shells did roister.

Like castanets fitting ; While limpets moved clearly, And rocks very nearly

With laughter were splitting.

Never was such an ullabulloo in this world, before or since; 'twas as if heaven and earth were coming together; and all out of Maurice Connor's wonderful tune!

In the height of all these doings, what should there be dancing among the outlandish set of fishes but a beautiful young woman—as beautiful as the dawn of day! She had a cocked hat upon her head; from under it her long green hair—just the colour of the sea—fell dovpn behind, without hinderance to her dancing. Her teeth were like rows of pearl; her lips for all the world looked like red coral; and she had an elegant gown, as white as the foam of the wave, with little rows of purple and red sea-weeds settled out upon it; for you never yet saw a lady, under the water or over the water, who had not a good notion of dressing herself out.

Up she danced at last to Maurice, who was flinging his feet from under him as fast as hops— for nothing in this world could keep still while that tune of his was going on—and says she to him, chaunting it out with a voice as sweet as honey—

" I'm a lady of honour Who live in the sea; Come down, Maurice Connor, And be married to me.

" Silver plates and gold dishes You shall have, and shall be Tlie king of the fishes.

When you're married to me."

Drink was strong in Maurice's head, and out he chaunted in return for her great civility. It is

not every lady, may be, that would be after making such an offer to a blind piper; therefore 'twas only right in him to give her as good as she gave herself—so says Maurice,

" I'm obliged to you, madam: Off a gold dish or plate, If a king, and I had 'em, I could dine in great state.

" With your own father's daughter I'd be sure to agree; But to drink the salt water Wouldn't do 80 with me!"

The lady looked at him quite amazed, and swinging her head from side to side like a great scholar, " Well," says she, " Maurice, if you're not a poet, where is poetry to be found ?"

In this way they kept on at it, framing high compliments ; one answering the other, and their feet going with the music as fast as their tongues. All the fish kept dancing too : Maiarice heard the clatter, and was afraid to stop playing lest it might be displeasing to the fish, and not knowing what so many of them may take it into their heads to do to him if they got vexed.

Well, the lady with the green hair kept on coaxing of Maurice with soft speeches, till at last she overpersuaded him to promise to marry her, and be king over the fishes, great and small. Maurice was well fitted to be their king, if they wanted one that could make them dance; and he surely would drink, barring the salt water, with any fish of them all.

When Maurice's mother saw him, with that unnatural thing in the form of a green-haired lady as his guide, and he and she dancing down together so lovingly to the water s edge, through the thick of the fishes, she called out after him to stop and come back. " Oh then," says she, " as if I was not widow enough before, there he is going away from me to be married to that scaly woman. And who knows but 'tis grandmother I may be to a hake or a cod—Lord help and pity me, but 'tis a mighty unnatural thing!—and may be 'tis boiling and eating my own grandchild I'll be, with a bit of salt butter, and I not knowing it!—Oh Maurice, Maurice, if there's any love or nature left in you, come back to your own ould mother, who reared you like a decent Christian !"

Then the poor woman began to cry and uUa-goane so finely that it would do any one good to hear her.

Maurice was not long getting to the rim of the water; there he kept playing and dancing on as if nothing was the matter, and a great thundering wave coming in towards him ready to swallow him up alive ; but as he could not see it, he did not fear it. His mother it was who saw it plainly through the big tears that were rolling down her cheeks; and though she saw it, and her heart was aching as much as ever mother's heart ached for a son, she kept dancing, dancing, all the time for the bare life of her. Certain it was she could not help it, for JMau-rice never stopped playing that wonderful tune of his.

He only turned the bothered ear to the sound of his mother's voice, fearing it might put him

out in his steps, and all the answer he made back was—

" Whisht with you, mother—sure I'm going to be king over the fishes down in the sea, and for a token of luck, and a sign that I am alive and well, I'll send you iii, every twelvemonth on this day, a piece of burned wood to Trafraska." Maurice had not the power to say a word more, for the strange lady with the green hair, seeing the wave just upon them, covered him up with herself in a thing like a cloak with a big hood to it, and the wave curling over twice as high as their heads, burst upon the strand, with a rush and a roar that might be heard as far as Cape Clear.

That day twelvemonth the piece of burned wood came ashore in Trafraska. It was a queer thing for Maurice to think of sending all the way from the bottom of the sea. A gown or a pair of shoes would have been something like a present for his poor mother; but he had said it, and he kept his word. The bj^ of burned wood regularly came ashore on the appointed day for as good, ay, and better than a hundred years. The day is now forgotten, and may be that is the reason why people say how Maurice Connor has stopped sending the luck - token to his mother. Poor woman, she did not live to get as much as one of them; for what through the loss of ^laurice, and the fear of eating her own grandchildren, she died in three weeks after the dance—some say it was the fatigue that killed her, but whichever it was, Mrs. Connor was decently buried with her own people.

Seafaring men have often heard, off the coast of Kerry, on a still night, the sound of music coming up from the water; and some, who have had good ears, could plainly distinguish Maurice Coimor's voice singing these words to his pipes :—

Beautiful shore, with thy spreading strand. Thy crystal water, and diamond sand ; Never would I have parted from thee But for the sake of my fair ladie.»

* This is almost a literal translation of a lUurn in the well-known song of Deardra.

The Irish Merrow, correctly written ?r)0ftUA8 or ?t)OTtUAC, answers exactly to the English Mermaid, being compounded of ^U]t\, the Sea, and O]^, a maid. It is also used to express a sea-monster, like the Armoric and Cornish Morhuch, to which it evidently bears analogy.

In Irish, ?t)uTt"Uc;!vt), ?f)u?n-5eilc, Sj^TP5UbA, and S\x\\\e are various names for sea-nymphs or mermaids. I'he romantic historians of Ireland describe the Suit e as playing round the ships of the Milesians when on their passage to that Island.

FAIRY LEGENDS.
THE DULLAHAN.

' Then wonder not at headiest folk. Since every day you greet 'em ; Nor treat old stories as a joke, When fools you daily meet 'em."—2^< Legendary.

'■ Says the friar, 'tis strange headless horses should trot."
Old So.ng.

THE DULLAHAN.
THE GOOD WOMAN.
XXVI.

In a pleasant and not unpicturesque valley of the White Knight's country, at the foot of the Galtee mountains, lived Larry Dodd and his wife Nancy. They rented a cabin and a few acres of land, which tliey cultivated with great care, and its crops rewarded their industry. They were independent and respected by their neighbours ; they loved each other in a marriageable sort of way, and few couples had altogether more the appearance of comfort about them.

Larry was a hard working, and, occasionally, a hard drinking, Dutch-built, little man, with a fiddle head and a round stern; a steady-going straight-forward fellow, barring when he carried too much whiskey, which, it must be confessed, might occasionally prevent his walking the chalked line with perfect philomathical accuracy. He had a moist ruddy countenance, rather inclined to an expression of gi'avity, and particularly so in the morning; but, taken all together, he was generally looked upon as a marvellously proper pex'son, P

notwithstanding he had, every day in the year, a sort of unholy dew upon his face, even in the coldest weather, which gave rise to a supposition (amongst censorious persons, of course), that Larry was apt to indulge in strong and frequent potations. However, all men of talents have their faults,—indeed, who is without them ?—and as Larry, setting aside his domestic virtues and skill in farming, was decidedly the most distinguished breaker of horses for forty miles round, he must be in some degree excused, considering the inducements of " the stirrup cup," and the fox-hunting society in which he mixed, if he had also been the greatest drunkard in the county: but, in truth, this was not the case.

Larry was a man of mixed habits, as well in his mode of life and his drink, as in his costume. His dress accorded well with his character—a sort of half-and-half between farmer and horse-jockey. He wore a blue coat of coarse cloth, with short skirts, and a stand -up collar ; his waistcoat was red, and his lower habiliments were made of leather, which in course of time had shrunk so much, that they fitted like a second skin; and long use had absorbed their moisture to such a degree, that they made a strange sort of crackling noise as he walked along. A hat covered witli oilskin ; a cutting-whip, all worn and jagged at the end ; a pair of second-hand, or, to speak more correctly, second-footed, greasy top-boots, that seemed never to have imbibed a refreshing draught of Wan-en's blacking of matchless lustre !—and one spur without a rowel, completed the every-day dress of Larry Dodd.

Thus equipped was Larry returning from Ca-shel, mounted on a rough-coated and wall-eyed nag, though, notwithstanding these and a few other trifling blemishes, a well-built animal; having just])urchased the said nag, with a fancy that he could make his own money again of his bargain, and, may be, turn an odd penny more by it at the ensuing Kildorrery fair. Well pleased with himself, lie trotted fair and easy along the road in the delicious and lingering twilight of a lovely June evening, thinking of nothing at all, only whistling, and wondering would horses always be so low. " If they go at this rate," said he to himself, *■' for half nothing, and that paid in butter buyer's notes, who would be the fool to walk ?" This very thought, indeed, was passing in his mind, when his attention Avas roused by a woman pacing quickly by the side of his horse and hurrying on as if endeavouring to reach her destination before the night closed in. Her figure, considering the long strides she took, appeared to be imder the common size — rather of the dumpy order; but further, as to whether the damsel was young or old, fair or bro\vn, pretty or ugly, Larry could form no precise notion, from her wearing a large cloak (the usual garb of the female Irish peasant), the hood of which was turned up, and completely concealed every feature.

Enveloped in this mass of dark and concealing drapery, the strange woman, without mucli exertion, contrived to keep up with Larry Dodd's steed for some time, when his master very civilly offered her a lift behind him, as far as he was going her way. " Civility begets civility," they say ; how-p 2

ever he received no answer; and thinking that the lidy's silence proceeded only from bash fulness, like a man of true gallantry, not a word more said Larry until he pulled up by the side of a gap, and then says he, "Jl/a colleen beg*, just jump up behind me, without a word more, though never a one have you spoke, and I'll take you save and sound through the lonesome bit of road that is before us."

She jumped at the offer, sure enough, and up with her on the back of the horse as light as a feather. In an instant there she was seated up behind Larrj', witli her hand and arm buckled round his waist holding on.

" I hope you're comfortable there, my dear," said Larry, in his own good-humoured way; but there was no answer; and on they went—trot, trot, trot—along the road; and all was so still and so quiet, that you might have heard the sound of the hoofs on the limestone a mile off: for that matter there was nothing else to hear except the moaning of a distant stream, that kept up a continued cronane'^, like a nurse hushoing. Larry, who had a keen ear, did not, however, require so profoimd a silence to detect the click of one of the shoes. " 'T is only loose the shoe is," said he to his companion, as they were just entering on the lonesome bit of road of which he had before spoken. Some old trees, with huge tnmks, all covered, and irregular branches festooned with ivy, grew over a dark pool of water, which had been formed as a drinking-place for cattle; and

* My little girl.

t A moDotonovis song ; a drowsy hummiDg noise.

in the distance was seen the majestic head of Gaultee-more. Here the liorse, as if in grateful recognition, made a dead halt; and Larry, not knowing wliat vicious tricks his new purchase might have, and unwilling that through any odd chance the young woman should get spilt in the water, dismounted, thinking to lead the horse quietly by the pool.

" By the piper's luck, that always found what he wanted," said Larry, recollecting himself, " I've a nail in my pocket: 'tis not the first time I've put on a shoe, and may be it won't be the last; for here is no want of paving-stones to make hammers in plenty."

No sooner was Larry off, than off with a spring came the young woman just at his side. Her feet touched the ground without making the least noise in life, and away she bounded like an ill-mannered wench, as she was, without saying, " by your leave," or no matter what else. She seemed to glide rather than run, not along the road, but across a field, up towards the old ivy-covered walls of Kilnaslattery church—and a pretty church it was.

" Not so fast, if you please, young woman— not so fast," cried Larry, calling after her: but away she ran, and Larry followed, his leathern garment, already described, crack, crick, crackling at every step he took. " Where's my wages ? " said Larry : " Thorum pog^ ma colleen oge ^,— sure I've earned a kiss from your pair of pretty lips—and I'll have it too!" But she went on faster and faster, regardless of these and other

» Give me a kiss, ray young girl.

flattering speeches from her pursuer; at last she came to the churchyard wall, and then over with her in an instant.

" Well, she's a mighty smart creature anyhow. To be sure, how neat she steps upon her pastenis ! Did any one ever see the like of that before;—r-but I'll not be baulked by any woman that ever wore a head, or any ditch either," exclaimed Larry, as with a desperate bound he vaulted, scrambled, and tumbled over the wall into the churchyard. Up he got from the elastic sod of a newly-made grave in which Tade Leary that morning was buried—rest his soul!—and on went Larry, stumbling over head-stones, and foot-stones, over old graves and new graves, pieces of coffins, and the skulls and bones of dead men—the Lord save us!—that were scattered about there as plenty as paving-stones; floundering amidst great overgrown dock-leaves and brambles that, with their long prickly arms, tangled round his limbs, and held him back with a fearful grasp. Mean time the merry wench in the cloak moved through all these obstructions as evenly and as gaily as if the churchyard, crowded up as it was with graves and gravestones (for people came to be buried there from far and near), had been the floor of a dancing-room. Round and round the walls of the old church she went. " I'll just wait," said Larry, seeing this, and thinking it all nothing but a trick to frighten him; " when she comes round again, if I don't take the kiss, I won't,, that's all, —and hero she is! " I>arry Dodd sprang forward with open arms, and clasped in them—a woman,

it is true—but a woman without any lips to kiss, by reason of her having no head !

"Murder!" cried he. "Well, that accounts for her not speaking." Having uttered these words, Larry himself became dumb with fear and astonishment; his blood seemed turned to ice, and a dizziness came over him ; and, staggering like a drunken man, he rolled against the broken window of the ruin, horrified at the conviction that he had actually held a Dullahan in his embrace !

When he recovered to something like a feeling of consciousness, he slowly opened his eyes, and then, indeed, a scene of wonder burst upon him. In the midst of the ruin stood an old wheel of torture, ornamented with heads, like Cork gaol, when the heads of Slurty Sullivan and other gentlemen were stuck upon it. This was plainly visible in the strange light which spread itself around. It was fearful to behold, but Larry could not choose but look, for his limbs were powerless through the wonder and the fear. Useless as it was, he would have called for help, but his tongue cleaved to the roof of his mouth, and not one word coidd he say. In short, there was Larry, gazing through a shattered window of the old church, with eyes bleared and almost starting from their sockets ; his breast resting on the thickness of the wall, over which, on one side, his head and outstretched neck projected, and on the other, although one toe touched the ground, it derived no support from thence: ten-or, as it were, kept him balanced. Strange noises assailed his ears, until at last they tingled painfully to the sharp

clatter of little bells, which kept up a continued ding — ding — ding ■— ding : marrowless bones rattled and clanked, and the deep and solemn sound of a great bell came booming on the night wind.

'Twos a spectre rung That ijeU when it swung—
Swing-swang! And the chain it squeaked, And the pulley creaked,
Swing-swang!
And with every roll Of the deep death toll
Ding-dong The hollow vault rang As the clapper went haag,
Dmg^Jong '

It was strange music to dance by; nevertheless, moving to it, round and round the wheel set with skulls, were well-dressed ladies and gentlemen, and soldiers and sailors, and priests and publicans, and jockeys and jennys, but all without tlieir heads. Some poor skeletons, whose bleached bones were ill covered by moth-eaten palls, and who were not admitted into the ring, amused themselves by bowling their brainless noddles at one another, which seemed to enjoy the sport beyond measure.

Larry did not know what to think ; his brains were all in a mist; and losing the balance which he had so long maintained, he fell liead foremost into the midst of the company of DuUahans.

" I'm done for and lost for ever," roared Larry, with his heels turned towards the stars, and souse down he came.

""Welcome, Larry Dodd, welcome," cried every liead, bobbing up and down in the air. "A drink for Larry Dodd," shouted they, as with one voice, that quavered like a shake on the bagpipes. No sooner said than done, for a player at heads, catching his own as it was bowled at him, for fear of its going astray, jumped up, put the head, without a word, under his left arm, and, with the right stretched out, presented a brimming cup to Larry, who, to show his manners, drank it off like a man.

" 'Tis capital stuff," he would have said, which surely it was, but he got no further than cap, when decapitated was he, and his head began dancing over his shoulders like those of the rest of the party. Larry, however, was not the first man who lost his head through the temptation of looking at the bottom of a brimming cup. Nothing more did he remember clearly,—for it seems body and head being parted is not very favourable to thought—but a gxeat hurry scarry with the noise of carriages and the cracking of whips.

When his senses returned, his first act was to put up his hand to where his head formerly grcAv, and to his great joy there he found it still. He then shook it gently, but his head remained firm enough, and somewhat assured at this, he proceeded to open his eyes and look around him. It was broad daylight, and in the old church of Kil-naslattery he found himself lying, with that head, the loss of which he had anticipated, qviietly resting, poor youth, " upon the lap of earth." Could it have been an ugly dream? "Oh no," said Larry, " a dream could never have brought me here,

stretched on the flat of my back, with that death's head and cross marrow bones forenentinw me on the fine old tombstone there that was faced by Pat Kearney * of Kilcrea—but where is the horse?" He got up slowly, every joint aching with pain from the bruises he had received, and went to the pool of water, but no horse was there. " 'Tis home I must go," said Larry, with a rueful countenance ; " but how will I face Nancy ?— what will I tell her about the horse, and tlie seven I.O.U.'s that he cost me?—'Tis them Dullahans that have made their-own of him from me—the horsestealing robbers of the world, that have no fear of the gallows!—but what's gone is gone, that's a clear case !"—so saying, he turned his steps homewards, and arrived at his cabin about noon without encountering any further adventures. There he found Nancy, who, as he expected, looked as black as a thundercloud at him for being oiit all night. She listened to the marvellous relation which he gave with exclamations of astonishment, and, when he had concluded, of grief, at the loss of the horse that he had paid for like an honest man with seven I.O.U.'s, three of which she knew to be as good as gold.

" But what took you up to the old church at all, out of the road, and at that time of the night, Larr)'?" inquired his wife.

Larry looked like a criminal for whom there was no reprieve; he scratched his head for an excuse, but not one could he muster up, so he knew not what to say.

• Faced, so written by the Chantrey of Kilcrea, for "fecit."

" Oh! Larry, Larry," muttered Nancy, after waiting some time for his answer, her jealous fears during the pause rising like barm; "'tis the very same way with you as with any other man — you are all alike for that matter — I've no pity for you—hut, confess the truth."

Larry shuddered at the tempest wliich he perceived was about to break upon his devoted head.

" Nancy," said he, " I do confess : — it was a young woman without any head that "

His wife heard no more. " A woman I knew it was," cried she; "but a woman without a head, Larry !—well, it is long before Nancy GoUagher ever thought it would come to that witli her!— that she would be left dissolute and alone here by her haste of a husband, for a woman without a head!—O father, father! and O mother, mother! it is well you are low to-day!—that you don't see this affliction and disgrace to your daughter that you reared decent and tender.

" O Larry, you villain, you'll be the death of your lawful wife going after such 0—0—O—"

" Well," says Larry, putting his hands in his coat-pockets, " least said is soonest mended. Of the young woman I know no more than I do of Moll Flanders : but this I know, that a woman without a head may well be called a Good Woman, because she has no tongue!"

How this remark operated on the matrimonial dispute history does not inform us. It is, however, reported that the lady had the last word.

•220

HANLON'S MILL.

XXVII.

One fine summer's evening Michael Noonan went over to Jack Brien's the shoemaker, at BallydufF, for the pair of brogues which Jack was mending for him. It was a pretty walk the way he took, but very lonesome; all along by the river side, down under the oak-wood, till he came to Hanlon's mill, that used to be, but that had gone to ruin many a long year ago.

Melancholy enough the walls of that same mill looked; the great old wheel, black with age, all covered over with moss and ferns, and the bushes all hanging down about it. There it stood, silent and motionless; and a sad contrast it was to its former busy clack, with the stream which once gave it use rippling idly along.

Old Hanlon was a man that had great knowledge of all sorts; there was not an herb that grew in the field but he could tell the name of it and its use, out of a big book he had written, every word of it in the real Irish karacter. He kept a school once, and could teach the Latin; that surely is a blessed tongue all over the wide world; and I hear tell as how "the great Burke" went to school to him. Master Edmund lived up at the old house there, which was then in the family, and it was the Nagles that got it afterwards, but they sold it.

But it was Michael Noonan's walk I was about speaking of. It was fairly between lights, the day was clean gone, and the moon was not yet up, when Mick was walking smartly across the Inch. Well, he heard, coming down out of the wood, such blowing of horns and hallooing, and the cry of all the hounds in the world, and he thought they were coming after him ; and the galloping of the horses, and the voice of the whipper-in, and he shouting out, just like the fine old song,

" Hallo Piper, Lilly, agiis Finder;"

and the echo over from the grey rock across the river giving back every word as plainly as it was spoken. But nothing could Mick see, and the shouting and hallooing following him every step of the way till he got up to Jack Brien's door; and he was certain, too, he heard the clack of old Hanlon's mill going, through all the clatter. To be sure, he ran as fast as fear and his legs could carry him, and never once looked behind him, well knowing that the Duhallow hounds were out in quite another quarter that day, and that nothing good could come out of the noise of Hanlon's mill.

Well, Michael Noonan got liis brogues, and well heeled they were, and well pleased was he with them; when who should be seated at Jack Brien's before him, but a gossip of his, one Darby Haynes, a mighty decent man, that had a horse and car of his own, and that used to be travelling with it, taking loads like the royal mail coach between Cork and Limerick; and when he was at

home, Darby was a near neighbour of Michael Noonan's.

"Is it home you're going with the brogues this blessed night ?" said Darby to him.

"Where else would it be?" replied Mick: " but, by my word, 'tis not across the Inch back again I'm going, after all I heard coming here; 'tis to no good that old Hanlon's mill is busy again."

" True, for you," said Darby; " and may be you'd take the horse and car home for me, Mick, by way of company, as 'tis along the road you go. I'm waiting here to see a sister's son of mine that I expect from Kilcoleman." " That same I'll do," answered Mick, " with a thousand welcomes." So Mick drove the car fair and easy, knowing that the poor beast had come off a long journey; and Mick—God reward him for it— was always tender-hearted and good to the dumb creatures.

The night was a beautiful one; the moon was better than a quarter old; and Mick, looking up at her, could not help bestowing a blessing on her beautiful face, shining down so sweetly upon the gentle Awbeg. He had now got out of the open road, and had come to where the trees grew on each side of it: he proceeded for some space in the chequered liglit which the moon gave through them. At one time, when a big old tree got between him and the moon, it was so dark, that he could hardly see the horse's head; then, as he passed on, the moonbeams would stream through the open boughs and varieofate the road with liwht and shade.

Mick was lying down in the car at his ease, having got clear of the plantation, and was watching the bright piece of a moon in a little pool at the road side, when he saw it disappear all of a sudden as if a great cloud came over the sky. He turned round on his elbow to see if it was so ; but how was JVIick astonished at finding, close along-side of the car, a gTeat high black coach drawn by six black horses, with long black tails reaching almost down to the ground, and a coachman dressed all in black sitting up on the box. But what surprised Mick the most was, that he could see no sign of a head either upon coachman or horses. It swept rapidly by him, and he could perceive the horses raising their feet as if they were in a fine slinging trot, the coachman touching them up with his long whip, and the wheels spinning round like hoddy-doddies; still he could hear no noise, only the regular step of his gossip Darby's horse, and the squeaking of the gudgeons of the car, that were as good as lost entirely for want of a little grease.

Poor Mick's heart almost died within him, but he said nothing, only looked on; and the black coach swept away, and was soon lost among some distant trees. Mick saw nothing more of it, or, indeed, of any thing else. He got home just as the moon was going down behind Mount Hillery— took the tackling off the horse, turned the beast out in the field for the night, and got to his bed.

Next morning, early, he was standing at the road-side, thinking of all that had happened the night before, when he saw Dan Madden, that was

Mr. Wrixon's huntsman, coming on the master's best horse down the hill, as hard as ever he went at the tail of the hounds. Mick's mind instantly misgave him that all was not right, so he stood out in the very middle of the road, and caught hold of Dan's bridle when he came up.

" Mick, dear—for the love of God! don't stop me," cried Dan.

" Why, what's the hurry ?" said Mick.

" Oh, the master!—he's oflf",—he's off—he'll never cross a horse again tUl the day of judgment !"

" Why, what would ail his honour ?" said Mick; " sure it is no later than yesterday morning that I was talking to him, and he stout and hearty ; and says he to me, Mick, says he—"

" Stout and hearty was he?" answered Madden; " and was he not out with me in the kennel last night, when I was feeding the dogs; and didn't he come out to the stable, and give a ball to Peg PuUaway with his own hand, and tell me he'd ride the old General to-day; and sure," said Dan, wiping his eyes with the sleeve of his coat, " who'd have thought that the first thing I'd see this morning was the mistress standing at my bed-side, and bidding me get up and ride off like fire for Doctor Galway; for the master had got a fit, and"—poor Dan's grief choked his voice—" oh, Mick ! if you have a heart in you, run over yourself, or send the gossoon for Kate Finnigan,the midwife; she's a cruel skilful woman, and may be she might save the master, till I get the doctor."

Dan struck his spurs into the hunter, and Mi-

chael Noonan flung ofi^ his newly-mended brogues, and cut acrosg the fields to Kate Finnigan s ; but neither the doctor nor Katty was of any avail, and the next night's moon saw Ballygibblin — and more's the pity — a house of mourning.

THE DEATH COACH.

XXVIII. -

'T IS midnight!—how gloomy and dark!

By Jupiter there's not a star !— 'Tis fearful!—'tis awful!—and hark !

What sound is that comes from afar ?

Still rolling and rumbling, that sound Makes nearer and nearer approach ;

Do I tremble, or is it the ground ?—

Lord save us!—what is it ?—a coach !—

A coach !—but that coach has no head ;

And the horses are headless as it: Of the driver the same may be said,

And the passengers inside who sit.

See the wheels! how they fly o'er the stones !

And whirl, as the whip it goes crack : Their spokes are of dead men's thigh bones.

And the pole is the spine of the back !

The hammer-cloth, shabby display, Is a pall rather mildew'd by damps ;

And to light this strange coach on its way, Two hollow skulls hang up for lamps !

From the gloom of Rathcooney church-yard, They dash down the hill of Glanmire ;

Pass Lota m gallop as hard As if horses were never to tire !

With people thus headless 't is fun

To drive in such furious career; Since headlong their horses can't run,

Nor coachman be heady from beer.

Very steep is the Tivoli lane,
But up-hill to them is as down; Nor the charms of Woodhill can detain
These DuUahans rushing to town.
Could they feel as I've felt—in a song—
A spell that forbade them depart; They'd a lingering visit prolong,
And after their head lose their heart!
No matter !—'tis past twelve o'clock ;
Through the streets they sweep on like the wind. And, taking the road to Blackrock,
Cork city is soon left behind.
Should they hurry thus reckless along,
To supper instead of to bed, The landlord will surely be wrong.
If he charge it at so much a head ! q2
Yet mine host may suppose them too poor To bring to his wealth an increase;
As till now, all who drove to his door, Possess'd at least one crown a-piece.
Up the Deadwoman's hill they are roll'd;
Boreenmannah is quite out of sight; Ballintemple they reach, and behold ! " At its
church-yard they stop and alight.
" Who's there ?" said a voice from the ground " We've no room, for the place is quite
fuU.'
" O ! room must be speedily found, For we come from the parish of Skull.
" Though Murphys and Crowleys appear On headstones of deep-letter'd pride ;
Though Scannels and Murleys lie here, Fitzgeralds and Toonies beside ;
" Yet here for the night we lie down, To-morrow we speed on the gale j
For having no heads of our own, We seek the Old Head of Kinsale."

THE HEADLESS HORSEMAN.
XXIX.

" God speed you, and a safe journey this night to you, Charley," ejaculated the master of
the little sheebeen house at Ballyhooley after his old friend and good customer, Charley Culnane,
who at length had turned his face homewards, with the prospect of as dreary a ride and as dark a
night as ever fell upon the Blackwater, along the banks of which he was about to journey.

Charley Culnane knew the country well, and moreover, was as bold a rider as any
Mallow-boy that ever rattled a four-year-old upon Drumrue race-course. He had gone to Fermoy
in the morning, as well for the purpose of purchasing some ingredients required for the
Christmas dinner by his wife, as to gratify his own vanity by having new reins fitted to his
snaffle, in which he intended showing off the old mare at the approaching St. Stephen's day hunt.

Charley did not get out of Fermoy until late; for although he was not one of your " nasty
particular sort of fellows" in any thing that related to the common occurrences of life, yet in all
the appointments connected with hunting, riding, leaping, in short, in whatever was connected
with the old mare, "Charley," the saddlers said, " was the devil to pldse." An illustration

of this fastidiousness was afforded by his going such a distance for his snaffle bridle. Mallow was full twelve miles nearer " Charley's fann" (which lay just three quarters of a mile below Carrick) than Fermoy; but Charley had quarrelled with all the Mallow saddlers, from hard-working and hard-drinking Tim Clancey, up to Mr, Ryan, who wrote himself " Saddler to the Duhallow Hunt;" and no one could content him in all particulars but honest Michael Twomey of Fermoy, who used to assert — and who will doubt it — that he could stitch a saddle better than the lord-lieutenant, although they made him all as one as king over Ireland.

This delay in the arrangement of the snaffle bridle did not allow Charley Culnane to pay so long a visit as he had at first intended to his old friend and gossip. Con Buckley, of the '^Harp of Erin." Con, however, knew the value of time, and insisted upon Charley making good use of what he had to spare. " I won't bother you waiting for water, Charley, because I think you'll have enough of that same before you get home; so drink off your liquor, man. It's as good parliament as ever a gentleman tasted, ay, and holy church too, for it will bear ' x waters^ and carry the bead after that, may be."

Charley, it must be confessed, nothing loth, drank success to Con, and success to the jolly " Harp of Erin," with its head of beauty and its strings of the hair of gold, .and to their better acquaintance, and so on, from the bottom of his soul, until the bottom of the bottle reminded him that Carrick was at the bottom of the hill on the other

side of Castletown Roche, and that he had got no further on his journey than his gossip's at Bally-hooley, close to the big gate of Conyamore. Catching hold of his oil-skin hat, therefore, whilst Con Buckley went to the cupboard for another bottle of the " real stuflF," he regularly, as it is termed, bolted from his friend's hospitality, darted to the stable, tightened his girths, and put the old mare into a canter towards home.

The road from Ballyhooley to Carrick follows pretty nearly the course of the Black water, occasionally diverging from the river and passing through rather wild scenery, when contrasted with the beautiful seats that adorn its banks. Charley cantered gaily, regardless of the rain, which, as his friend Con had anticipated, fell in torrents: the good woman's currants and raisins were carefully packed between the folds of his yeomanry cloak, which Charley, who was proud of showing that he belonged to the " Royal Mallow Light Horse Volunteers," always strapped to the saddle before him, and took care never to destroy the military eflFect of by putting it on.—Away he went singing like a thrush—

" Sporting, belleing, dancing, drinking. Breaking windows— (hiccup!) —sinking, Ever raking—never thinking.

Live tlie rakes of Mallow.

Spending faster than it comes, '

Beating— (hiccup, hie), and duns, Duhallow's true-begotten sons,

Live the rakes of Mallow.

Notwithstanding that the visit to the jolly " Harp of Erin" had a little increased the natural com-

placency of bis mind, the drenching of the new snaffle reins began to disturb him; and then followed a train of more anxious thoughts than even were occasioned by the dreaded defeat of the pride of his long-anticipated turn out on St. Stephen's day. In an hour of good fellowship, when his heart was warm, and his head not over cool, Charley had backed the old mare against Mr. Jephson's bay filly Desdemona for a neat hundred, and he now felt sore misgivings as to the prudence of the match. In a less gay tone he continued—

" Living short, but merry lives, Going where the devil drives, Keeping "

" Keeping" he muttered, as the old mare had reduced her canter to a trot at the bottom of Kil-cummer Hill. Charley's eye fell on the old walls that belonged, in former times, to the Templars : but the silent gloom of the ruin was broken only by the heavy rain which splashed and pattered on the gravestones. He then looked up at the sky, to see if there was, among the clouds, any hopes for mercy on his new snaffle reins; and no sooner were his eyes lowered, than his attention was arrested by an object so extraordinary as almost led him to doubt the evidence of his senses. The head, apparently, of a white horse, with short cropped ears, large open nostrils and immense eyes, seemed rapidly to follow him. No connexion with body, legs, or rider, could possibly be traced—the head advanced—Charley's old mare, too, was moved at this unnatural sight.

and snorting violently, increased her trot up the hill. The head moved forward, and passed on: Charley, pursuing it with astonished gaze, and wondering by what means, and for what purpose, this detached head thus proceeded through the air, did not perceive the corresponding body until he was suddenly startled by finding it close at his side. Charley turned to examine what was thus so sociably jogging on with him, when a most unexampled apparition presented itself to his view. A figure, whose height (judging as well as the obscurity of the night would permit him) he computed to be at least eight feet, was seated on the body and legs of a white horse full eighteen hands and a half high. In this measurement Charley could not be mistaken, for his own mare was exactly fifteen hands, and the body that thus jogged alongside he could at once determine, from his practice in horseflesh, was at least three hands and a half higher.

After the first feeling of astonishment, which found vent in the exclamation " I'm sold now for ever I " was over, the attention of Charley, being a keen sportsman, was naturally directed to this extraordinary body; and having examined it with the eye of a connoisseur, he proceeded to reconnoitre the figure so unusually mounted, who had hitherto remained perfectly mute. Wishing to see whether his companion's silence proceeded from bad temper, want of conversational powers, or from a distaste to water, and the fear that the opening of his mouth might subject him to have it filled by the rain, which was then drifting in violent gusts against them, Charley endeavoured

to catch a sight of his companion's face, in order to form an opinion on that point. But his vision failed in carrying him further than the top of the collar of the figure's coat, which was a scarlet single-breasted hunting frock, having a waist of a very old-fashioned cut reaching to- the saddle, with two huge shining buttons at about a yard distance behind. " I ought to see further than this, too," thought Charley, " although he is mounted on his high horse, like my cousin Darby, who was made barony constable last week, unless 'tis Con's whiskey that has blinded me entirely." However, see further he could not, and after straining his eyes for a considerable time to no purpose, he exclaimed, with pure vexation, " By the big bridge of Mallow, it is no head at all he has !"

" Look again, Charley Culnane," said a hoarse voice, that seemed to proceed from under the right arm of the figure.

Charley did look again, and now in the proper place, for he clearly saw, under the aforesaid right arm, that head from which the voice had proceeded, and such a head no mortal ever saw before. It looked like a large cream cheese hung round with black puddings; no speck of colour enlivened the ashy paleness of the depressed features; the skin lay stretched over the unearthly surface, almost like the parchment head of a drum. Two fiery eyes of prodigious circumference, with a strange and irregular motion, flashed like meteors upon Charley, and to complete all, a mouth reached from either extremity of two ears, which peeped forth from under a profusion of matted locks of lus-

treless blackness. This head, which the figure had evidently hitherto concealed from Charley's eyes, now burst upon his view in all its hideousness. Charley, although a lad of proverbial courage in the county of Cork, yet could not but feel his nerves a little shaken by this unexpected visit from the headless horseman, whom he considered his fellow traveller must be. The cropped-eared head of the gigantic horse moved steadily forward, always keeping from six to eight yards in advance. The horseman, unaided by whip or spur, and disdaining the use of stirrups, which dangled uselessly from the saddle, followed at a trot by Charley's side, his hideous head now lost behind the lappet of his coat, now starting forth in all its horror, as the motion of the horse caused his arm to move to and fro. The ground shook under tlie weight of its supernatural burden, and the water in the pools became agitated into waves as he trotted by them.

On they went—heads without bodies, and bodies without heads.—The deadly silence of night was broken only by the fearful clattering of hoofs, and the distant sound of thunder, which rumbled above the mystic hill of Cecaune a Mona Finnea. Charley, who was naturally a merry-hearted, and rather a talkative fellow, had hitherto felt tongue-tied by apprehension, but finding his companion showed no evil disposition towards him, and having become somewhat more reconciled to tlie'Patago-nian dimensions of the horseman and his headless steed, plucked up all his courage, and thus addressed the stranc^r:—

"Why, then, your honour rides mighty well without the stirrups !"

" Humph," growled the head from under the horseman's right arm.

" 'Tis not an over civil answer," thought Charley ; " but no matter, he was taught in one of them riding-houses, may be, and thinks nothing at all about bumping his leather breeches at the rate of ten miles an hour. I'll try him on the other tack. Ahem!" said Charley, clearing his throat, and feeling at the same time rather daimted at this second attempt to establish a conversation, " Ahem ! that's a mighty neat coat of your honour's, although 'tis a little too long in the waist for the present cut."

" Humph," growled again the head.

This second humph was a terrible thump in the face to poor Charley, who was fairly bothered to know what subject he could start that would prove more agreeable. " 'Tis a sensible head," thought Charley, " although an ugly one, for 'tis plain enough the man does not like flattery." A third attempt, however, Charley was determined to make, and ha^^ng failed in his observations as to the riding and coat of his fellow-traveller, thought he would just drop a trifling allusion to the wonderful headless horse, that was jogging on so sociably beside his old mare; and as Charley was considered about Carrick to be very knowing in horses, besides being a full private in the Royal Mallow Light Horse Volunteers, which were every one of them mounted like real Hessians, he felt rather sanguine as to the result of his third attempt.

" To be sure, that's a brave horse your honour rides," recommended the persevering Charley.

" You may say that, with your own ugly mouth," growled the head.

Charley, though not much flattered by the compliment, nevertheless chuckled at his success in obtaining an answer, and thus continued :—

" May be your honour wouldn't be after riding him across the country ?"

" Will you try me, Charley ?" said the head, >vith an inexpressible look of ghastly delight,

" Faith, and that's what I'd do," responded Charley, "only I'm afraid, the night being so dark, of laming the old mare, and I've every halfpenny of a hundred pounds on her heels."

This was true enough ; Charley's courage was nothing dashed at the headless horseman's proposal ; and there never was a steeple-chase, nor a fox-chase, riding or leaping in the country, that Charley Culnane was not at it, and foremost in it. •

" Will you take my word," said the man who carried his head so snugly under his right arm, " for the safety of your mare ?"

" Done," said Charley; arid away they started, helter skelter, over every thing, ditch and wall, pop, pop, the old mare never went in such style, even in broad daylight: and Charley had just the start of his companion, when the hoarse voice called out " Charley Culnane, Charley, man, stop for your life, stop !"

Charley pulled up hard. " Ay," said he, " you may beat me by the head, because it always goes so much before you; but if the bet was neck-and-

neck, and that's the go between the old mare and Desdemona, I'd win it hollow!"

It appeared as if the stranger was well aware of what was passing in Charley's mind, for he suddenly broke out quite loquacious.

" Charley Culnane,"isays he, " you have a stout soul in you, and are every inch of you a good rider. I've tried you, and I ought to know; and that's the sort of man for my money. A hundred years it is since my horse and I broke our necks at the bottom of Kilcummer hill, and ever since I have been trying to get a man that dared to ride with me and never found one before. Keep, as you have always done, at the tail of the hounds, never baulk a ditch, nor turn away from a stone wall, arid the headless horseman will never desert you nor the old mare."

Charley, in amazement, looked towards the stranger's right arm, for the purpose of seeing in his face whether or not he was in earnest, but behold ! the head was snugly lodged in the huge pocket of the horseman's scarlet hunting-coat. The horse's head had ascended perpendicularly above them, and his extraordinary companion, rising quickly after his avant-coureur, vanished from the astonished gaze of Charley Culnane.

Charley, as may be supposed, was lost in wonder, delight, and perplexity; the pelting rain, the wife's pudding, the new snaffle—even the match against squire Jephson—all were forgotten; nothing could he think of, nothing could he talk of, but the headless horseman. He told it, directly that he got home, to Judy; he told it the following morning to all the neighbours; and he told

THE HEADLESS HORSEMAN.

239

it to the hunt on St. Stephen's day: but what provoked him after all the pains he took in describing the head, the horse, and the man, was that one and all attributed the creation of the headless horseman to his friend Con Buckley's " X water parliament." This, however, should be told, that Charley's old mare beat Mr. Jephson s bay filly, Desdemona, by Diamond, and Charley pocketed his cool hundred; and if he didn't win by means of the headless horseman, I am sure I don't know any other reason for his doing so.

<-;::tj^'«^^

Dullahan or DuLACHAN (bublACA)) signifies a dark sullen person. The word Durrachan or Dullahan, by which in some places the goblin is known, has the same Eignification. U comes from Dorr or Durr, anger, or Durrach, malicious, fierce, &c.— MS. communicatioH from the lale Mr. Edward O'Reilly.

The correctness of this last etymology may be questioned, as t)u5 black, is evidently a component part of the word.

The Death Coach, or Headless Coach and Horses, is called in Ireland " Coach a bower ;" and its appearance is generally regarded as a sign of death, or an omen of some misfortune.

The belief in the appearance of headless people and horses appears to be, like most popular superstitions, widely extended.

In England, see the Spectator (No. 110) for mention of a spirit that had appeared in the shape of a black horse without a head.

In Wales, the apparition of " Fenyuj keb un pen," the headless woman, and " Ceffyl heb un pen," the headless horse, are generally accredited.— MS. communication from Miss Williams.

" The Irish Dullahan puts mc in mind of a spectre at Drumlanrig Castle, of no less a person than the Duchess of Queensberry,^'Fair Kilty, blooming, youug, and gay,*—who, instead of setting fire to the world in mamma's chariot, amuses herself with wheeling her own bead in a weeel-barrow through the great gallery."— MS. communication from Sib Walter Scott.

In Scotland, so recently as January, 1826, that veritable paper, the Glasgow Chronicle, records, upon the occasion of some siik-weavers being out of employment at Paisley, that " Visions have been seen of carls, caravans, and coaches, going up Gleniffer braes without horses, with horses without heads," &c.

Cervantes mentions tales of the " Caballo tin cabepa among the euentot de vi^)at con que *e entretienen al/ueffo la* dilatada* noche* del inviemo," &c.

" The people of Basse Br^tagne believe, that when the death of any person is al hand, a hearse drawn by skeletons (which they call carriquet au nankon), and covered with a white sheet, pastes by the bouse where the sick person lies, and the creaking of the wheels may be plainly heard."— Journal de* Science*, 1826, communicated by Dr. William Grimm.

See also Thiele't Dan*ke Folke*agn, vol. iv. p. C6, &c.

FAIRY LEGENDS.

THE FIR DARRIG.

Whene'er such wanderers I meete, "
Ab from their night-sports they trudge home,'; With counterfeiting voice I greete,
And call them on, with me to roame ,

Tlirough woods, through lakes,' Through bogs, through brakes ; Or else, unseene, with
them I go, All in the nicke. To play some tricke, And frolicke it, with ho, ho, ho \—Oli Song,
DIARMID BAWN, THE PIPER.

One stormy night Patrick Burke was seated in the chimney comer, smoking his pipe quite
contentedly after his hard day's work ; his two little boys were roasting potatoes in the ashes,
Avhile his rosy daughter held a splinter* to her mother, who, seated on a siesteenf, was mending
a rent in Patrick's old coat; and Judy, the maid, was singing merrily to the sound of her wheel,
that kept up a beautiful humming noise, just like the sweet drone of a bagpipe. Indeed they all
seemed quite contented and happy ; for the storm howled without, and they were warm and snug
within, by the side of a blazing turf fire. " I was just thinking," said Patrick, taking the dudeen
from his mouth and giving it a rap on his thumb-nail to shake out the ashes—" I was just
thinking how thankful we ought to be to have a snug bit of a cabin this pelting night over our
heads, for in all my born days I never heard the like of it."

" And that's no lie for you, Pat," said his wife; "but, whisht! what noise is that I hard'?"
and she dropped her work upon her knees, and looked

• A splinter, or slip of bog-deal, which, bein? dipped in tallow, it used as a candle.
t Siestecu is a low block-like seat, made of straw bands firmly sewed or bound together.
R 2

fearfully towards the door. " The Vargin herself defend us all!" cried Judy, at the same
time rapidly making a pious sign on her forehead, " if 'tis not the banshee !"

" Hold your tongue, you fool," said Patrick, "it's only the old gate swinging in the wind;"
and he had scarcely spoken, when the door was assailed by a violent knocking. Molly began to
mumble her prayers, and Judy proceeded to mutter over the muster-roll of saints; the youngsters
scampered off to hide themselves behind the settle-bed ; the storm howled louder and more
fiercely than ever, and the rapping was renewed with redoubled violence.

" Whisht, whisht! " said Patrick—" what a noise ye're all making about nothing at all.
Judy a-roon, can't you go and see who's at the door ? " for, notwithstanding his assumed bravery,
Pat Burke preferred that the maid should open the door.

" Why, then, is it me you're speaking to ?" said Judy in the tone of astonishment; " and is it cracked mad you are. Mister Burke; or is it, may be, that you want me to be rund away with, and made a horse of, like my grandfather was ?— the sorrow a step will I stir to open the door, if you were as great a man again as you are, Pat Burke."

" Bother you, then! and hold your tongue, and I'll go myself." So saying, up got Patrick, and made the best of his way to the door. " Who's there ?" said he, and his voice trembled mightily all the while. " In the name of Saint Patrick, who's there ? " " 'Tis I, Pat," answered a voice

■which he immediately knew to be the young squire's. In a moment the door was opened, and in walked a young man, with a gun in his hand, and a brace of dogs at his heels^ " Your honour s honour is quite welcome, entirely," said Patrick; who was a very civil sort of a fellow, especially to his betters. " Your honour's honour is quite welcome; and if ye'll be so condescending as to demean yourself by taking off your wet jacket, Molly can give ye a bran new blanket, and ye can sit forenent the fire while the clothes are drying." " Thank you, Pat," said the squire, as he wrapt himself, like Mr. Weld, in the proffered blanket*.

" But what made you keep me so long at the door?"

" Why then, your honour, 'twas all along of Judy, there, being so much afraid of the good people; and a good right she has, after what happened to her grandfather—the Lord rest his soul!"

" And what was that, Pat ?" said the squire.

" Why, then, your honour must know that Judy had a grandfather; and he was oidd Diarmid Bawn, the piper, as personable a looking man as any in the five parishes he was; and he could play the pipes so sweetly, and make them spake to such perfection, that it did one's heart good to hear him. We never had any one, for that matter, in this side of the country like him, before or since, except James Gandsey, that is own piper to Lord Headley—his honour's lordship is the real good gentleman—and 'tis Mr.

• See Weld's Killaniey, 8vo ed. p. 228.

Gandsey's music that is the pride of Killamer lakes. Well, as I was saying, Diarmid was Judy's grandfather, and he rented a small mountainy farm; and he was walking about the fields one moonlight night, quite melancholy-like in himself for want of the tohaccy; because why, the river w^as flooded, and he could not get across to buy any, and Diarmid would rather go to bed without his supper than a whiff of the dudeen. Well, your honour, just as he came to the old fort in the far field, what should he see ?—^the Lord preserve us!—but a large army of the good people, 'coutered for all the world just like the dragoons ! ' Are ye all ready ?' said a little fellow at their head dressed out like a general. ' No,' said a little curmudgeon of a chap all dressed in red, from the crown of his cocked hat to the sole of his boot. ' No, general,' said he: 'if you don't get the Fir darrig a horse he must stay behind, arid yell lose the battle.'

" ' There's Diarmid Bawn,' said the general, pointing to Judy's grandfather, your honour, ' make a horse of him.'

" So with that master Fir darrig comes up to Diarmid, who, you may be sure, was in a mighty great fright; but he determined, seeing there was no help for him, to put a bold face on the matter ; and so he began to cross himself, and to say some blessed words, that nothing bad could stand before.

" ' Is that what you'd be after, you spalpeen ?' said the little red imp, at the same time grinning a horrible grin ; ' I'm not the man to care a straw for either your words or your crossings.' So, without more to do, he gives poor Diarmid a rap with the flat side of his sword, and in a moment he was changed into a horse, with little Fir darrig stnck fast on his back.

" Away they all flew over the wide ocean, like so many wild geese, screaming and chattering all the time, till they came to Jamaica; and there they had a murdering fight with the good people of that country. Well, it was all very well with them, and they stuck to it manfully, and fought it out fairly, till one of the Jamaica men made a cut with his sword under Diarmid's left eye. And then, sir, you see, poor Diamiid lost his temper entirely, and he dashed into the very middle of them, with Fir darrig mounted upon his back, and he threw out his heels, and he whisked his tail about, and wheeled and turned round and round at such a rate, that he soon made a fair clearance of them, horse, foot, and dragoons. At last Diarmid's faction got the better, all through his means ; and then they had such feasting and rejoicing, and gave Diarmid, who was the finest horse amongst them all, the best of every thing.

" ' Let every man take a hand of tohaccy for Diarmid Bawn,' said the general; and So they did ; and away they flew, for 'twas getting near morning, to the old fort back again, and there they vanished like the mist from the mountain.

" When Diarmid looked about, the sun was rising, and he thought it was all a dream, till he saw a big rick of tohaccy in the old fort, and felt the blood running from his left eye : for sure enough he was wounded in the battle, and would have been kilt entirely, if it wasn't for a gospel composed by father Murphy that hung about his

neck ever since he had the scarlet fever; and for certain, it was enough to have given him another scarlet fever to have had the little red man all night on his back, whip and spur for the bare life. However, there was the tohaccy heaped up in a great heap by his side; and he heard a voice, although he could see no one, telling him, ' That 'twas all his own, for his good behaviour in the battle ; and that whenever Fir darrig would want a horse again he'd know where to find a clever beast, as he never rode a better than Diarmid Bawn.' That's what he said, sir."

" Thank you, Pat," said the squire; " it certainly is a wonderful story, and I am not surprised at Judy's alarm. But now, as the storm is over, and the moon shining brightly, I'll make the best of my way home." So saying, he disrobed himself of the blanket, put on his coat, and whistling his dogs, set off across the movmtain; while Patrick stood at the door, bawling after him, " May God and the blessed Virgin preserve your honour, and keep ye from the good people ; for 'twas of a moonlight night like this that Diarmid Bawn was made a horse of, for the Fir darriff to ride."

TEIGUE OF THE LEE*
XXXI.

" I can't stop in the house—I won't stop in it for all the money that is buried in the old castle of Carrigrohan. If ever there was such a thing in the world!—to be abused to my face night and day, and nobody to the fore doing it! and then^ if I'm angry, to be laughed at with a great roaring ho, ho, ho ! I won't stay in the house after to-night, if there was not another place in the country to put my head under." This angry soliloquy was pronounced in the hall of the old manor-house of Carrigrohan by John Sheehan. John was a new servant: he had been only three days in the house, which had the character of being haunted, and in that short space of time he had been abused and laughed at by a voice which sounded as if a man spoke with his head in a cask ; nor could he discover who was the speaker, or from whence the voice came. " I'll not stop here," said John ; " and that ends the matter."

" Ho, ho, ho ! be quiet, John Sheehan, or else worse will happen to you."

John instantly ran to the hall window, as the words were evidently spoken by a person immediately outside, but no one was visible. He had scarcely placed his face at the pane of glass, when he heard another loud " Ho, ho, ho!" as if behind

him in the hall; as quick as lightning he turned his head, but no living thing was to be seen.

" Ho, ho, ho, John !" shouted a voice that appeared to come from the lawn before the house; " do you think you'll see Teigue ?—oh, never ! as long as you liA'e ! so leave alone looking after him, and mind your business; there's plenty of company to dinner from Cork to be here to-day, and 'tis time you had the cloth laid."

" Lord bless us ! there's more of it!—I'U never stay another day here," repeated John.

" Hold your tongue, and stay where you are quietly, and play no tricks on Mr. Pratt, as you did on Mr. Jervois about the spoons."

John Sheehan was confounded by this address from his invisible persecutor, but nevertheless he mustered courage enough to say—" Who are you ?—come here, and let me see you, if you are a man;" but he received in reply only a laugh of unearthly derision, which was followed by a " Good-bye—I'll watch you at dinner, John !"

" Lord between us and harm! this beats all! —I'll watch you at dinner!—maybe you will; —'tis the broad daylight, so 'tis no ghost ; but this is a terrible place, and this is the last day I'll stay in it. How does he know about the spoons ?—if he tells it, I'm a ruined man !— there was no living soul could tell it to him but Tim Barrett, and he's far enough ofiF in the wilds of Botany Bay now, so how could he know it— I can't tell for the world ! But what's that I see there at the comer of the wall ?—'tis not a man!—oh, what a fool I am ! 'tis only the old

stump of a tree!—But this is a shocking place —I'll never stop in it, for I'll leave the house tomorrow ; the very look of it is enough to frighten any one."

The mansion had certainly an air of desolation; it was situated in a lawn, which had nothing to break its uniform level, safe a few tufts of narcisuses and a couple of old trees coeval with the building. The house stood at a short distance from tlie road; it was upwards of a century old, and Time was doing his work upon it; its walls were weather-stained in all colours, its roof showed various white patches, it had no look of comfort; all was dim and dingy without, and within there was an air of gloom, of departed and departing greatness, which harmonised well with the exterior. It required all the exuberance of youth and of gaiety to remove the impression, almost amounting to awe, with which you trod the huge square hall, paced along the gallery which surrounded the hall, or explored the long rambling passages below stairs. The ball-room, as the large drawing-room was called, and several other apartments, were in a state of decay : the walls were stained with damp; and I remember well the sensation of awe which I felt creeping over me when, boy as I was, and full of bojnsh life, and -wild and ardent spirits, I descended to the vaults; all without and within me became chilled beneath their dampness and gloom—their extent, too, terrified me; nor could the merriment of my two schoolfellows, whose father, a respectable clergyman, rented the dwelling for a time, dispel the feelings of a romantic imagination, until I once again ascended to the upper regions.

John had pretty well recovered himself as the dinner-hour approached, and the several guests arrived. They were all seated at table, and had begun to enjoy the excellent repast, when a voice was heard from the lawn :—

" Ho, ho, ho, Mr. Pratt, won't you give poor Teigue some dinner ? ho, ho, a fine company you have there, and plenty of everything that's good; sure you won't forget poor Teigue ?"

John dropped the glass he had in his hand.

" Who is that ?" said Mr. Pratt's brother, an officer of the artillery.

" That is Teigue," said Mr. Pratt, laughing, " whom you must often have heard me mention."

" And pray, Mr. Pratt," inquired another gentleman, " who is Teigue ?"

" That," he replied, " is more than I can tell. No one has ever been able to catch even a glimpse of him. I have been on the watch for a whole evening with three of my sons, yet, although his voice sometimes sounded almost in my ear, I could not see him. I fancied, indeed, that I saw a man in a white frieze jacket pass into the door from the garden to the lawn, but it could be only fancy, for I found the door locked, while the fellow, vrhoever he is, was laughing at our trouble. He visits us occasionally, and sometimes a long interval passes between his visits, as in the present case; it is now nearly two years since we heard that hollow voice outside the window. He has never done any injury that w^e know of, and once

when he broke a plate, he brought one back exactly like it."

"It is very extraordinary," said several of the company.

" But," remarked a gentleman to young Mr. Pratt, " your father said he broke a plate; how did he get it without your seeing him ?"

" When he asks for some dinner, we put it outside the window and go away; whilst we watch he will not take it, but no sooner have we withdrawn, than it is gone."

" How does he know that you are watching?"

" That's more than I can tell, but he either knows or suspects. One day my brothers Robert and James with myself were in our back parlour, which has a window into the garden, when he came outside and said, ' Ho, ho, ho! master James, and Robert, and Henry, give poor Teigue a glass of whiskey.' James went out of the room, filled a glass with whiskey, vinegar, and salt, and brought it to him. ' Here, Teigue,' said he, ' come for it now.' ' Well, put it down, then, on the step outside the window.' This was done, and we stood looking at it. ' There, now, go away,' he shouted. We retired, but still watched it. ' Ho, ho ! you are watching Teigue; go out of the room, now, or I won't take it.' We went outside the door and returned; the glass was gone, and a moment after we heard him roaring and cursing frightfully. He took away the glass, but the next day the glass was on the stone step under the window, and there were crumbs of bread in the inside, as if he had put it in his pocket; from that time he was not heard till to-day."

" Oh," said the colonel, " I'll get a sight of him; you are not used to these things; an old soldier has the best chance; and as I shall finish my dinner with this wing, I'll be ready for him when he speaks next.—Mr. Bell, will you take a glass of wine with me?"

" Ho, ho! Mr. Bell," shouted Teigue. " Ho, ho! Mr. Bell, you were a quaker long ago. Ho, ho ! Mr. Bell, you 're a pretty boy ;—a pretty quaker you were; and now you're no quaker, nor any thing else:—ho, ho! Mr. Bell. And there's Mr. Parkes: to be sure, Mr. Parkes looks mighty fine to-day, with his powdered head, and his grand silk stockings, and his bran new rakish-red waistcoat.—And there's Mr. Cole,—did you ever see such a fellow ? a pretty company you've brought together, Mr. Pratt: kiln-dried quakers, butter-buying buckeens from Mallow-lane, and a drinking exciseman from the Coal-quay, to meet the great thundering artillery-general that is come out of the Indies, and is the biggest dust of them all."

" You scoundrel!" exclaimed the colonel: " I'll make you show yourself;" and snatching up his sword from a comer of the room, he sprang out of the window upon the lawn. In a moment a shout of laughter, so hollow, so unlike any human sound, made him stop, as well as Mr. Bell, wha with a huge oak stick was close at the colonel's heels; others of the party followed on the lawn, and the remainder rose and went to the windows. " Come on, colonel," said Mr. Bell; " let us catch this impudent rascal."

" Ho, ho! Mr. Bell, here I am—here's Teigue

—why don't you catch him ?—Ho, ho ! colonel Pratt, what a pretty soldier you are to draw your sword upon poor Teigue, that never did any body harm."

" Let us see your face, you scoundrel," said the colonel.

" Ho, ho, ho !—look at me—look at me r da you see the wind, colonel Pratt ? — you'll see Teigue as soon; so go in and finish your dinner."

" If you're upon the earth I'll find you, you villain !" said the colonel, whilst the sane unearthly shout of derision seemed to come from behind an angle of the building. " He's round that comer," said Mr. Bell—" run, run."

They followed the sound, which was continued at intervals along the garden wall, but could discover no human being; at last both stopped to draw breath, and in an instant, almost at their ears, sounded the shout.

" Ho, ho, ho 1 colonel Pratt, do you see Teigue now ?—do you hear him ?—Ho, ho, ho I you're a fine colonel to follow the wind."

" Not that way, Mr. Bell—not that way; come here," said the colonel.

" Ho, ho, ho! what a fool you are; do you think Teigue is going to show himself to you in the field, there ? Biit colonel, follow me if you can : — you a soldier ! — ho, ho, ho !" The colonel was enraged—he followed the voice over hedge and ditch, alternately laughed at and tavmt-ed by the unseen object of his pursuit—(Mr. Bell, who was heavy, was soon thrown out), until at length, after being led a weary chase, he found himself at the top of the cliff, over tliat part of the

river Lee which, from its great depth, and the blackness of its water, has received the name of Hell-hole. Here, on the edge of the cliff, stood the colonel out of breath, and mopping his forehead with his handkerchief, while the voice, which seemed close at his feet, exclaimed — " Now, colonel Pratt — now, if you're a soldier, here's a leap for you ; — now look at Teigue — why don't you look at him ?—Ho, ho, ho ! Come along: you're warm, I'm sure, colonel Pratt, so come in and cool yourself; Teigue is going to have a swim !" The voice seemed as descending amongst the trailing ivy and brushwood which clothes this picturesque cliff nearly from top to bottom, yet it was impossible that any human being could have found footing. " Now, colonel, have you courage to take the leap ?—Ho, ho, ho ! what a pretty soldier you are. Good-bye — I'll see you again in ten minutes above, at the house—look at your watch, colonel:—there's a dive for you !" and a heavy plunge into the water was heard. The colonel stood still, but no sound followed, and he walked slowly back to the house, not quite half a mile from the Crag.

"Well, did you see Teigue ?" said his brother, whilst his nephews, scarcely able to smother their laughter, stood by.—" Give me some wine," said the colonel. " I never was led such a dance in my life: the fellow carried me all round and round, till he brought me to the edge of the cliff, and then down he went into Hell-hole, telling me he'd be here in ten minutes: 'tis more than that now, but he's not come."

"Ho, ho, ho! colonel, isn't he here?—Teigue

never told a lie in his life : but, Mr. Pratt, give me a drink and my dinner, and then good night to you all, for I'm tired; and that's the colonel's doing." A plate of food w^as ordered: it was placed by John, with fear and trembling, on the lawn under the window. Every one kept on the watch, and the plate remained undisturbed for some time.

" Ah ! Mr. Pratt, will you starve poor Teigue ? Make every one go away from the windows, and master Henry out of the tree, and master liichard off the garden-wall."

The eyes of the company were turned to the tree and the garden-wall; the two boys' attention was occupied in getting down : the visiters were looking at them ; and " Ho, ho, ho !—^good luck to you, Mr. Pratt!—'tis a good dinner, and there's the plate, ladies and gentlemen— good-bye to you, colonel—good-bye, Mr. Bell !—good-bye to you all!"—brought their attention back, when they saw the empty plate lying on the grass; and Teigue's voice was heard no more for that evening. IMany visits were afterwards paid by Teigue; but never was he seen, nor was any discovery ever made of his person or character.

NED SHEEHY'S EXCUSE.

XXXII.

Ned Sheeiiy was servant-man to Richard Gum-bleton, esquire, of Mountbally, Gumbletonmore, in the north of the county of Cork ; and a better servant than Ned was not to be found in that honest county, from Cape Clear to the Kihvorth Mountains; for nobody—no, not his worst enemy —could say a word against him, only that he was rather given to drinking, idling, lying, and loitering, especially the last; for send Ned of a five-minute message at nine o'clock in the morning, and you were a lucky man if you saw him before dinner. If there happened to be a public-house in the way, or even a little out of it, Ned was sure to mark it as dead as a pointer; and, knowing everybody, and everybody liking him, it is not to be wondered at he had so much to say and to hear, that the time slipped away as if the sun somehow or other had knocked two hours into one.

But when he came home, he never was short of an excuse: he had, for that matter, five hundred ready upon the tip of his tongue; so much so, that I doubt if even the very reverend doctor Swift, for many years Dean of St. Patrick's, in Dublin, could match him in that particular, though his reverence had a pretty way of his own of

writing things which brought him into very decent company. In fact, Ned would fret a saint, but then he was so good-humoured a fellow, and really so handy about a house,—for, as he said himself, he was as good as a lady's-maid,—that his master could not find it in his heart to part with him.

In your grand houses—not that I am saying that Richard Gumbleton, esquii-e, of ilountbaUy, Gumbletonmore, did not keep a good house, but a plain country gentleman, although he is second-cousin to the last high-sheriiF of the county, cannot have all the army of servants that the lord-lieutenant has in the castle of Dublin—I say, in your grand houses, you can have a servant for every kind of thing, but in Mountbally, Gumbletonmore, Ned was expected to please master and mistress; or, as counsellor Curran said,—by the same token the counsellor was a little dark man—(jne day that he dined there, on his way to the Clonmel assizes—Ned was minister for the home and foreign departments.

But to make a long story short, Ned Sheehy was a good butler, and a right good one too, and as for a groom, let him alone with a horse: he could dress it, or ride it, or shoe it, or physic it, or do anything wnth it but make it speak—he was a second whisperer ! — there was not his match in the barony, or the next one neither. A pack of hounds he could manage well, ay, and ride after them with the boldest man in the land. It was Ned who leaped the old bounds' ditch at the turn of the boreen of the lands of Reenascreena, after the English captain pulled up on looking at it, and cried out it was " No go." Ned rode that s 2

day Brian Boro, Mr. Gumbleton's famous chesnut, and people call it Ned Sheehy's Leap to this hour.

So, you see, it was hard to do without him : however, many a scolding he got; and although his master often said of an evening, " I'll turn off Ned," he always forgot to do so in the morning. These threats mended Ned not a bit; indeed, he was mending the other way, like bad fish in hot weatlier.

One cold winter's day, about three o'clock in the afternoon, Mr. Gumbleton said to him,

" Ned," said he, " go take Modderaroo down to black Falvey, the horse-doctor, and bid him look at her knees; for Doctor Jenkinson, who rode her home last night, has hurt her somehow. I suppose he thought a parson's horse ought to go upon its knees; but, indeed, it was I was the fool to give her to him at all, for he sits twenty stone if he sits a pound, and knows no more of riding, particularly after his third bottle, than I do of preaching. Now mind and be back in an hour at furthest, for I want to have the plate cleaned up properly for dinner, as sir Augustus O'Toole, you know, is to dine here to-day.—Don't loiter, for your life."

" Is it I, sir?" says Ned. "Well, that beats anything; as if I'd stop out a minute!" So, mounting Modderaroo, off he set.

Four, five, six o'clock came, and so did sir Augustus and lady O'Toole, and the four misses O'Toole, and Mr. O'Toole, and Mr. Edward O'Toole, and Mr. James O'Toole, which were all the young O'Tooles that were at home, but no Ned Sheehy appeared to clean the plate, or

to lay the tablecloth, or even to put dinner on. It is needless to say how Mr. and Mrs. Dick Gumbleton fretted and fumed ; but it was all to no use. They did their best, however, only it was a disgrace to see long Jem the stable-boy, and Bill the gossoon that used to go of errands, waiting, without anybody to direct them, when there was a real baronet and his lady at table; for sir Augustus was none of your knights. But a good bottle of claret makes up for much, and it was not one only they had that night. However, it is not to be concealed that Mr. Dick Gumbleton went to bed very cross, and he awoke still Grosser.

He heard that Ned had not made his appearance for the whole night; so he dressed himself in a great fret, and, taking his horsewhip in his hand, he said,

" There is no further use in tolerating this scoundrel; I'll go look for him, and if I find him, I'll cut the soul out of his vagabond body 1 I will, by "

" Don't swear, Dick, dear," said Mrs. Gumbleton (for she was always a mild woman, being daughter of fighting Tom Crofts, who shot a couple of gentlemen, friends of his, in the cool of the evening, after the Mallow races, one after the other), " don't swear, Dick, dear," said she ; " but do, my dear, oblige me by cutting the flesh off his bones, for he richly deserves it. I was quite ashamed of lady O'Toole, yesterday, I was, 'pon honour."

Out sallied Mr. Gumbleton; and he had not far to walk ; for, not more than two hundred yards

firom the house, he found Ned lying fast asleep under a ditch (a hedge), and Modderaroo standing by him, poor beast, shaking every limb. The loud snoring of Ned, who was lying with his head upon a stone as easy and as comfortable as if it had been a bed of down or a hop-bag, drew him to the spot, and Mr, Gumbleton at once perceived, from the disarray of Ned's face and person, that he had been engaged in some perilous adventure during the night. Ned appeared not to have descended in the most regular manner; for one of his shoes remained sticking in the stirrup, and his hat, having rolled down a little slope, was embedded in green mud. Mr. Gumbleton, however, did not give himself much trouble to make a curious siirvey, but with a vigorous application of his thong, soon banished sleep from the eyes of Ned Sheehy.

" Ned!" thundered his master in great indignation,—and on this occasion it was not a word and blow, for with that one word came half a doBen: " Get up, you scoundrel," said he.

Ned roared lustily, and no wonder, for his master's hand was not one of the lightest; and he cried out, between sleeping and waking—" O, sir! —don't be angry, sir!—don't be angry, and I'll roast you easier—easy as a lamb !"

"Roast me easier, you vagabond!" said Mr. Gumbleton; "what do you mean?—I'll roast you, my lad. Where were you all night ?—!Mod-deraroo will never get over it.—Pack out of my service, you worthless villain, this moment; and, indeed, you may give God thanks that I don't get you transported,

" Thank God, master dear," said Ned, who was now perfectly awakened —" it's yourself anyhow. There never was a gentleman in the whole county ever did so good a turn to a poor man as your honour has been after doing to me: the Lord reward you for that same. Oh ! but strike me again, and let me feel that it is yourself, master dear;—may whiskey be my poison—"

" It will be your poison, you good-for-nothing scoundrel," said Mr. Gumbleton.

" AVell, then vnay whiskey be my poison," said Ned, " if 'twas not I was — God help me !—in the blackest of misfortunes, and they were before me, whichever way I turned 'twas no matter. Your honour sent me last night, sure enough, with Modderaroo to mister Falvey's—I don't deny it —why should I ? for reason enough I have to remember what happened."

" Ned, my man," said Mr. Gumbleton, " I'll listen to none of your excuses: just take the mare into the stable and yourself off, for I vow to—"

" Begging your honour's pardon," said Ned earnestly, "for interrupting your honoiir; but, master, master ! make no vows — they are bad things : I never made but one in all my life, which was, to drink nothing at all for a year and a day, and 'tis myself repmted of it for the clean twelvemonth after. But if your honour would only listen to reason: I'll just take in the poor baste, and if your honour don't pardon me this one time may I never see another day's luck or grace."

" I know you, Ned," said Mr. Gumbleton.

" Whatever your luck has been, you never had any grace to lose: but I don't intend discussing the matter with you. Take in the mare, sir."

Ned obeyed, and his master saw him to the stables. Here he reiterated his commands to quit, and Ned Sheehy's excuse for himself began. That it was heard uninterruptedly is more than I can affirm; but as interruptions, like explanations, spoil a story, we must let Ned tell it his own way.

" No wonder your honour," said he, " should be a bit angry—grand company coming to the house and all, and no regular serving-man to wait, only long Jem ; so I don't blame your honour the least for being fretted like ; but when all's heard, you will see that no poor man is more to be pitied for last night than myself. Fin Mac Coul never went through more in his born days than I did, though he was a great joint (giant), and I only a man.

" I had not rode half a mile from the house, when it came on, as your honour must have perceived clearly, mighty dark all of a sudden, for aU the world as if the sun had tumbled down plump out of the fine clear blue sky. It was not so late, being only four o'clock at the most, but it was as black as your honour's hat. Well, I didn't care much, seeing I knew the road as well as I knew the way to my mouth, whether I saw it or not, and I put the mare into a smart canter; but just as I turned down by the corner of Terence Leahy's field—sure your honour ought to know the place well—^just at the very spot the fox was killed when your honour came in first out of a whole field of a hundred and fifty gentlemen, and may be more, all of them brave riders."

(Mr. Gumbleton smiled.)

" Just then, there, I heard the low cry of the good people wafting upon the wind. ' How early you are at your work, my little fellows!' says I to myself; and, dark as it was, having no wish for such company, I thought it best to get out of their way ; so I turned the horse a little up to the left, thinking to get down by the boreen, that is that way, and so round to Falvey's; but there I heard the voice plainer and plainer close behind, and I could hear these words:—

• Ned ! Ned! By my cap so red '. You 're as good, Ned, As a man that is dead.'

' A clean pair of spurs is all that's for it now,' said I; so off I set, as hard as I could lick, and in my hurry knew no more where I was going than I do the road to the hill of Tarah. Away I galloped on for some time, until I came to the noise of a stream, roaring away by itself in the darkness. ' What river is this ?' said I to myself—for there ^as nobody else to ask—'I thought,' says I, 'I knew every inch of ground, and of water too, within twenty miles, and never the river surely is there in this direction.' So I stopped to look about; but I might have spared myself that trouble, for I could not see as much as my hand. I didn't know what to do ; but I thought in myself, it's a queer river, surely, if somebody does not live near it; and I shouted out as loud as I could,

Murder! murder!—fire !—robbery !—anything that would be natural in such a place— but not a sound did I hear except my own voice echoed back to me, like a hundred packs of hounds in full cry above and below, right and left. This didn't do at all; so I dismounted, and guided myself along the stream, directed by the noise of the water, as cautious as if I was treading upon aggfi, holding poor Modderaroo by the bridle, who shook, the poor brute, all over in a tremble, like my old grandmother, rest her soul anyhow! in the ague. "Well, sir, the heart was sinking in me, and I was giving myself up, when, as good luck would have it, I saw a light. ' Maybe,' said I, ' my good fellow, you are only a jacky lantern, and want to bog me and Modderaroo.' But I looked at the light hard, and I thought it was too studt/ (steady) for a jacky lantern. ' I'll try you,' says I—' so here goes;' and, walking as quick as a thief, I came towards it, being very near plumping into the river once or twice, and being stuck up to my middle, as your honour may perceive cleanly the marks of, two or three times in the slob*. At last I made the liorht out, and it coming from a bit of a house by the roadside; so I went to the door and gave three kicks at it, as strong as I could.

" ' Open the door for Xed Sheehy,' said a voice inside. Now, besides that I could not, for the life of me, make out how any one inside should know me before I spoke a word at all, I did not like the sound of that voice, 't was so hoarse and so hollow,

* Or slaib; mire on the sea strand or river's bank.— O'Brien.

just like a dead man's!—so I said nothing immediately. The same voice spoke again, and said, ' Why don't you open the door to Ned Sheehy ?' ' How pat my name is to you,' said I, without speaking out,' on tip of your tongue, like hutter;' and I was between two minds about staying or going, when what should the door do but open, and out came a man holding a candle in his hand, and he had upon him a face as white as a sheet.

"' "Why, then, Ned Sheehy,' says he, ' how grand you're grown, that you won't come in and see a friend, as you're passing by.'

"' Pray, sir,' says I, looking at him—though that face of his was enough to dumbfounder any honest man like myself—' Pray, sir,' says I,' may I make so bold as to ask if you are not Jack Myers that was drowned seven years ago, next Martinmas, in the ford of Ah-na-foiirish ?'

"' Suppose I was,' says he: ' has not a man a right to be drowned in the ford facing his own cabin-door any day of the week that he likes, from Sunday morning to Saturday night ?'

" ' I'm not denying that same, Mr. Myers, sir,' says I, ' if 't is yourself is to the fore speaking to me.'

" ' Well,' says he, ' no more words about that matter now : sure you and I, Ned, were friends of old; come in, and take a glass; and here's a good fire before you, and nobody shall hurt or harm you, and I to the fore, and myself able to do it.'

" Now, your honour, though 't was much to drink with a man that was drowned seven years

before, in the ford of Ah-na-fourish, facing his own door, yet the glass was hard to be withstood —to say nothing of the fire that was blazing within—for the night was mortal cold. So tying Modderaroo to the hasp of the door—if I don't love the creatnre as I love my own life—I went in with Jack Myers.

" Civil enough he was—I'll never say otherwise to my dying hour—for he handed me a stool by the fire, and bid me sit down and make myself comfortable. But his face, as I said before, was as white as the snow on the hills, and his two eyes fell dead on me, like the eyes of a cod without any life in them. Just as I was going to put the glass to my lips, a voice—^"twas the same that I heard bidding the door be opened—spoke out of a cupboard that was convenient to the left-hand side of the chimney, and said, ' Have you any news for me, Ned Sheehy V

" ' The never a word, sir,' says I, making answer before I tasted the whiskey, all out of civility; and, to speak the truth, never the least could I remember at that moment of what had happened to me, or how I got there; for I was quite bothered with the fright.

" ' Have you no news,' says the voice, ' Ned, to tell me, from [Mountbally Gumbletonmore; or from the 31ill; or about Moll Trantum that was married last week to Bryan Oge, and you at the wedding ?'

" ' No, sir,' says I, ' never the word.'

"' What brought you in here, Ned, then V says the voice. I could say nothing; for, whatever other people might do, I never could frame

an excuse; and I was loth to say it was on account of the glass and the fire, for that would be to speak the truth.

" ' Turn the scoundrel out,' says the voice; and at the sound of it, who would I see but Jack Myers making over to me with a lump of a stick in his hand, and it clenched on the stick so Avicked. For certain, I did not stop to feel the weight of the blow; so, dropping the glass, and it full of the stuff too, I bolted out of the door, and never rested from running away, for as good, I believe, as twenty miles, till I found myself in a big wood.

" ' The Lord preserve me ! what will' become of me now !' says I. ' Oh, Ned Sheehy!' says I, speaking to myself, ' my man, you're in a pretty hobble; and to leave poor Modderaroo after you !' But the words were not well out of my mouth, when I heard the dismallest uUagoane in the world, enough to break any one's heart that was not Ijroke before, with the grief entirely ; and it was not long till I could plainly see four men coming towards me, with a great black coffin on their shoulders. ' I'd better get up in a tree,' says I, ' for they say 'tis not lucky to meet a corpse: I'm in the way of misfortune to-night, if ever man was.'

" I could not help wondering how a berrin (funeral) should come there in the lone wood at that time of night, seeing it could not be far from the dead hour. But it was little good for me thinking, for they soon came under the very tree I was roosting in, and down they put the coffin, and began to make a fine fire under me. I'll be smothered alive now, thinks I, and that will be the end of me ; but I was afraid to stir for the life, or-to speak out to bid them just make their fire under some other tree, if it would be all the same thing to them. Presently they opened the coffin, and out they dragged as fine-looking a man as you'd meet with in a day's walk.

" ' Where's the spit ?' says one.

" ' Here 'tis,' says another, handing it over; and for certain they spitted him, and began to turn him before the fire.

" If they are not going to eat him, thinks I, like the Hannihals father Quinlan told us about in his sarmint last Sunday.

" ' Who'll turn the spit while we go for the other ingredients V says one of them that brought the coffin, and a big ugly-looking blackguard he was.

"'Who'd turn the spit but Ned Sheehy?' says another.

" Burn you ! thinks I, how should you know that I was here so handy to you up in the tree ?

" ' Come down, Ned Sheehy, and turn the spit,' says he.

" ' I'm not here at all, sir,' says I, putting my hand over my face that he may not see me.

" ' That won't do for you, my man,' says he; ' you'd better come down, or maybe I'd make you.'

" ' I'm coming, sir,' says I; for 'tis always right to make a virtue of necessity. So down I came, and there they left me turning the spit in the middle of the wide wood.

" ' Don't scorch me, Ned Sheehy, you vagabond,' says the man on the spit.

" ' And my lord, sir, and ar'n't you dead, sir,' says I, ' and your honour taken out of the coffin and all ?'

" ' I ar'n't,' says he.

" ' But surely you are, sir,' says I, ' for 'tis to no use now for me denying that I saw your honour, and I up in the tree.'

" ' I ar'n't,' says he again, speaking quite short and snappish.

" So I said no more, until presently he called, out to me to turn him easy, or that maybe 'twould be the worse turn for myself.

" ' Will that do, sir ?' says I, turning him as easy as I could.

" ' That's too easy,' says he: so I turned him faster.

" ' That's too fast,' says he; so finding that, turn him which way I would, I could not please him, I got into a bit of a fret at last, and desired him to turn himself, for a grumbling spalpeen as he was, if he liked it better.

" Away I ran, and away he came hopping, spit and all, after me, and he but half-roasted, ' IMur-der !' says I, shouting out; ' I'm done for at long last — now or never !' — when all of a sudden, and 'twas really wonderful, not knowing where I was rightly, I found myself at the door of the very little cabin by the roadside that I had bolted out of fi'om Jack]Myers; and there was

Modderaroo standing hard by.

" ' Open the door for Ned Sheehy,' says the voice,—for 'twas shut against me,—and tlie door flew open in an instant. In I ran, without stop or stay, thinking it better to be beat by Jack Myers, he being an old friend of mine, than to be spitted like a Michaelmas goose by a man that I knew nothing about, either of him or his family, one or the other.

" ' Have you any news for me ?' says the voice, putting just the same question to me that it did before.

" ' Yes, sir,' says I, ' and plenty.' So I mentioned all that had happened to me in the big wood, and how I got up in the tree, and how I was made come down again, and put to turning the spit, roasting the gentleman, and how I could not please him, turn him fast or easy, although I tried my best, and how he ran after me at last, spit and all.

" ' If you had told me this before, you would not have been turned out in the cold,' said the voice.

" ' And how could I tell it to you, sir,' says I, ' before it happened ?'

'• ' Xo matter,' says he, ' you may sleep now till morning on that bundle of hay in the comer there, and only I was your friend, you'd have been kilt entirely.' So down I lay, but I was dreaming, dreaming all the rest of the night, and when you, master dear, woke me with that blessed blow, I thought 'twas the man on the spit had hold of me, and could hardly believe my eyes when I found myself in your honour's presence, and poor Modderaroo safe and sound by my side; but how I came tliere is more than I can say, if 'twas not Jack Myers, although he did make the offer to strike me, or some one among the good people that befriended me."

" It is all a drunken dream, you scoundrel," said Mr, Gmnbleton; " have I not had fifty such excuses from you?"

" But never one, your honour, that really happened before," said Ned, w^ith unblushing front. " Howsomever, since your honour fancies 'tis drinking I was, I'd rather never drink again to the world's end, than lose so good a master as yourself, and if I'm forgiven this once, and get another trial "

" Well," said Mr. Gumblcton, " you may, for this once, go into Moiintbally Gumbletonmore again; let me see that you keep your promise as to not drinking, or mind the consequences; and, above all, let me hear no more of the good people, for I don't believe a single word about them, whatever I may do of bad ones."

So saying, jNIr. Gumblcton turned on his heel, and Ned's countenance relaxed into its usual expression,

" Now I would not be after saying about the good people what the master said last," exclaimed Peggy, the maid, who was within hearing, and who, by the way, had an eye after Ned: " I would not be after saying such a thing; the good people, maybe, will make him feel the differ (diflFerence) to his cost."

Nor was Peggy wrong; for whether Ned Sheehy dreamt of the Fir Darrig or not, wnthin a fortnight after, two of]\fr. Gumbleton's cows, the best milkers in the parish, ran dry, and before the week was out, Modderaroo was lying dead in the stone quarry.

THE LUCKY GUEST.

XXXIII.

TflE kitchen of some country houses in Ireland presents in no ways a bad modem translation of the ancient feudal hall. Traces of clanship still linger round its hearth in the numerous dependants on " the master s" bounty. Nurses, foster-brothers, and other hangers-on, are there as matter of right, while the strolling piper, full of mirth and music, the benighted traveller, even the passing beggar, are received with a hearty welcome, and each contributes planxty, song, or superstitious tale, towards the evening's amusement. An assembly, such as has been described, had collected round the kitchen fire of BalljTahen-house, at the foot of the Galtee mountains, when, as is ever the case, one tale of wonder called forth another; and with the advance of the evening each succeeding story was received with deep and deeper attention. The history of Cough na Looba's dance with the black friar at Rahill, and the fearful tradition of Coum an 'ir morriv (the dead man's hollow), were listened to in breathless silence. A pause followed the last relation, and all eyes rested on thc narrator, an old nurse who occupied the post of honour, that next the fireside. She was seated in that peculiar position which the Irish name " Currigguih" a position

generally assumed by a veteran and detennined story-teller. Her haunches resting upon the ground, and her feet bundled under the body; her arms folded across and supported by her knees, and the outstretched chin of her hooded head pressing on the upper arm; which compact arrangement nearly reduced the whole figure into a perfect triangle.

Unmoved by the general gaze, Bridget Doyle made no change of attitude, while she gravely asserted the truth of the marvellous tale concerning the Dead Man's HoUow; her strongly-marked countenance at the time receiving what painters term a fine chiaro-obscuro efifect from the fire-light.

*' I have told you," she said, " what happened to my own people, the Butlers and the Doyles, in the old times; but here is little Ellen Connell from the county Cork, who can speak to what happened under her own father and mother s roof —the Lord be good to them !"

Ellen, a young and blooming girl of about sixteen, was employed in the dairy at Bally-rahen. She was the picture of health and rustic beauty; and at this hint from nurse Doyle, a deep blush mantled over her countenance; yet, although " unaccustomed to public speaking," she, without further hesitation or excuse, proceeded as follows:—

" It was one May-eve, about thirteen years ago, and that is, as everybody knows, the airiest day in all the twelve months. It is the day above all other days," said Ellen, with her large dark eyes cast down on the ground, and drawing a deep sigh, T 2

" when the young boys and the young girls go looking after the Drutheen, to learn from it rightly the name of their sweethearts.

" My father, and my mother, and my two brothers, with two or three of the neighbours, were sitting round the turf fire, and were talking of one thing or Smother. My mother was husho-ing my little sister, striving to quieten her, for she was cutting her teeth at the time, and was mighty uneasy through the means of them. The day, which was threatening all along, now that it was coming on to dusk, began to rain, and the rain increased and fell fast and faster, as if it was pouring through a sieve out of the wide heavens ; and when the rain stopped for a bit there was a wind which kept up such a whistling and racket, that you would have thought the sky and the earth were coming together. It blew and it blew, as if it had a mind to blow the roof off the cabin, and that would not have been very hard for it to do, as the thatch was quite loose in two or three places. Then the rain began again, and you could hear it spitting and hissing in the fire, as it came down through the big chimhley.

" ' God bless us,' says my mother, ' but 'tis a dreadful night to be at sea,' says she, ' and God be praised that we have a roof, bad as it is, to shelter us.'

" I don't, to be sure, recollect all this, mistress Doyle, bvit only as my brothers told it to me, and other people, and often have I heard it; for I was so little then, that they say I could just go under the table without tipping my head. Anyway, it was in the very height of the pelting and whistling that we heard something speak outside the door. My father and all of us listened, but there was no more noise at that time. We waited a little longer, and then we plainly heard a sound like an old man's voice, asking to be let in, but mighty feeble and weak. Tim bounced up, without a word, to ask us whether we'd like to let the old man, or whoever he was, in—havii\g always a heart as soft as a mealy potato before the voice of sorrow. When Tim pulled back the bolt that did the door, in marched a little bit of a shrivelled, weather-beaten creature, about two feet and a half high.

" We were all watching to see who'd come in, for there was a wall between us and the door ; but when the sound of the undoing of the bolt stopped, we heard Tim give a sort of a screech, and instantly he bolted in to us. He had hardly time to say a word, or we either, when the little gentleman shuffled in after him, without a God save all here, or by your leave, or any other sort of thing that any decent body might say. We all, of one accord, scrambled over to the furthest end of the room, where we were, old and young, every one trying who'd get nearest the wall, and farthest from him. All the eyes of our body were stuck upon him, but he didn't mind us no more than that frying-pan there does now. He walked over to the fire, and squatting himself doAvn like a frog, took the pipe that my father dropped from his mouth in the hurry, put it into his own, and then began to smoke so liearty, that he soon filled the room of it.

" We had plenty of time to observe him, and

my brothers say that he wore a sugar-loaf hat that was as red as blood : he had a face as yellow as a kite's claw, and as long as to-day and tomorrow put together, with a mouth all screwed and puckered up like a washerwoman's hand, little blue eyes, and rather a highish nose; his hair was quite grey and lengthy, appearing under his hat, and flowing over the cape of a long scarlet coat, which almost trailed the ground behind him, and the ends of which he took up and planked on his knees to dry, as he sat facing the fire. He had smart corduroy breeches, and woollen stockings drawn up over the knees, so as to hide the kneebuckles, if he had the pride to have them; but, at any rate, if he hadn't them in his knees he had buckles in his shoes, out before his spindle legs. When we came to ourselves a little we thought to escape from the room, but no one would go first, nor no one would stay last; so we huddled ourselves together and made a dart out of the room. My little gentleman never minded anything of the scrambling, nor hardly stirred himself, sitting quite at his ease before the fire. The neighbours, the very instant minute they got to the door, although it still continued pelting rain, cut gutter as if Oliver Cromwell himself was at their heels ; and no blame to them for that, anyhow. It was my father, and my mother, and my brothers, and myself, a little hop-of-my-thumb midge as I was then, that were left to see what would come out of this strange visit; so we all went quietly to the labhig*^ scarcely daring to throw an eye at

• ioftW^—bed, from leoba.—Vide O'Bbibn and O'Reiilt.

him as we passed the door. Never the wink of sleep could they sleep that live-long night, though, to he sure, I slept like a top, not knowing better, while they were talking and thinking of the little man.

"When they got up in the morning, every thing was as quiet and as tidy about the place as if nothing had happened, for all that the chairs and stools were tumbled here, there, and everywhere, when we saw the lad enter. Now, indeed, I forget whether he came next night or not, but anyway, that was the first time we ever laid eye upon him. This I know for certain, that, about a month after that he came regularly every night, and used to give us a signal to be on the move, for 'twas plain he did not like to be observed. This sign was always made about eleven o'clock ; and then, if we'd look towards the door, there was a little hairy arm thrust in through the keyhole, which would not have been big enough, only there was a fresh hole made near the first one, and the bit of stick between them had been broken away, and so 'twas just fitting for the little arm.

" The Fir Darrig continued his visits, never missing a night, as long as we attended to the signal; smoking always out of the pipe he made his own of, and warming himself till day dawned before the fire, and tlien going no one living knows where : but there was not the least mark of him to be found in the morning; and 'tis as true, nurse Doyle, and honest people, as you are all here sitting before me and by the

side of me, that the family continued thriving, and my father and brothers rising in the world while ever he came to us. "When we observed this, we used always look for the very moment to see when the arm would come, and then we'd instantly fly off with ourselves to our rest. But before we found the luck, we used sometimes sit still and not mind the arm, especially when a neighbour would be with my father, or that two or three or four of them would have a drop among them, and then they did not care for all the arms, hairy or not, that ever were seen. No one, however, dared to speak to it or of it insolently, except, indeed, one night that Davy Kennane—but he was drunk—walked over and hit it a rap on the back of the wrist: the hand was snatched off like lightning ; but every one knows that Davy did not live a month after this happened, though he was only about ten days sick. The like of such tricks are ticklbh things to do.

" As sure as the red man would put in his arm for a sign through the hole in the door, and that we did not go and open it to him, so sure some mishap befel the cattle: the cows were elf-stoned, or overlooked, or something or another went wrong with them. One night my brother Dan refused to go at the signal, and the next day, as he was cutting turf in Crogh-na-drimina bog, within a mile and a half of the house, a stone was thrown at him which broke fairly, with the force, into two halves. Now, if that had happened to hit him he'd be at this hour as dead as my great-great-grandfather. It came

whack slap against the spade he had in his hand, and spht at once in two pieces. He took them np and fitted them together, and they made a perfect heart. Some way or the other he lost it since, but he still has the one which was shot at the spotted mUch cow, before the little man came near us. Many and many a time I saw that same; 'tis just the shape of the ace of hearts on the cards, only it is of a dark red colour, and polished up like the grate that is in the grand parlour within. "When this did not kill the cow on the spot, she swelled up ; but if you took and put the elf-stone under her udder, and milked her upon it to the last stroking, and then made her drink the milk, it would cure her, and she would thrive with you ever after.

" But, as I said, we were getting on well enough as long as we minded the door and watched for the hairy arm, which we did sharp enough when we found it was bringing luck to us, and we were now as glad to see the little red gentleman, and as ready to open the door to him, as we used to dread his coming at first and be frightened of him. But at long last we throve so well that the landlord—God forgive him—took notice of us, and envied us, and asked my father how he came by the penny he had, and wanted him to take more ground at a rack-rent tliat was more than any Christian ought to pay to another, seeing there was no making it. When my father—and small blame to him for that—refused to lease the ground, he turned us ofi" the bit of land we had, and out of

the house and all, and left us in a wide and wicked world, where my father, for he was a soft innocent man, was not up to the roguery and the trickery that was practised upon him. He was taken this way by one and that way by another, and he treating them that were working his downfall. And he used to take bite and sup with them, and they with him, free enough as long as the money lasted; but when that was gone, and he had not as much ground, that he could call his own, as would sod a lark, they soon shabbed him ofiP. The landlord died not long after; and he now knows whether he acted right or wrong in taking the house from over our heads.

" It is a bad thing for the heart to be cast down, so we took another cabin, and looked out with great desire for the Fir Darrig to come to us. But ten o'clock came and no arm, although we cut a hole in the door just the moral (model) of the other. Eleven o'clock !—twelve o'clock !— no, not a sign of him : and every night we watched, but all would not do. We then travelled to the other house, and we rooted up the hearth, for the landlord asked so great a rent for it from the poor people that no one could take it; and we carried away the very door off the hinges, and we brought every thing with us that we thought the little man was in any I'espect partial to, but he did not come, and we never saw him again.

" My father and my mother, and my young sister, are since dead, and my two brothers, who could tell all about this better than myself, are

THE LUCKY GUEST.

283

both of them gone out with Ingram in liis last voyage to the Cape of Good Hope, leaving me behind without kith or kin."

Here young Ellen's voice became choked with sorrow, and bursting into tears, she hid her face in her apron.

Fitt Dabrig, correctly written l^eAtl iPeAftS, means the red man, and is a member of the fairy community of Ireland, who bears a strong resemblance to the Shakspearian Puck, or Robin Goodfellow. Like that merry goblin, his delight is in mischief and mockery ; and this Irish spirit is doubtless the same as the Scottish Red Cap ,- which a writer in the Quarterly Review (No. XLIV. p. 358), tracing national analogies, asserts, is the Robin Hood of England, and the Saxon spirit Hudkin or Hodeken, so called from the hoodakiu or little hood wherein be appeared,—a spirit similar to the Spanish Duende. The Fir Darrig has also some traits of resemblance in common with the Scotch Brownie, the German Kobold (particularly the celebrated one, Hinzel-man), the English Hobgoblin (Milton's" Lubber Fiend"),and the FoUet of Gervase of Tilbury, who says of the Folletos, " Verba utique hu-mano more audiuntur et effigies non comparent. De istis pleraque miracula memini me in vita abbreviata et miraculis beatissimi Antoiiit reperisse."— Otia fmperialia.

The red dress and strange flexibility of voice possessed by the Fir Darrig form his peculiar characteristics; the latter, according to Irish tall-tellers, is like f^itAfn) nA bCOQ, the sound of the waves; and again it is compared to Ceol i)A T)A]t)5eAl, the music of angels; CejleAbAtt tlA tjeAtJ, the warbling of birds, &c. ; and the usual address to this fairy is, Na ftCAtJ t:oct1)0]& fu]^, Do not mock us. His entire dress, when he is seen, is invariably described as crimson ; whereas, Irish fairies generally appear in ?)aca 6uB, cuIaIo 5lAf, rrocAi5 bAtjA, A5UT bftoSA beAttSA; a black hat, a green suit, white stockings, and red shoes.

FAIRY LEGENDS.
TREASURE LEGENDS.

' Bell, book, and candle, shall not drive me back When gold and silver becks me to come on."

King John.

'This is fairy gold, boy, and 'twill prove so."

Winter's Tale.

TREASURE LEGENDS.

DREAMING TIM JARVIS.

Timothy Jarvis was a decent, honest, quiet, hard-working man, as everybody knows that knows Balledehob.

Now Balledehob is a small place, about forty miles west of Cork. It is situated on the summit of a hill, and yet it is in a deep valley; for on all sides there are lofty mountains that rise one above another in barren grandeur, and seem to look down with scorn upon the little busy village which they surround with their idle and unproductive magnificence, Man and beast have alike deserted them to the dominion of the eagle, who soars majestically over them. On the highest of those mountains there is a small, and as is commonly believed, unfathomable lake, the only inhabitant of which is a huge serpent, who has been sometimes seen to stretch its enormovis head above the waters, and frequently is heard to utter a noise which shakes the very rocks to their foundation.

But, as I was saying, everybody know Tim Jarvis to be a decent, honest, quiet, hard-working man, who was thriving enough to be able to give his daughter Nelly a fortune of ten pounds ; and Tim himself would have been snug enough besides, but that he loved the drop sometimes. However, he was seldom backward on rent-day. His ground was never distrained but twice, and both times through a small bit of a mistake ; and his landlord had never but once to say to him— " Tim Jarvis, you're all behind, Tim, like the cow's tail." Now it so happened that, being heavy in himself, through the drink, Tim took to sleeping, and the sleep set Tim dreaming, and he dreamed all night, and night after night, about crocks full of gold and other precious stones ; so much so, that Norah Jarvis his wife could get no good of him by day, and have little comfort with him by night. The grey dawn of the morning would see Tim digging away in a bog-hole, maybe, or rooting under some old stone walls like a pig. At last he dreamt tliat he found a mighty great crock of gold and silver — and where do you think ? Every step of the way upon London-bridge, itself! Twice Tim dreamt it, and three times Tim dreamt the same thing ; and at last he made up his mind to transport himself, and go over to London, in Pat Mahoney's coaster —and so he did !

"Well, he got there, and found the bridge without much difficulty. Every day he walked up and down looking for the crock of gold, but never the find did he find it. One day, however, as he was looking over the bridge into the water,

a man, or something like a man, with great black whiskers, like a Hessian, and a black cloak that reached down to the ground, taps him on the shoulder, and says he—" Tim Jarvis, do you see me ? "

" Surely I do, sir," said Tim; wondering that any body should know him in the strange place.

" Tim," says he, " what is it brings you here in foreign parts, so far away from your own cabin by the mine of grey copper at Balledehob ?"

" Please your honour," says Tim, " I'm come to seek my fortune."

" You're a fool for your pains, Tim, if that's all," remarked the stranger in the black cloak; " this is a big place to seek one's fortune in, to be sure, but it's not so easy to find it."

Now Tim, after debating a long time with himself, and considering, in the first place, that it might be the stranger who was to find the crock of gold for him; and in the next, that the sti-angtr might direct him where to find it, came to the resolution of telling him all.

" There's many a one like me comes here seeking their fortunes," said Tim.

" True," said the stranger.

" But," continued Tim, looking up, " the body and bones of the cause for myself leaving the woman, and Nelly, and the boys, and travelling so far, is to look for a crock of gold that I'm told is lying somewhere hereabouts."

" And who told you that, Tim ?"

" Why then, air, tliat's what I can't tell myself rightly—only I dreamt it."

" Ho, ho! is that all, Tim!" said the stranger, laughing; " I had a dream myself; and I dreamed that I found a crock of gold, in the Fort field, on Jerry Driscoll's ground at Balledehob; and by the same token, the pit where it lay was close to a large furze bush, all full of yellow blossom."

Tim knew Jerry Driscoll's ground well; and, moreover, he knew the Fort field as well as he knew his own potato garden ; he was certain, too, of the very furze bush at the north end of it—so, swearing a bitter big oath, says he—

" By all the crosses in a yard of check, I always thought there was money in that same field!"

The moment he rapped out the oath, the stranger disappeared, and Tim Jarvis, wondering at all that had happened to him, made the best of his way back to Ireland. Norah, as may well be supposed, liad no very warm welcome for her runaway husband—the dreaming blackguard, as she called him—and so soon as she set eyes upon him, all the blood of her body in one minute was into her knuckles to be at him ; but Tim, after his long journey, looked so cheerful and so happylike, that she could not find it in her heart to give him the first blow ! He managed to pacify his wife by two or three broad hints about a new cloak and a pair of shoes, tliat, to speak honestly, were much wanting for her to go to chapel in; and decent clothes for Nelly to go to the patron with her sweetheart, and brogues for the boys, and some corduroy for himself. " It wasn't for nothing," says Tim, " I went to foreign pai-ts all

the ways; and you'll see what'U come out of it —mind my words."

A few days afterwards Tim sold his cabin and his garden, and bought the Fort field of Jerry Di'iscoll, that had nothing in it, but was full of thistles, and old stones, and blackberry bushes; and all the neighbours—as well they might— thought he was cracked !

The first night that Tim could summon courage to begin his work, he walked ofi"to the field with his spade upon his shoulder; and away he dug all night by the side of the furze bush, till he came to a big stone. He struck his spade against it, and he lieard a hollow sound; but as the morning had begun to dawTi, and the neighbours would be going out to their work, Tim, not wishing to have the thing talked about, went home to the little hovel, where Norah and the children were huddled together under a lieap of straw; for he had sold every thing he had in the world to purchase DriscoU's field, though it was said to be " the back-bone of the world, picked by the devil."

It is impossible to describe the epithets and reproaches bestowed by the poor woman on her unlucky husband for bringing her into such a way. Epithets and reproaches, which Tim had but one mode of answering, as thus :—" Norah, did you see e'er a cow you'd like ?"—or, " Norah, dear, hasn't Poll Deasy a feather-bed to sell ?" '—or, " Norah, honey, wouldn't you like your sUver buckles as big as Mrs. Doyle's ?"

As soon as night came Tim stood beside the furze-bush, spade in hand. The moment he u

2

jumped down into the pit he heard a strange rumbling noise under him, and so, putting his ear against the great stone, he listened, and overheard a discourse that made the hair on his head stand up like bulrushes, and every limb tremble.

" How shall we bother Tim ?" said one voice.

" Take him to the mountain, to be sure, and make him a toothful for the ould sarpint; 'tis long since he has had a good meal," said another voice.

Tim shook like a potato-blossom in a storm.

" No," said a third voice ; " plunge him in the bog, neck and heels."

Tim was a dead man, barring the breath.*

" Stop!" said a fourth ; but Tim heard no more, for Tim was dead entirely. In about an hour, however, the life came back into him, and he crept home to Norah.

"SVhen the next night arrived, the hopes of the crock of gold got the better of his fears, and •taking care to arm himself with a bottle of potheen, away he went to the field. Jumping into the pit, he took a little sup from the bottle to keep his heart up—he then took a big one— and then, with desperate wrench, he wrenched up the stone. All at once, up rushed a blast of wind, wild and fierce, and down fell Tim—down, down and down he went—until he thumped upon what seemed to be, for all the world, like a floor of sharp pins, which made him bellow out

* " r non mori, e non riraasi viro:

Pensa oraniai per te, a' hal fior d' ingegno Qual io divetini d' uno e d' altro privo."

Dantb, Inferno, canto 34.

in earnest. Then he liearcl a whisk and a hurra, and instantly voices beyond number cried out—

" Welcome, Tim Jarvis, dear .' Welcome, down here!"

Though Tim's teeth chattered like magpies with the fright, he continued to make answer—" I'm he-he-hSr-ti-ly ob-ob-liged to-to you all, gen-gentlemen, fo-for your civility to-to a poor stranger like myself." But though he had heard all the voices about him, he could see nothing, the place was so dark and so lonesome in itself for want of the light. Then something pulled Tim by the hair of his head, and dragged him, he did not know how far, but he knew he was going faster than the wind, for he heard it behind him, trying to keep up with him, and it could not. On, on, on, he went, till all at once, and suddenly, he was stopped, and somebody came up to him, and said, " Well, Tim Jarvis, and how do you like your ride ?"

" Mighty well! I thank your honour," said Tim ; " and't was a good beast I rode, surely !"

There was a great laugh at Tim's answer; and then there was a whispering, and a great cugger mugger, and coshering; and at last a pretty little bit of a voice said, " Shut your eyes, and you '11 see, Tim."

" By my word, then," said Tim, " that is the queer way of seeing; but I'm not the man to gainsay you, so I'll do as you bid me, any how," Presently he felt a small warm hand rubbed over his eyes with an ointment, and in the next

minute he saw himself in the middle of thousands of little men and women, not half so high as his brogue, that were pelting one another with golden guineas and lily-white thirteens*, as if they were 80 much dirt. The finest dressed and the biggest of them all went up to Tim, and says he, " Tim Jarvis, because you are a decent, honest, quiet, civil, well-spoken man," says he, " and know how to behave yourself in strange company, we've altered our minds about you, and will find a neighbour of yours that will do just as well to give to the old serpent."

"Oh, then, long life to you, sir!" said Tim, " and there's no doubt of that."

" But what will you say, Tim," inquired the little fellow, " if we fill your pockets with these yellow boys ? What will you say, Tim, and what will you do with them ?"

*' Your honour s honour, and your honour's glory," answered Tim, " I'll not be able to say my prayers for one month with thanking you— and indeed I've enough to do with them. I'd make a grand lady, you see, at once of Norah— she has been a good wife to me. We'll have a nice bit of pork for dinner ; and, maybe, I'd have a glass, or maybe two glasses; or sometimes, if 't was with a friend, or acquaintance, or gossip, 5'ou know, three glasses every day ; and I'd build a new cabin ; and I'd have a fresh egg every morning, myself, for my breakfast; and I'd snap my fingers at the 'squire, and beat his hounds, if they'd come coxirsing through my fields; and I'd

* An English shilling'wu thirteen pence, Irish currency.

have a new plough ; and Norah, your honour, would have a new cloak, and the boys would have shoes and stockings as well as Biddy Leary's brats — that's my sister that was — and Nelly would marry Bill Long of Affadown ; and, your honour, I'd have some corduroy for myself to make breeches, and a cow, and a beautiful coat with shining buttons, and a horse to ride, or maybe two, I'd have everything," said Tim, " in life, good or bad, that is to be got for love or money—hurra-whoop !—and that's what I'd do."

" Take care, Tim," said the little fellow, " your money would not go faster than it came, with your hurra-whoop."

But Tim heeded not this speech : heaps of gold were around him, and he filled and filled away as hard as he could, his coat and his waistcoat and his breeches pockets; and he thought himself very clever, moreover, because he stuffed some of the guineas into his brogues. When the little people perceived this, they cried out — " Go home, Tim Jarvis, go home, and think yourself a lucky man."

" I hope, gentlemen," said he, " we won't part for good and all; but maybe ye'U ask me to see you again, and to give you a fair and square account of what I've done with your money."

To this there was no answer, only another shout—" Go home, Tim Jarvis—go home—fair play is a jewel; but shut your eyes, or ye'U never see the light of day again,"

Tim shut his eyes, knowing now that was the yray to see clearly ; and away he was whisked as

before—away, away he went till he again stopped all of a sudden.

He nibbed his eyes with his two thumbs— and where was he ? Where, but in the very pit in the field that was Jer DriscoU's, and his wife Norah above with a big stick ready to beat " her dreaming blackguard." Tim roared out to tlie woman to leave the life in him, and put his hands in his pockets to show her the gold; but he pulled out nothing only a handful of small stones mixed with yellow furze blossoms. The bush was under him, and the great flag-stone that he had wTenched up, as he thought, was lying, as if it was never stirred, by his side: the whiskey bottle was drained to the last drop ; and the pit was just as his spade had made it.

Tim Jarvis, vexed, disappointed, and almost heart-broken, followed his wife home: and, strange to say, from that night he left off drinking, and dreaming, and delving in bog-holes, and rooting in old caves. He took again to his hard working habits, and was soon able to buy back his little cabin and former potato-garden, and to get all the enjoyment he anticipated from the fairy gold.

Give Tim one, or at most two, glasses of whiskey punch (and neither friend, acquaintance, nor gossip can make him take more), and he will relate the story to you much better than you have it here. Indeed, it is worth going to Balledehob to hear him tell it. He always pledges himself to the truth of every word with his fore-fingers crossed; and when he comes to speak of the loss of his guineas, he never fails to console himself

by adding—" If they stayed with me I wouldn't have hick with them, sir; and father O'Shea told nie 'twas as well for me they were changed, for if they hadn't, they'd have burned holes in my pocket, and got out that way."

I shall never forget his solemn countenance, and the deep tones of his warning voice, when he concluded his tale, by telling me, that the next day after his ride with the fairies, Mick Dowling was missing, and he believed him to be given to the sarpint in his place, as he had never been heard of since. " The blessing of the saints be between all good men and harm," was the concluding sentence of Tim Jarvis's narrative, as he flung the remaining drops from his glass upon the green sward.

RENT-DAY.

XXXV.

" Oil ullagone, uUagone! this is a wide world, but what will we do in it, or where will we. go?" muttered Bill Doody, as he sat on a rock by the Lake of Killamey. " What will we do ? tomorrow's rent-day, and Tim the Driver swears if we don't pay up our rent, he'll cant every ha'perth we have : and then, sure enough, there's Judy and myself, and the poor little graich*^ will be turned out to starve on the high road, for the never a halfpenny of rent have I!—Oh hone, that ever I should live to see this day!"

Thus did Bill Doody bemoan his hard fate, pouring his son'ows to the reckless waves of the most beautiful of lakes, which seemed to mock his misery as they rejoiced beneath the cloudless sky of a May moraing. That lake, glittering in sunshine, sprinkled with fairy isles of rock and verdure, and bounded by giant hills of ever-varying hues, might, with its magic beauty, charm all sadness but despair; for alas,

" How ill the scene that offers rest, And heart that cannot rest, agree !"

Yet Bill Doody was not so desolate as he supposed ; there was one listening to him he little

• Children.

thought of, and help was at hand from a quarter he could not have expected.

" What's the matter with you, my poor man ? " said a tall portly-looking gentleman, at the same time stepping out of a furze-brake. Now Bill was seated on a rock that commanded the view of a large field. Nothing in the field could be concealed from him, except this furze-brake, which grew in a hollow near the margin of the lake. He was, therefore, not a little surprised at the gentleman's sudden appearance, and began to question whether the personage before him belonged to this world or not. He, however, soon mustered courage sufficient to tell him how his crops had failed, how some bad member had channed away his butter, and how Tim the Driver threatened to turn him out of the farm if he didn't pay up every penny of the rent by twelve o'clock next day.

" A sad story indeed," said the stranger; " but surely, if you represented the case to your landlord's agent, he won't have the heart to turn you out."

" Heart, your honour ! where would an agent get a heart!" exclaimed Bill. " I see your honour does not know him : besides, he has an eye on the farm this long time for a fosterer of his own; so I expect no mercy at all at all, only to be turned out."

" Take this, my poor fellow, take this," said the stranger, pouring a purse full of gold into Bill's old hat, which in his grief he had flung on the ground. " Pay the fellow your rent, but I'll take care it shall do him no good. I remember

the time when things went otherwise in this country, when I would have hung up such a fellow in the twinkling of an eye !"

These words were lost upon Bill, who was insensible to every thing but the sight of the gold, and before he could unfix his gaze, and lift up his head to pour out his hundred thousand blessings, the stranger was gone. The bewildered peasant looked around in search of his benefactor, and at last he thought he saw him riding on a white horse a long way off on the lake.

" O'Donoghue, O'Donoghue !" shouted Bill; " the good, the blessed O'Donoghue !" and he ran capering like a madman to show Judy the gold, and to rejoice her heart with the prospect of wealth and happiness.

The next day Bill proceeded to the agent's; not sneakingly, with his hat in his hand, his eyes fixed on the ground, and his knees bending under him ; but bold and upright, like a man conscious of his independence.

" Why don't you take off your hat, fellow; don't you know you are speaking to a magistrate ?" said the agent.

" I know I'm not speaking to the king, sir," said Bill; " and I never takes off my hat but to them I can respect and love. The Eye that sees aU knows I've no right either to respect or love an agent!"

" You scoundrel 1" retorted the man in office, biting his lips with rage at such an unusual and unexpected opposition, " I'll teach you how to be insolent again — I have the power, remember."

RENT-DAY. SOI

"To the cost of the country, I know you have," said Bill, who still remained with his head as firmly covered as if he was the lord Kingsale himself,

" But come," said the magistrate ; " have you got the money for me ? — this is rent-day. If there's one penny of it wanting, or the running gale that's due, prepare to turn out before night, for you shall not remain another hour in possession."

" There is your rent," said Bill, with an unmoved expression of tone and countenance; "you'd better count it, and give me a receipt in full for the running gale and all."

The agent gave a look of amazement at the gold ; for it was gold—real guineas! and not bits of dirty ragged small notes, that are only fit to light one's pipe with. However willing the agent may have been to ruin, as he thought, the unfortunate tenant, he took up the gold, and handed the receipt to Bill, who strutted off with it as proud as a cat of her whiskers.

The agent going to his desk shortly after, was confounded at beholding a heap of gingerbread cakes instead of the money he had deposited there. He raved and swore, but all to no purpose ; the gold had become gingerbread cakes, just marked like the guineas, with the king's head, and Bill had the receipt in his pocket; so he saw there was no use in saying anything about the affair, as he would only get laughed at for his pains.

From that hour Bill Doody grew rich ; all his undertakings prospered; and he often blesses

RENT-DAY.

the day that he met with O'Donoghue, the great prince that lives down under the lake of Killamey.

Like the butterfly, the spirit of Donoghue closely hovers over the perfume of the hills and flowers it loves ; while, as the reflection of a star in the waters of a pure lake, to those who look not above, that glorious spirit is believed to dwell beneath.

LINN-NA-PAYSHTHA.

Travellers go to Leinster to see Dublin and the Dargle; to Ulster, to see the Giant's Causeway, and, perhaps, to do penance at Lough Dearg; to Munster, to see Killarney, the beautiful city of Cork, and half a dozen other fine things ; but who ever thinks of the fourth province?—who ever thinks of going—

—" westward, where Dick Martin rultd The houseleiis wilds of Cunnemara ? "

The Ulster-man's ancient denunciation " to Hell or to Connaught," has possibly led to the supposition that this is a sort of infernal place above ground—a kind of terrestrial Pandenioniunx —in short, that Connaught is little bettor than hell, or hell little worse than Connaught; but let any one only go there for a month, and, as the natives say, " I'll warrant he'll soon see the differ, and learn to understand that it is mighty like the rest o'green Erin, only something poorer ;" and yet it might be thought that in this particular '• worse would be needless;" but so it is.

"My gracious me," said the landlady of the Inn at Sligo, " I wonder a gentleman of your teeste and curosity would think of leaving Ireland without making a toirer (tour) of Connaught, if it was nothing more than spending a day at

Ilazlewood, and up the lake, and on to the ould abbey at Friarstown, and tlie castle at Droma-haii\"

Polly M'Bride, my kind hostess, might not in this remonstrance have been altogether disinterested ; but her advice prevailed, and the dawn of the following morning found me in a boat on the unruffled surface of Lough Gill. Arrived at the head of that splendid sheet of water, covered with rich and wooded islands with their ruined buildings, and bounded by towering mountains, noble plantations, grassy slopes, and precipitous rocks, which give beauty, and, in some places, sublimity to its shores, I proceeded at once up the wide river which forms its principal tributarj'. The " old abbey" is chiefly remarkable for having been built at a period nearer to the Reformation than any other ecclesiastical edifice of the same class. Full within view of it, and at the distance of half a mile, stands the shattered remnant of Breffhi's princely hall. I strode forward with the enthusiasm of an antiquary, and the high-beating heart of a patriotic Irishman. I felt myself on classic ground, immortalised by the lays of Swift and of Moore. I pushed my way into the hallowed precincts of the grand and venerable edifice. I entered its chambers, and, oh my countrj'men, I found them converted into the domicile of pigs, cows, and poultrj-! But the exterior of " O'Kourke's old haU," grey, frowning, and ivy-covered, is well enough; it stands on a beetling precipice, round which a noble river wheels its course. The opposite bank is a very steep ascent, thickly wooded, and rising

to a height of at least seventy feet; and, for a qiiarter of a mile, this beautiful copse follows the course of the river.

The first individual I encountered was an old cowherd ; nor was I unfortunate in my cicerone, for he assured me there were plenty of old stories about strange things that used to be in the place ; " but," continued he, " for my own share, I never met anything worse nor myself. If it bees ould stories that your honour's after, the story about Linn-na-Payshtha and Poul-maw-GuUyawn is the only thing about this place that's worth one jack-straw. Docs your honour see that great big black hole in the river yonder below ?" He pointed my attention to a part of the river about fifty yards from the old hall, where a long island occupied the centre of the wide current, the water at one side running shallow, and at the other assuming every appearance of unfathomable depth. The spacious pool, dark and still, wore a deathlike quietude of surface. It looked as if the speckled trout would shun its rriurky precincts—as if even the daring pike would shrink from so gloomy a dwelling-place. " That's Linn-na-Payshtha, sir," resumed my guide, " and Poul-maw-GuUyawn is just the very moral of it, only that it's round, and not in a river, but standing out in the middle of a green field, about a short quarter of a mile from this. Well, 'tis as good as fourscore years—I often hard my father, God be merciful to him! tell the story— since Manus O'Rourke, a great buckeen, a cock-fighting, drinking blackguard that was long ago, went to sleep one night and had a dream about Linn-na-Payshtha. This Manus, the dirty spalpeen, there was no ho with him; he thought to ride rough-shod over his betters tlu-ough the whole country, though he was not one of the real stock of the O'Rourkes. Well, this fellow had a dream that if he dived in Linn-na-Payshtha at twelve o'clock of a Hollow-eve night, he'd find more gold than would make a man of him and his wife, whUe grass grew or water ran. The next night he had the same dream, and sure enough if he had it the second night, it came to him the third in the same form. Manus, well becomes him, never told mankind or womankind, but sworc to himself, by all the books that were ever shut or open, that, any how, he would go to the bottom of the big hole. What did he care for the Payshtha-more that was lying there to keep guard on the gold and silver of the old ancient family that was buried there in the wars, packed up in the brewing-pan ? Sure he was as good an O'Rourke as the best of them, taking care to forget that his grandmother's father was a cow-boy to the earl O'Donnel. At long last Hollow-eve comes, and sly and silent master Manus creeps to bed early, and just at midnight steals down to the river side. When he came to the bank his mind misgave him, and he wheeled up to Frank M'Clure's —the old Frank that was then at that time—and got a bottle of whiskey, and took it with him, and 'tis unknown how much of it he drank. He walked across to the island, and down he went gallantly to the bottom like a stone. Sure enough the Payshtha was there afore him, lying like a great big conger eel, seven yards

long, and as thick as a bull in the body, with a mane upon his neck like a horse. The Payshtha-more reared himself up ; and, looking at the poor man as if he'd eat him, says he, in good English,

" ' Arrah, then, Manus,' says he, ' what brought you here ? It would have been better for you to have blown your brains out at once with a pistol, and have made a quiet end of yourself, than to have come down here for me to deal with you.'

" ' Oh, plase your honour,' says Manus, ' I beg my life:' and there he stood shaking like a dog in a wet sack.

" ' Well, as you have some blood of the O'Rourkes in you, I forgive you this once; but, by this and by that, if ever I see you, or any one belonging to you, coming about this place again, I'll hang a quarter of you on every tree in the wood.*

" ' Go home,' says the Payshtha—' go home, Manus,' says he; ' and if you can't make better use of your time, get drunk; but don't come here, bothering me. Yet, stop! since you are here, and have ventured to come, I'll show you something that you'll remember till you go to your grave, and ever after, while you live.'

" With that, my dear, he opens an iron door in the bed of the river, and never the drop of water ran into it; and there Manus sees a long dry cave, or imder-ground cellar like, and the Payshtha drags him in, and shuts the door. It wasn't long before the baste besan to get smaller, and smaller, and smaller; and at last he grew as little as a taughn of twelve years old ; and there x2

he was a brownish little man, about four feet high."

" ' Plase your honour,' says Manus^ ' if I might make so bold, maybe you are one of the good people V

" ' Maybe I am, and maybe I am not; but, anyhow, all you have to understand is this, that I'm bound to look after the Thiemas * of BreflFni, and take care of them through every generation ; and that my present business is to watch this cave, and what's in it, till the old stock is reigning over this country once more,'

" ' Maybe you are a sort of a banshee ?'

" ' I am not, you fool,' said the little man. ' The banshee is a woman. j\Iy business is to live in the form you first saw me in, guarding this spot. And now hold your tongue, and look about you.'

" Manus nibbed his eyes, and looked right and left, before and behind; and there was the vessels of gold and the vessels of silver, the dishes, and the plates, and the cups, and the punch-bowls, and the tankards: there was the golden mether, too, that every Thiema at his wedding used to drink out of to the kerne in real usquebaugh. There was all the money that ever was saved in the family since they got a grant of this manor, in the days of the Firbolgs, down to the time of their outer ruination. He then brought Manus on with him to where there was arms for three hundred men; and the sword set with diamonds, and the golden helmet of the O'Rourke ; and he showed him the staff made out of an elephant's

* Tigheama —a lord. Vide O'Bkihn.

tooth, and set with nibies and gold, that the Thiema used to hold while he sat in his great hall, giving justice and the laws of the Brehons to all his clan. The first room in the cave, ye see, had the money and the plate, the second room had the arms, and the third had the books, papers, parchments, title-deeds, wills, and everything else of the sort belonging to the family.

" ' And now, Manus,' says the little man, ' ye seen the whole o' this, and go your ways; but never come to this place any more, or allow any one else. I must keep watch and ward till the Sassanach is dmv out of Ireland, and the Thiernas o' Breffni in their glory again.' The little man then stopped for a while and looked up in Manus's face, and says to him in a great passion, ' Arrah! bad luck to ye, Manus, why don't ye go about your business ?'

'^ ' How can I ?—sure you must show me the way out,' says Manus, making answer. The little man then pointed forward with his finger.

" ' Can't we go out the way we came ?' says Manus.

" ' No, you must go out at the other end— that's the rule o' this place. Ye came in at Linn-na-Payshtha, and you must go out at Poul-maw-GuUyaviTi: ye came down like a stone to the bottom of one hole, and ye must spring up like a cork to the top of the other.' With that the little man gave him one hoise^ and all that Manus remembers was the roar of the water in his ears; and sure enough he was found the next morning, high and dry, fast asleep, with the empty bottle beside him, but far enough from the place

he thought he landed, for it was just below yonder on the island that his wife found him. My father, God be merciful to him! heard Manus swear to every word of the story."

As tliere are few things which exdte human desire throughout all nations more than wealth, the legends concerning the concealment, discovery, and circulation of money, are, as may be expected, widely extended; yet in all the circumstances, which admit of so much fanciful embellishment, there everywhere exists a striking similarity.

Like the golden apples of the Hesperides, treasure is guarded by a dragon or serpent. Vide Creuzer, Keligions de I'Antiquit^, traduction de Guigniaut, i. 248. Paris, 1825. Stories of its discovery in consequence of dreams or spiritual agency are so numerous, that, if collected, they would fill many volumes, yet they vary little in detail beyond the actors and locality. Vide Grimm's Deutsche Sagen, i. 200. Thielc's Danske Folkesagn, i. 112, ii. 24. Kirke's Secret Commonwealth, p. 12, &c.

The circulation of money bestowed by the fairies or supernatural personages, like that of counterfeit coin, is seldom extensive. See story, in the Arabian Nights, of the old rogue whose fine-lookiug money turned to leaves. When Waldemar, Holgar, and Groen Jette, in Danish tradition, bestow money upon the boors whom they meet, their gift sometimes turns to fire, sometimes to pebbles, and sometimes is so hot, that the receiver drops it from his hand, when the gold, or what appeared to be so, sinks into the ground.

In poor Ireland, the wretched peasant contents himself by soliloquising—" Money is the devil, they say ; and God is good that He keeps it from us."

FAIRY LEGENDS.
ROCKS AND STONES.

---ti<t.^.^^*^'
Forms in silence frown'd,
Shapeless and nameless ; and to mine eyo
Sometimes tliey rolled off cloudily,
Wedding themselves with gloom—or grew
Gigantic to my troubled view,
And seem'd to gather roimd me."
Banim'8 Cell's Paradite.

ROCKS AND STONES.
THE LEGEND OF CAIRN THIERNA.

From the town of Fem^oy, famous for the excellence of its bottled ale, you may plainly see the mountain of Cairn Thierna. It is crowned with a great heap of stones, which, as the country people remark, never came there without " a crooked thought and a cross job." Strange it is, that any work of the good old times should be considered one of labour; for round towers then sprung up like mushrooms in one night, and people played marbles with pieces of rock, that can now no more be moved than the hills themselves.

This great pile on the top of Cairn Thierna was caused by the words of an old woman, whose bed still remains— Labacally^ the hag's bed— not far from the village of Glanworth. She

Avas certainly far wiser than any woman, either old or young, of my immediate acquaintance.

Jove defend me, however, from making an envious comparison between ladies; but facts are stubborn things, and the legend will prove my assertion.

O'Keefe was Lord of Fermoy before the Roches came into that part of the country; and he had an only son—never was there seen a finer child ; his young face filled with innocent joy was enough to make any heart glad, yet his father looked on his smiles with sorrow, for an old hag had foretold that this boy should be drowned before he grew up to manliood.

Now, although the prophecies of Pastorini were a failure, it is no reason why prophecies should altogether be despised. The art in modern times may be lost, as well as that of making beer out of the mountain heath, which the Danes did to great perfection. But I take it, the malt of Tom Walker is no bad substitute for the one ; and if evil prophecies were to come to pass, like the old woman's, in my opinion we are far more comfortable without such knowledge.

" Infanl heir of proud Fermoy, Fear not fields of slaughter ; Storm and fire frar not, my boy. But shuu the fatal water."

These were the warning words which caused the chief of Fermoy so much unhappiness. His infant son was carefully prevented all approach to the river, and anxious watch was kept over every plajiFul movement. The child grew up in strength

and in beauty, and every day became more dear to his father, who, hoping to avert the doom, which, however, was inevitable, prepared to build a castle far removed from the dreaded element.

The top of Cairn Thiema was the place chosen ; and the lord's vassals were assembled, and employed in collecting materials for the purpose. Hither came the fated boy; with delight he viewed the laborious work of raising mighty stones from the base to the summit of the mountain, imtil the vast heap which now forms its rugged crest was accumulated. The workmen were about to commence the building, and the boy, who was considered in safety when on the moun -tain, was allowed to rove about at will. In his case how true are the words of the great dramatist :

" Put but a little water In a spoon,

And it shall be, as all the ocean. Enough to stifle such a being up."

A vessel which contained a small supply of water, brought there for the use of the workmen, attracted the attention of the child. lie saw, with wonder, the glitter of the sunbeams within it; he approached more near to gaze, when a fonn resembling his own arose before him. He gave a cry of joy and astonishment, and drew back ; the image drew back also, and vanished. Again he approached; again the form appeared, expressing in every feature delight corresponding with his own. Eager to welcome the young stranger, he bent over the vessel to press his lips ; and

THE LEGEND OF CAIRN THIERNA.

losing his balance, the fatal prophecy was accomplished.

The father in despair abandoned the commenced building; and the materials remain a proof of the folly of attempting to avert the course of fate.

THE ROCK OF THE CANDLE.

XXXVIII.

A PEW miles west of Limerick stands the once formidable castle of Carrio-oounnel. Its riven

tower and broken archway remain in mournful evidence of the sieges sustained by that city. Time, however, the great soother of all things, has destroyed the painful eflPect which the view of recent violence produces on the mind. The ivy creeps around the riven tower, concealing its injuries, and upholding it by a tough swathing of stalks. The archway is again united by the long-anned briar which grows across the rent, and the shattered buttresses are decorated witli wild-flowers, which gaily spring from their crevices and broken places.

Boldly situated on a rock, the ruined walls of Carrigogunnel now forai only a romantic feature in the peaceful landscape. Beneath them, on one side, lies the flat marshy ground called Cor-cass land, which borders the noble river Shannon ; on the other side is seen the neat parish church of Kilkeedy, with its glebe-house and surrounding improvements; and at a short distance appear the irregular mud cabins of the little village of Ballybrown, with the venerable trees of Tervoo.

On the rock of Carrigogunnel, before the castle

318 THE ROCK OF THE CANDLE,

was built, or Brien Boro bom to build it, dwelt a hag named Grana, who made desolate the surrounding country. She was gigantic in size, and frightful in appearance. Her eye\'7d)rows grew into each other with a grim curve, and beneath their matted bristles, deeply sunk in her head, two small grey eyes darted forth baneful looks of evil. From her deeply-wrinkled forehead issued forth a hooked beak, dividing two shrivelled cheeks. Her skinny lips curled with a cruel and malignant expression, and her prominent chin was studded with bunches of grisly hair.

Death was her sport. Like the angler with his rod, the hag Grana would toil, and watch, nor think it labour, so that the death of a victim rewarded her vigils. Every evening did she light an enchanted candle upon the rock, and whoever looked upon it died before the next morning's sun arose. Numberless were the victims over whom Grana rejoiced; one after the other had seen the light, and their death was the consequence. Hence came the country round to be desolate, and Carrigogunnel, the Rock of the Candle, by its dreaded name.

These were fearful times to live in. But the Finnii of Erin were the avengers of the oppressed. Their fame had gone forth to distant shores, and their deeds were sung by a hundred bards. To tlicm the name of danger was as an invitation to a rich banquet. The web of enchantment stopped their course as little as the swords of an enemy. Many a mother of a son— many a wife of a husband—many a sister of a brother, had the valour of the Finnian heroes bereft. Dismembered limbs quivered, and heads bounded on the ground before their progress in battle. They rushed forward with the strengih of the furious wind, tearing vip the trees of the forest by their roots. Loud was their war-cry as the thunder, raging was their impetuosity above that of common men, and tierce was their anger as the stormy waves of the ocean!

It was the mighty Finn liimself who lifted up his voice, and commanded the fatal candle of the hag Grana to be extinguished. " Thine, Regan, be the task," he said, and to him he gave a cap thrice charmed by the magician Luno of Lochlin.

With the star of the same evening the candle of death burned on the rock, and Regan stood beneath it. Had he beheld the slightest glimmer of its blaze, he, too, would have perished, and the liag Grana, with the morning's dawn, rejoiced over his corse. When Regan looked towards the light, the charmed cap fell over his eyes and prevented his seeing. The rock was steep, but he climbed up its craggy side with such caution and dexterity, that, before the hag was aware, the warrior, with averted head, had seized the candle, and flung it with prodigious force into the river Shannon; the hissing waters of which quenched its light for ever !

Then flew the charmed cap from the eyes of Regan, and he beheld the enraged hag, with outstretched arms, prepared to seize and whirl him after her candle. Regan instantly bounded westward from the rock just two miles, with a wild and wondrous spring. Grana looked for a moment at the leap, and then tearing up a huge

fragment of the rock, flung it after Regan with such tremendous force, that her crooked hands trembled and her broad chest heaved with heavy puffs, like a smith's labouring bellows, from the exertion.

The ponderous stone fell harmless to the ground, for the leap of Regan far exceeded the strength of the furious hag. In triumph he returned to Fin;

" The hero valiant, renowned, and learned ; White-looth'd, graceful, magnanimous, and active." •

The hag Grana was never heard of more; but the stone remains, and, deeply imprinted in it, is still to be seen the mark of the hag's fingers. That stone is far taller than the tallest man, and the power of forty men would fail to move it from the spot where it fell.

The grass may wither around it, the spade and plough destroy dull heaps of earth, the walls of castles fall and perish, but the fame of the Finnii of Erin endures with the rocks themselves, and Clough -a-Regaun is a monument fitting to preserve the memory of the deed !

'210 n)ili» AfimAc ATijtDneAc eolAc; (Deu&5eAl, ftCAlbcAc, n)e.A^tx)r)A.c ctieoftAc."

CLOUGH NA CUDDY.

XXXIX.

Above all tlie islands in the lakes of Killamey give rae Innisfallen —" sweet Innisfallen," as the melodious Moore calls it. It is, in truth, a fairy isle, although I have no fairy story to tell you about it; and if I had, these are such unbelieving times, and people of late have grown so sceptical, that they oiJy smile at my stories, and doubt them.

However, none will doubt that a monastery once stood upon Innisfallen island, for its ruins may still be seen; neither, that within its walls dwelt certain pious and learned persons called Monks. A very pleasant set of fellows they were, I make not the smallest doubt; and I am sure of this, that they had a very pleasant «pot to enjoy themselves in after dinner—the proj)er time, believe me, and I am no bad judge of such matters, for the enjoyment of a fine prospect.

Out of all the monks you could not pick a better fellow nor a merrier soul than Father Cuddy; he sung a good song, he told a good story, and had a jolly, comfortable-looking paimch of his 'Own, that was a credit to any refectory-table. He was distinguished above all the rest by the name of " the fat father." Now

there are many that will take huflF at a name; but father Cuddy liad no nonsense of that kind about him; he laughed at it—and well able he was to laugh, for his mouth nearly reached from one ear to the other: his might, in truth, be called an open countenance. As his paunch was no disgrace to his food, neither was his nose to his drink. 'Tis a doubt to me if there were not more carbuncles upon it than ever were seen at the bottom of the lake, which is said to be full of them. His eyes had a right merry twinkle in them, like moonshine dancing on the water; and his cheeks had the roundness and crimson glow of ripe arbutus berries.

I,. " He ate, and dran'k, and prayed, and slept—What then ? He ate, and drank, and prayed, and slept again ! "

Such was the tenor of his simple life: but when he prayed, a certain drowsiness would come upon him, which, it must be confessed, never occurred when a well-filled "black-jack" stood before him. Hence his prayers were short and his draughts were long. The world loved him, and he saw no good reason why he should not in return love its venison and its usquebaugh. But, as times went, he must have been a pious man, or else what befel him never would have happened.

Spiritual affairs — for it was respecting the importation of a tun of wine into the island monastery— demanded the presence of one of the brotherhood of Innisfallen at the abbey of Irelagh, now called Mucruss. The superintendence of this important matter was committed to father

Cuddy, who felt too deeply interested in the future welfare of any community of which he was a member, to neglect or delay such mission. "With the morning's light he was seen guiding his shallop across the crimson waters of the lake towards the peninsula of Mucruss; and having moored his little bark in safety beneath the shelter of a wave-worn rock, he advanced with becoming dignity towards the abbey.

The stillness of the bright and balmy hour was broken by the heavy footsteps of the zealous father. At the sound the startled deer, shaking the dew from their sides, sprung up from their lair, and as they bounded off —" Hah!" exclaimed Cuddy, " what a noble haunch goes there!—how delicious it would look smoking upon a goodly platter!"

As he proceeded, the mountain-bee hummed his tune of gladness around the holy man, save when buried in the foxglove bell, or revelling upon a fragrant bunch of thyme; and even then the little voice munnured out happiness in low and broken tones of voluptuous delight. Father Cuddy derived no small comfort from the sound, for it presaged a good metheglin season, and me-theglin he regarded, if well manufactured, to be no bad liquor, particularly when there was no stint of usquebaugh in the brewing.

Arrived within the abbey garth, he was rfe-ceived with due respect by the brethren of Ire-lagh, and arrangements for the embarkation of the wine were completed to his efitire satisfaction. " Welcome, father.Cuddy," said the prior: " grace be on you."

T 2

" Grace before meat, then," said Cuddy, " for a lonpr walk always makes me hungry, and I am certain I have not walked less than half a mile this morning, to say nothing of crossing the water."

A pasty of choice flavour felt the truth of this assertion, as regarded father Cuddy's appetite. After such consoling repast, it would have been a reflection on monastic hospitality to depart without partaking of the grace-cup; moreover, father Cuddy had a particular respect for the antiquity of that custom. He liked the taste of the grace-cup well: — he tried another, — it was no k'ss excellent; and when he had swallowed the third he found his heart expand, and put forth its fibres, willing to embrace all mankind. Surely, then, there is Christian love and charity in wine! ^

I said he sung a good song. Now though psalms are good songs, and in accordance ^ith his vocation, I did not mean to imply that he was a mere psalm-singer. It was well known to the brethren, that wherever father Cuddy was, mirth and melody were with him;—mirth in his eye and melody on his tongue; and these, from experience, are equally well known to be thirsty com -modities ; but he took good care never to let them run dry. To please the brotherhood, whose excellent -vWne pleased him, he sung, and as ^^in tfino Veritas" his song will well become this veritable history.

CANTAT MONACHIJS.*

Hoc erat in votis, Et bene sufficerit totis Si dum porto sacculum Boniun esset ubique jentnculum ! Et si parvus In arvis Nullam Invenero pullam, Ovum gentiliter prsebebit recons

Puella decens. 3Ianu nee dabislnvita Flos vallium harum, Decus puellanim, Candida ^larguerita '.

• THE FRIAR'S SONG.

My vows I can never fulfil, UntU 1 have breakfasted, one way or other ; And I freely protest. That I never can rest, 'Till I borrow or beg An egg. Unless I can come at the ould hen, its mother. But Maggy, my dear. While you're here, I don't fear To want eggs that have just been laid newly; For och : you're a pearl Of a girl. And you're called so in Latin most truly.

Me hora juconda cans

Dilectat bene, Et rerura sine dubio grandium Maxima est pranditun:

Sed mihi crede,

In hie sede^ Mnlto magis gaudeo. Cum gallicantum audio.

In sinu tuo

Videns ova duo. Oh semper me tractes ita !

Panibus de hordeo factis,

Et copia lactis, Candida Margarita !

II.

There is most to my mind something that is still upper

Than supper, The' it most be admitted I feel no way thinner

After dinner ; But soon as I hear the cock crow

In the morning, That eggs yon are bringing full surely I know,

By that warning, AMiile yonr buttermilk helps me to float

Down my throat Those sweet cakes made of oat.

I don't envy an earl.

Sweet girl, Ocb, 'tis you are a beautiful pearl.

Such was his song. Father Cuddy smacked his lips at the recollection of Margery's delicious fried eggs, which always imparted a peculiar relish to his liquor. The very idea provoked Cuddy to

raise the cup to his mouth, and with one hearty pull thereat he finished its contents.

This is, and ever was a censorious world, often construing what is only a fiair allowance into an excess : but I scorn to reckon up any man's drink, like an unrelenting host; therefore, I cannot tell how many brimming draughts of wine, bedecked with the venerable Bead, father Cuddy emptied into his " soul-case," so he figuratively termed the body.

His respect for the goodly company of the monks of Irelagh detained him until their adjournment to vespers, when he set forward on his return to Innisfallen. Whether his mind was occupied in philosophic contemplation or wrapped in pious musings, I cannot declare, but the honest father wandered on in a different direction from that in which his shallop lay. Far be it from me to insinuate that the good liquor which he had so commended caused him to foi-get his road, or that his track was irregular and unsteady. Oh no !— he caiTied his drink bravely, as became a decent man and a good Christian; yet, somehow, he thought he could distinguish two moons. " Bless my eyes," said Father Cuddy, " every thing is changing now-a-days!—the very stars are not in the same places they used to be ; I think Catn-ceachta (the Plough) is driving on at a rate I never saw it before to-night; but I suppose the driver is drunk, for there are blackguards everywhere."

Cuddy had scarcely uttered these words, when he saw, or fancied he saw, the form of a young woman, who holding up a bottle, beckoned him towards her. The night was extremely beautiful,

and the white dress of the girl floated gracefully in the moonlight as with gay step she tripped on before the worthy father, archly looking back upon him over her shoulder.

" Ah, Margery, merry Margery!" cried Cuddy, " you tempting little rogue!

' Flos vallium harum, Decus puellarum, Candida Margarita.'

I see you, I see you and the bottle ! let me but catch you, Candida Margarita!" and on he followed, panting and smiling, after this alluring apparition.

At length his feet grew weary, and his breath failed, which obliged him to give up the chase ; yet such was his piety, that unwilling to rest in any attitude but that of prayer, down dropped father Cuddy on his knees. Sleep, as usual, stole upon his devotions; and the morning was far advanced, when he awoke from dreams, in which tables groaned beneath their load of viands, and wine poured itself free and sparkUng as the mountain spring.

Rubbing his eyes, he looked about him, and the more he looked the more he wondered at the alteration which appeared in tlie face of the country. " Bless my soul and body !" said the good father, " I saw the stars changing last night, but here is a change !" Doubting his senses, he looked again. The hills bore the same majestic outline as on the preceding day, and tlie lake spread itself beneath his view in the same tranquil beauty, and studded ■vN^ith the same number of islands;

but every smaller feature in the landscape was strangely altered. What had been naked rocks, were now clothed with holly and arbutus. Whole woods had disappeared, and waste places had become cultivated fields; and, to complete the work of enchantment, the very season itself seemed changed. In the rosy dawn of a summer s morning he had left the monastery of Innisfallen, and he now felt in every sight and sound the dreariness of winter. The hard ground was covered with withered leaves; icicles depended from leafless branches; he heard the sweet low note of the robin, who familiarly approached him; and he felt his fingers numbed from the nipping frost. Father Cuddy found it rather difficult to account for such sudden transformations, and to convince himself it was not the illusion of a dream, he was about to arise, when lo ! he discovered that both his knees were buried at least six inches in the solid stone; for, notwithstanding all these changes, he had never altered his devout position.

Cuddy was now wide awake, and felt, when he got up, his joints sadly cramped, which it was only natural they should be, considering the hard texture of the stone, and the depth his knees had sunk into it. But the great difficulty was to explain how, in one night, summer had become winter, whole woods had been cut down, and well-grown trees had sprouted up. The miracle, nothing else could he conclude it to be, urged him to hasten his return to Innisfallen, Avhere he might learn some explanation of these marvellous events.

Seeing a boat moored within reach of the shore, he delayed not, in the midst of such wonders, to

seek his own bark, but, seizing the oars, pulled stoutly towards the island; and here new wonders awaited him.

Father Cuddy waddled, as fast as cramped limbs could carry his rotund corporation, to the gate of the monastery, where he loudly demanded admittance.

" Holloa! whence come you, master monk, and what's your business?" demanded a stranger who occupied the porter's place.

" Business !—my business!" repeated the confounded Cuddy,—" why, do you not know me ? Has the wine arrived safely?"

" Hence, fellow!" said the porter's representative, in a surly tone; " nor think to impose on me with your monkish tales."

" Fellow !" exclaimed the father: " mercy upon us, that I should be so spoken to at the gate of my own house !—Scoundrel!" cried Cuddy, raising his voice, " do you not see my garb— my holy garb ?"

" Ay, fellow," replied he of the keys—" the garb of laziness and filthy debauchery, which has been expelled from out these walls. Know you not, idle knave, of the suppression of this nest of superstition, and that the abbey lands and possessions were granted in August last to Master Robert CoUam, by oru* Lady Elizabeth, sovereign queen of England, and paragon of all beauty— whom God preserve!"

"Queen of England!" said Cuddy; "there never was a sovereign queen of England—this is but a piece witli the rest. I saw how it was going with the stars last night—the world's turned up-

side down. But surely this is Innisfallen island, and I am the father Cuddy who yesterday morning went over to the abbey of Irelagh, respecting the tun of wine. Do you not know me now ?"

*' Know you !—how should I know you ? " said the keeper of the abbey. " Yet, true it is, that I have heard my grandmother, whose mother remembered the man, often speak of the fat father Cuddy of Innisfallen, who made a profane and godless ballad in praise of fresh eggs, of which he and his vile crew knew more than they did of the word of God; and who, being drunk, it is said, tumbled into the lake one night, and was drowned; but that must have been a hundred, ay, more than a hundred years since."

" 'Twas I who composed that song in praise of Margery's fresh eggs, which is no profane and godless ballad—no other father Cuddy than myself ever belonged ta Innisfallen," earnestly exclaimed the holy man. " A hundred years!—what was your great-grandmother's name?"

" She was a Mahony of Dunlow—Margaret ni Mahony; and my grandmother—"

What! merry Margery of Dunlow your great-grandmother!" shouted Cuddy. " St. Brandon help me!—the wicked wench, with that tempting bottle !—why, 'twas only last night— a hundred years!—your great-grandmother, said you?— God bless us! there has been a strange torpor over me; I must have slept all this time !"

That father Cuddy had done so, I think is sufficiently proved by the changes which occurred during his nap. A reformation, and a serious one it was for him, had taken place. Pretty Margery's fresh eggs were no longer to be had in Innisfallen; and with a heart as heavy as his footsteps, the worthy man directed his course towards Dingle, where he embarked in a vessel on the point of sailing for Malaga. The rich wine of that place had of old impressed him with a high respect for its monastic establishments, in one of which he quietly wore out the remainder of his days.

The stone impressed with the mark of father Cuddy's knees may be seen to this day. Should any incredulous persons doubt my story, I request them to go to Killarney, where Clough na Cuddy —80 is the stone called—^remains in Lord Ken-mare's park, an indisputable evidence of the fact. Spillane, the bugle-man, will be able to point it out to them, as he did so to me; and here is my sketch by which they may identify it.

THE GIANTS STAIRS.

On the road between Passage and Cork there is an old mansion called Ronayne's Court, It may be easily known from the stack of chimneys and the gable ends, which are to be seen, look at it which way you will. Here it was that Maurice Ronayne and his wife Margaret Gould kept house, as may be learned to this day from the great old chimney-piece, on which is carved their arms. They were a miglity worthy couple, and had but one son, who was called Philip, after no less a person than the king of Spain.

Immediately on his smelling the cold air of this world the child sneezed; and it was naturally taken to be a good sign of having a clear head; but the subsequent rapidity of his learning was truly amazing ; for on the xery first day a primer was put into his hand, he tore out the A, B, C page, and destroyed it, as a thing quite beneath his notice. No wonder then that both father and mother were proud of their heir, who gave such indisputable proofs of genius, or, as they call it in that part of the world, '•'• genus."

One morning, however, Master Phil, who was then just seven years old, was missing, and no one ■could tell what had become of him : servants were sent in all directions to seek him, on horseback

and on foot, but they returned without any tidings of the boy, whose disappearance altogether was most unaccountable. A large reward was offered, but it produced them no intelligence, and years rolled away without Mr. and Mrs. Ronayne having obtained any satisfactory account of the fate of their lost child.

There lived, at this time, near Carigaline, one Robert Kelly, a blacksmith by trade. He was what is termed a handy man, and his abilities were held in much estimation by the lads and the lasses of the neighbourhood : for, independent of shoeing horses, which he did to great perfection, and making plough-irons, he interpreted dreams for the young women, sung Arthur O'Bradley at their weddings, and was so good-natured a fellow at a christening, that he was gossip to half the country round.

Now it happened that Robin had a dream himself, and young Philip Ronayne appeared to him in it at the dead hour of the night. Robin thought he saw the boy mounted upon a beautiful white horse, and that he told him how he was made a page to the giant Mahon Mac Mahon, who had carried him off, and who held his court in the hard heart of the rock. " The seven years—my time of ser^^ce,—are clean out, Robin," said he, " and if you release me this night, I will be the making of you for ever after."

" And how will I know," said Robin—cunning enough, even in his sleep—" but this is all a dream ?"

"Take that," said the boy, "for a token"— and at the word the white horse struck out with

one of his hind legs, and gave poor Robin such a kick in the forehead, that thinking he was a dead man, he roared as loud as he could after his brains, and woke up calling a thousand murders. He found himself in bed, but he had the mark of the blow, the regular print of a horse-shoe upon his forehead as red as blood ; and Robin Kelly, who never before found himself puzzled at the dream of any other person, did not know what to think of his o'wn.

Robin was well acquainted with the Giant's Stairs, as, indeed, who is not that knows the harbour ? They consist of great masses of rock, which, piled one above another, rise like a flight of steps, from very deep water, against the bold cliff of Carrigmahon. Nor are they badly suited for stairs to those who have legs of sufficient length to stride over a moderate sized house, or to enable them to clear the space of a mile in a hop, step, and jump. Both these feats the giant Mac Mahon was said to have performed in the days of Finnian glory; and the common tradition of the country placed his dwelling within the cliff up whose side the stairs led.

Such was the impression which the dream made on Robin, that he determined to put its truth to the test. It occurred to him, however, before setting out on this adventure, that a plough-iron may be no bad companion, as, from experience, he knew it was an excellent knock-down argument, having, on more occasions than one, settled a little disagreement very quietly: so, putting one on his shoulder, off he marched in the cool of the evening through Glaun a Thowk (the

Hawk's Glen) to Monkstown. Here an old gossip of his (Tom Clancey by name) lived, who, on hearing Robin's dream, promised him the use of his skiff, and moreover offered to assist in rowing it to the Giant's Stairs,

After a supper which was of the best, they embarked. It was a beautiful still night, and the little boat glided swiftly along. The regular dip of the oars, the distant song of the sailor, and sometimes the voice of a belated traveller at the ferry of Carrigaloe, alone broke the quietness of the land and sea and sky. The tide was in their favour, and in a few minutes Robin and his gossip rested on their oars under the dark shadow of the Giant's Stairs. Robin looked anxiously for the entrance to the Giant's Palace, which, it was said, may be found by any one seeking it at midnight; but no such entrance could he see. His impatience had hurried him there before that time, and after waiting a considerable space in a state of suspense not to be described, Robin, with pure vexation, could not help exclaiming to his companion, " 'Tis a pair of fools we are, Tom Clancey, for coming here at all on the strength of a dream."

" x\nd whose doing is it," said Tom, " but your own ?"

At the moment he spoke they perceived a faint glimmering light to proceed from tlie cliff", which

Gradually increased until a porch big enoiigh for a ing's palace unfolded itself almost on a level with the water. They pulled the skiff directly towards the opening, and Robin Kelly, seizing his plough-iron, boldly entered with a strong hand and a

stout heart. Wild and strange was that entrance; the wliole of which appeared formed of grim and grotesque faces, blending so strangely each with the other that it was impossible to define any : the chin of one formed the nose of another : what appeared to be a fixed and stem eye, if dwelt upon, changed to a gaping mouth ; and the lines of the lofty forehead grew into a majestic and flowing beard. The more Robin allowed himself to contemplate the forms around him, the more terrific they became; and the stony expression of this crowd of faces assumed a savage ferocity as his imagination converted feature after feature into a different shape and character. Losing the twilight in which these indefinite forms were visible, he advanced through a dark and devious passage, whilst a deep and rumbling noise sounded as if the rock was about to close upon him and swallow him up alive for ever. Now, indeed, poor Robin felt afraid.

" Robin, Robin," said he, " if you were a fool for coming here, what in the name of fortune are you now?" But, as before, he had scarcely spoken, when he saw a small light twinkling through the darkness of the distance, like a star in the midnight sky. To retreat was out of the question; for so many turnings and windings were in the passage, that he considered he had but little chance of making his way back. He therefore proceeded towards the bit of light, and came at last into a spacious chamber, from the roof of which hung the solitary lamp that had guided him. Emerging from such profound gloom, the single lamp afforded Robin abimdant light to

discover several gigantic figures seated round a massive stone table as if in serious deliberation, but no word disturbed the breathless silence vv'hich prevailed. At the head of this table sat Mahon Mac Mahon himself, whose majestic beard had taken root, and in the course of ages grown into the stone slab. He was the first who perceived Robin ; and instantly starting up, drew his long beard from out the huge lump of rock in such haste and with so sudden a jerk, that it was shattered into a thousand pieces.

" What seek you ?" he demanded in a voice of thunder.

" I come," answered Robin, with as much boldness as he could put on—for his heart was almost fainting within him—" I come," said he, " to claim Philip Ronayne, whose time of service is out this night."

" And who sent you here ?" said the giant.

" Twas of my own accord I came," said Robin.

" Then you must single him out from among my pages," said the giant; " and if you fix on the wrong one your life is the forfeit. Follow me." He led Robin into a hall of vast extent and filled with lights ; along either side of which were rows of beautiful children all apparently seven years old, and none beyond that age, cb-essed in green, and every one exactly dressed alike.

" Here," said Mahon, " you are free to take Philip Ronayne, if you will; but, remember, I give but one choice."

Robin was sadly perplexed; for there were hundreds upon hundreds of children ; and he had no very clear recollection of the boy he sought.

But he walked along the hall, by the side of Ma-hon, as if nothing was the matter, although his great iron dress clanked fearfully at every step, sounding louder than Robin's own sledge battering on his anvil.

They had nearly reached the end of the hall without speaking, when Robin, seeing that the only means he had was to make friends with the giant, determined to try what effect a few soft words might have upon him.

" 'Tis a fine wholesome appearance the poor children carry," remarked Robin, " although they have been here so long shut out from the fresh air and tlie blessed light of heaven. 'Tis tenderly your honour must have reared them ! "

" Ay," said the giant, " that is true for you ; 80 give me your hand; for you are, I believe, a very honest fellow for a blacksmith."

Robin at the first look did not much like the huge size of the hand, and therefore presented his plough-iron, which the giant seizing,^twisted in his grasp round and round again as if it had been a potato-stalk; on seeing this all the children set up a shout of laughter. In the midst of their mirth Robin thought he heard his name called ; and, all ear and eye, he put hie hand on the boy who he fancied had spoken, crying out at the same time, " Let me live or die for it, but this is young Phil Ronayne."

" It is Philip Ronayne—happy Philip Ronayne," said his young companions; and in an instant the hall became dark. Crashing noises were heard, and all was in strange confusion: but Robin held fast his prize, and found himself

lying in the grey dawn of the morning at the head of the Giant's Stairs, with the boy clasped in his arms.

Robin had plenty of gossips to spread the story of his wonderful adventure—Passage, Monks-town, Ringaskiddy, Seamount, Carrigaline—the whole barony of Kerricurrihy rung with it.

" Are you quite sure, Robin, it is young Phil Ronayne you have brought back with you ?" was the regular question; for although the boy had been seven years away, his appearance now waa just the same as on the day he was missed. He had neither grown taller nor older in look, and he spoke of things which had happened before he was carried off as one awakened from sleep, or as if they had occurred yesterday.

" Am I sure ? Well, that's a queer question," was Robin's reply ; " seeing tlie boy has the blue eyes of the mother, with the foxy hair of the father; to say nothing of the purtt/ wart on the right side of his little nose."

However Robin Kelly may have been questioned, the worthy couple of Ronayne's court doubted not that he was the deliverer of their child from the power of the giant Mac]\Iahon; and the reward they bestowed upon him equalled their gratitude.

Philip RonavTie lived to be an old man; and he was remarkable to the day of his death for his skill in working brass and iron, which it was believed he had learned during his seven years' apprenticeship to the giant Mahon Mac Mahon.

And now, farewell! the fairy dream is o'er ; The tales my infancy had loved to hear. Like blissful visions fade and disappear.

Such tales Momonia's peasant tells no more !

Vanisli'd are mkrjiaids from the sea-beat shore;

Check'd is the Headless horseman's strange career ; Fir Darkio's voice no longer mocks the ear,

Nor nocKS bear wondrous imprints as of yore I

Such is " the march of mind." But did the fays (Creatures of whim—the gossamers of will) In Ireland work such soitow and such ill

As stormier spirits of our modern days ? Oh land beloved ! no angry voice I raise ; My constant prayer—" May peace be with thee still I"

^ppetttiix.

letter from sir walter scott to the author of the irish fairy legends.

Sir,

I HAVE been obliged by the courtesy which sent me your very interesting work on Irish Superstitions, and no less by the amusement which it has afforded me, both from the interest of the stories, and the lively manner in which they are told. You are to consider this, Sir, as a high compliment from one, who holds him on the subject of elves, ghosts, visions, &c. nearly as strong as William Chume of Staffordshire—

*' Who every year can mend your cheer Wiih tales both old and new."

The extreme similarity of your fictions to ours in Scotland is very striking. The Cluricaune (which is an admirable subject for a pantomime) is not known here. I suppose the Scottish cheer was not sufficient to tempt to the hearth either him, or that singular demon called by Hey-wood the Buttery Spirit, which diminished the profits of an unjust landlord by eating up all that he cribbed for his guests.

The beautiful superstition of the Banshee seems in a great measure peculiar to Ireland, though in some Highland families there is such a spectre, particularly in that of Mac Lean of Lochbuy; but I think I could match all your other tales with something similar.

I can assure you, however, that the progress of philosophy has not even yet entirely " pulled the old woman out of our hearts," as Addison expresses it. Witches are still held in reasonable detestation, although we no longer burn or even score above the breath. As for the water bull, they live who will take their oaths to having seen him emerge from a small lake on the boundary of my property here, scarce large enough to have held him, I should think. Some traits in his description seem to answer the hippopotamus, and these are always mentioned both in highland and lowland story: strange if we could conceive there existed, under a tradition so universal, some shadowy reference to those fossil bones of animals which are so often found in the lakes and bogs.

But to leave antediluvian stories for the freshest news from fairy land, I cannot .resist the temptation to send you an account of King Oberon's court, which was verified before me as a magistrate, with all the solemnities of a court of justice, within this fortnight past. A young shepherd, a lad of about eighteen years of as^e, well brought up, and of good capacity, and, that I may be perfectly accurate, in the service of a friend, a most respectable farmer, at Oak-wood, on the estate of Hugh Scott, Esq. of Harden, made oath and said, that going to look after some sheep which his master had directed to be put upon turnips, and passing in the grey of the morning a small copse-wood adjacent to the river Etterick, he was surprised at the sight of four or five little personages, about two feet or thirty inches in height, wlio were seated under the trees, and apparently in deep conversation. At this singular appearance he paused till he had refreshed his noble courage with a prayer and a few recollections of last Sunday's sermon, and then advanced to the little party. But observing that, instead of disappearing, they seemed to become yet more magnificently distinct than before, and now doubting nothing, from their foreign dresses and splendid decorations, that they were the choice ornaments of the fairy court, he fairly turned tail and went " to raise the water," as if the South'ron had made a raid. Others came to the rescue, and yet the fairy cortege awaited their arrival in still and silent dignity. I wish I could stop here, for the devil take all explanations, they stop duels and destroy the credit of apparitions, neither allow ghosts to be made in an honourable way, or to be believed in (poor souls!) when they revisit the glimpses of the moon.

I must however explain, like other honourable gentlemen, elsewhere. You must know, that, like our neighbours, we have a school of arts for our mechanics at

G , a small manu&cturing town in this country, and

that the tree of knowledge there as elsewhere produces its

usual crop of good and evil. The day before this avatar of Oberon was a fair-day at Selkirk, and amongst other popular divertisements, was one which, in former days, 1 would have called a puppet-show, and its master a puppet-showtnan. He has put me right, however, by informing me, that he writes himself artist from Vauxhall, and that he exhibits/an/occi»«,* call them what you will, it seems they gave great delight to the unwashed artificers of G Formerly they would have been contented to wonder and applaud, but not so were they satisfied in our modem days of investigation, for they broke into Punch's sanctuarj-forcibly, after he had been laid aside for the evening, made violent seizure of his person, and carried off him, his spouse, and heaven knows what captives besides, in their plaid nooks, to be examined at leisure. All this they literally did (forcing a door to accomplish their purpose) in the spirit of science alone, or but slightly stimulated by that of malt whiskey, with which last we have been of late deluged. Cool reflection came as they retreated by the banks of the Etterick ; they made the discovery that they could no more

make Punch move than Lord could make him speak ;

and recollecting, I believe, that there was such a person as the Sheriff in the world, they abandoned their prisoners, in hopes, as they pretended, that they would be found and restored in safety to their proper owner.

It is only necessary to add that the artist had his losses made good by a subscription, and the scientific inquirers escaped with a small fine, as a warning not to indulge such an irregular spirit of research in future.

As this somewhat tedious story contains the very last news from fairy land, I hope you will give it acceptance, and beg you to believe me very much

Your obliged and thankful servant.

Waiter Scott, J7th April, 1825.

Abbotsfohd, Melrose.

The End

Made in the USA
Columbia, SC
11 August 2023